In memory of my dear friend Trish.

Title: The House
Author: Margaret Lygnos
ISBN: 978-1-7640500-2-9
©Margaret Lygnos 2025

Margaret Lygnos, a retired paediatric nurse, lives in the Macedon Ranges with her husband. A mother of four children and grandmother to six, she now writes, paints, sews and spends time in the garden.

Her previous books are
POPPY
GROUP THERAPY
LADDER ON THE FENCE
ORCHARD LANE

Contents

Prologue

I have so many things stored in my memory, some I can see as clearly as if they happened just last week. Good memories, bad memories, sad and happy memories always there and when I least expect it one will burst out from where it's been hiding. That's okay if it's a positive memory but others can really bite and kick, causing anxiety, sorrow, anger or pain.

The first time I saw my baby brother asleep in the canvas bassinet my father had made for him. He looked so sweet, his long eye lashes closed against his plump cheeks, his rosebud lips closed tightly. My mother's tear-stained face as she returned from a phone call next door telling her that her elderly mother had died. The tall firemen who arrived in a fire truck to put out a fire in the laundry at our house. The night I went to the MCG to see the American evangelist Billy Graham preaching his American Christianity to us. All normal memories I suppose for a woman of my age.

Later, as a nurse, I remember the first time I saw a baby fighting for breath as he died, a man who was so badly burnt he was black all over; he died. I could go on and relate some awful stories but I won't. All nurses have unpleasant memories of injured, dead and dying patients and their loved ones suffering, and we coped with these memories sometimes, somewhat, somehow.

For me there are other memories and stories of mistreated women and children, not things that have happened to me but things I have been told or heard about or seen. Unfortunately mostly these abuses happened at the hands of an evil male of our species.

I have a memory of my first son at the age of four asking me, "Mum what is the most dangerous animal that could hurt us?" It was an awakening for me as I faced for the first time the reality of the cruelty and unfairness of life for some people and the enormous responsibility I had taken on as a parent.

Thinking just a little, the answer popped into my head like a bolt of lightning and I answered him wishing it was not true. "It's very bad men."

I believe we need to be aware of these things because knowledge is power and power can help to prevent some people some suffering.

That's why I have written this and other stories relating what has happened to some women. The characters (all fictional) and their lives have been pieced together from here and there, bits and pieces I have gleaned from word of mouth, newspapers, over the fence whispers, unhappy disclosures from women I hardly knew or women I knew well, things I have seen or invented. They are not biographical and there is quite a lot of imagination involved.

The truth will set you free but first it will piss you off.
— Gloria Steinem

PART ONE

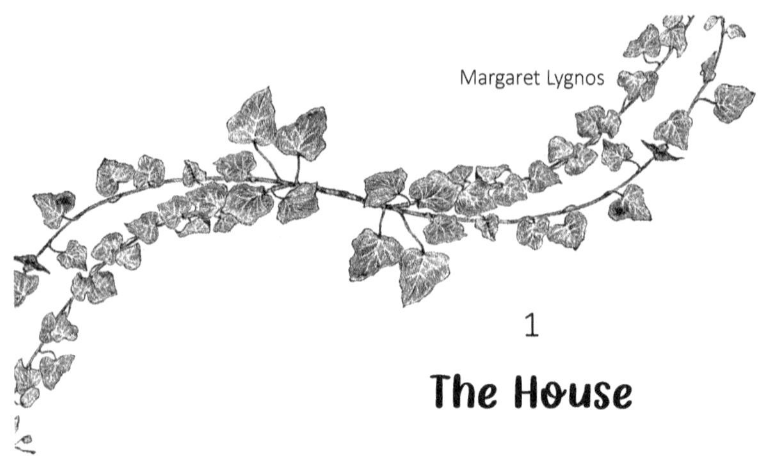

1

The House

It was one of those houses that children typically like to draw. A front door flanked by equal-sized windows on either side, a chimney or two, and a central gate in a picket fence. If you viewed the house from the street you would be right in assuming it was forgotten and unloved. Several pickets were missing from the shabby fence, the paint almost non-existent, and the mail box which was lacking a lid hung at an awkward angle. A rusty iron gate emitted a loud screech when it was forced opened. A weed-ridden brick path led towards two uneven wooden steps rising to the wide veranda. Timber decking across the front of the house had a few loose boards and the front door and windows which were draped with spider webs had not seen a broom or a duster for years. In the upper corner of the right side window a fat black spider lived only emerging occasionally to grab an unfortunate insect caught in her web.

The weatherboard house sat forlornly sad and empty crying out for attention most particularly new paint. Any real estate agent would call it a doer upper or a developers' delight. Fortunately the house was in an area where the Victorian houses were valued and permission from the local council had to be obtained for demolition of an old house, so there it stood unfortunately not in its former glory. Even so, and in spite of its present state, if the sun shone on the front of the house the windows managed a sparkle and a wink to any passing observer. It was as if it was saying don't give up on me yet, don't judge a house by its lack of paint, I can still be useful.

When the house was first built it would probably have been occupied by a middle class family where the father may have worked in an office or perhaps as a teacher. His wife would have been at home caring for her children, husband and house. She could have had a vegetable garden in the back yard and most likely some chickens to provide eggs and a roast chicken now and then. To do the weekly washing she would have boiled water in the copper in the laundry and hung the washing on an elevated rope line. The copper in the outside laundry was a large deep copper bowl bricked in above a small oven where a fire was lit to warm the water for the washing. The dirty clothes and linen were boiled in the copper then rinsed in a cement trough before being pulled with a long wooden paddle and pushed through a mangle into the adjoining trough. The mangle squeezed the water out between two rollers flattening and preparing the items for drying. The wet items were taken outside to a rope clothes line suspended between two very tall poles where the washing was hung. Another long pole was used to hoist the rope up higher so that it was out of the way and the washing which was pegged with wooden dolly pegs could flap in the breeze to dry.

Wood had to be chopped to fuel the open fires which were lit to warm the house and keep the oven in the kitchen going. Everything took longer in those days and the woman of the house was always busy. It was quite common for the eldest daughter to leave school in her early teens to help her mother at home. She would have been expected to assist her mother with the daily chores and maybe help care for the younger children.

In the more than one hundred years since it was built the house had been the home of only two different families. The last of these families, the Cuthberts, lived there for over eighty years. When the elderly couple died they left the dwelling to their only son who lived there until he recently died. His only living relative, an unmarried sister called Marcia Cuthbert, inherited the house and contents from him.

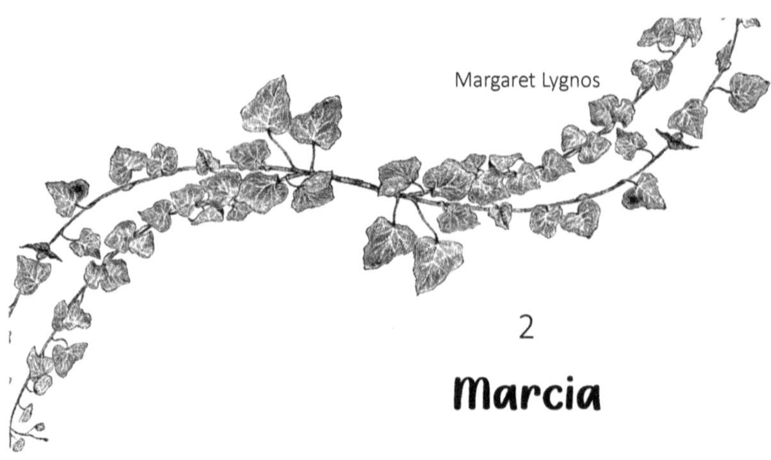

2

Marcia

Marcia Cuthbert a successful lawyer worked in a large law firm in Melbourne. A well dressed middle aged woman of average height and slim build she kept her blonde hair cut into a long bob and emanated an air of confidence and success. Having worked all her life and having no dependents she was very well off financially. Her life had been full and rewarding in many ways, aside from her career she'd had several long term relationships and many lovers but no children. Sometimes she thought wistfully about the child she could have given birth to but as she had been young, still studying and not well off at the time she had the pregnancy terminated. That child would have been in his or her forties now and she always remembered the awful details of the abortion on the anniversary of the day it had been carried out. It was before abortion was legal in Victoria and with the help of her boy friend she had just enough money to pay an obstetrician to carry out the illegal procedure in his consulting rooms in Collins street Melbourne. Memories of the sound of the toilet flushing the foetus away still haunted her.

Marcia was now living in a luxurious penthouse apartment in the centre of Melbourne which provided wonderful scenic views from Port Phillip Bay in the south to the Macedon Ranges in the north. Sitting in her living room she could look out to the Bay and enjoy the sunset reflecting on the westerly side of the bay and in the morning from her bedroom she could enjoy the sun rising from the east. Possessing everything she needed and having travelled extensively she felt that because she had been so privileged it was time for her to give back to society.

Through one of her junior colleagues who had worked in a fairly new organisation as a student she became aware of a not for profit charity which concentrated on assisting women in crisis. Marcia made an appointment and when being interviewed made an offer the manager couldn't refuse.

Marcia began work in a voluntary capacity one day a week as a trial with a view to maybe increasing her hours in the future. She knew there were always women in need of help or support of one sort or another, she was also aware of the increasing numbers of older homeless women in Melbourne but she was surprised at how many there were and the reasons for them becoming homeless. The reasons were as varied as the people themselves and the increasing number of women with nowhere to live she found alarming. She was not opposed to helping homeless men but for the moment she decided she would work for this establishment called Assisting Women In Crisis.

Some of the clients were in need of straight forward legal advice and guidance with separation issues and child custody, others in dividing the few meagre assets they had between them and one even deciding who would have the family dog. But the biggest problem was finding safe affordable housing for women and their children. There was never enough government housing available and the waiting list was very long. After the first day at AWIC Marcia realised this could easily be a full time job for her.

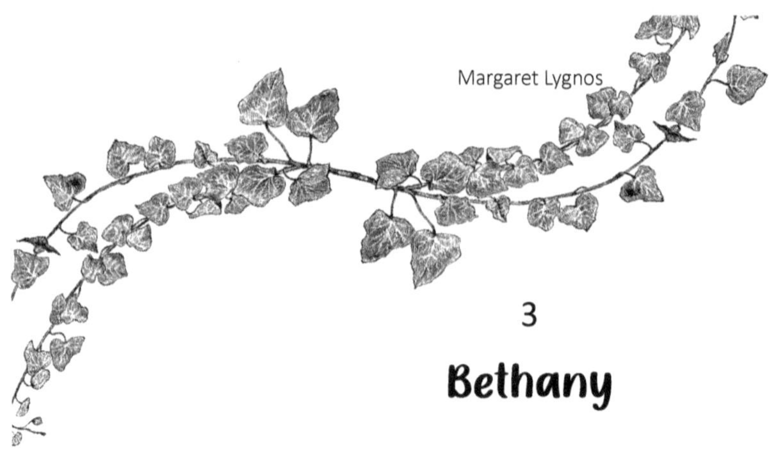

3

Bethany

One day after several busy weeks of appointments had passed, Marcia welcomed Bethany, a woman of about forty, into her office for a consultation. Sitting opposite Marcia, Bethany related a horrific tale of abuse and misunderstanding which had ruined her marriage and her life as she had known it. Marcia watched as Bethany, a tall, attractive dark-haired woman, spoke nervously. Looking unwell and in need of a hair-cut, her pretty blue eyes were underlined by dark skin. Bethany told Marcia she had almost no money and only a part-time job three hours a day five days a week. She didn't own a car and rarely saw her two children. She had been married for ten years and had known her husband for five years before they wed. They had met through friends where they had been involved in a trivia quiz group. The group, which took itself very seriously, became competent, successful and well known. Taking part in or organising as many quizzes as they could they were often hard to beat. Bethany's husband (Joe) and one of the other participants made a part-time business out of conducting trivia quizzes and were in high demand, even going interstate at the weekends to carry out their quizzes. They had earned a good reputation and were in demand so most weekends Joe was away. Bethany said she had not minded Joe being away because he was doing what he loved and was earning extra money which made him happy, so she was happy for him.

As Bethany told her story she began to stumble over her words and Marcia could see she was finding it difficult to continue so, resisting the urge to reach out to the woman's hands, she instead suggested they have a small break.

"Would you like a cup of coffee Bethany?'

With obvious relief she accepted, "Yes thank you, I did rush to get here and skipped my morning coffee."

Returning to her desk where Bethany was seated, Marcia carried a tray holding a pretty, fine china tea set, a steaming plunger of coffee and two almond croissants.

Passing the plate of pastries to Bethany she said. "These are my favourite and the reason I'm getting a bit thick around the waist."

"Mmm, lovely."

"Milk and sugar in your coffee?"

"Just milk."

They sat gazing out of the window to a pleasant little courtyard and garden which was outside Marcia's office. A young man who was sweeping leaves back onto the garden stopped and turned to see them watching him. He smiled and waved, Marcia raised her hand and waved back to him.

"Not only do I have a pretty garden to admire but also a good-looking young man who is young enough to be my son to remind me that although I'm ageing, I'm still well and truly alive. He keeps the garden in good shape. I suppose we could have been out there enjoying the garden instead of here in the office." Marcia said thoughtfully "Maybe next time. More coffee?"

"No thank you but I really needed that," Bethany said as she returned her cup to the tray.

"Okay, shall we continue?" Marcia asked.

Bethany sat back in her chair and, feeling a little more relaxed, resumed her story where she had left off. Having stopped work towards the end of her first pregnancy she had not gone back to her career in nursing because she became pregnant with her second child. Both of these children were wanted and dearly loved by both she and Joe. Having more than five years away from nursing meant that she couldn't go back without doing a refresher course. She was quite prepared to do the refresher course at sometime but not until the children were a little older. She had a job which she shared with another woman working as a cleaner in a nursing home. It was a far cry from the work she had done as a nurse but she liked the elderly patients at the nursing home and they liked her as she always had time to have a little chat as she swept and mopped around their beds and chairs. Joe was not impressed with her doing such a lowly job but Bethany was able to fit it in around the children at kinder and school and as the woman she shared the job with also had young children, they were able to cover for each other if the need arose. It suited her for the time being.

Joe's parents lived in New Zealand and had come over for the wedding, stayed for a few weeks then returned home to Auckland. Because of this Bethany did not know them very well until they moved from their house in Auckland and travelled to Melbourne to live close to Joe and his young family. Bethany was delighted her in-laws had moved to Melbourne because Joe was happy and it meant her children would have grandparents in their lives. In the back of her mind she hoped that once they were settled, her mother in-law would be willing to help out with child care and perhaps even help out if she enrolled in the nursing refresher course.

Joe's mother, Margery. a tall heavily built woman, had an air of confidence and authority, unlike her husband Bill who was thin and as quiet as a mouse. They rented a house a few miles away from Bethany and Joe's house so they were close enough to see them often but not too close to be popping in all the time. It wasn't long before Margery made it very clear she would not be doing any childminding.

"I've already brought up my own children I'm not going to bring up my grandchildren, that's your job," she told Bethany.

Bethany was shocked by the directness of her mother-in-law who was adamant about not caring for her grandchildren even occasionally, so she decided she certainly wouldn't lower herself to raise the issue again. The only time they saw Joe's parents was when Margery rang saying, "We will come for dinner," on a certain night that she nominated. Bethany was equally shocked by this; she thought it rude as they were never invited back to the in-laws home for a meal. When Bethany knew Margery and Bill were coming for dinner she naturally became nervous and worried about what she should cook because it turned out they were very plain eaters and pushed things to the side of their plates if it was something they didn't like the look of. Bethany had tried the first time to please them by serving them something different— moussaka, a tasty dish of layered eggplant and mince topped with béchamel sauce. Neither of them ate any of it because Margery said as she pulled a face, "it doesn't look very nice. What's this weird-looking vegetable in our meal?" She also said it was wrong to serve such strange food to young children.

"It will upset their stomachs. They won't be able to digest such unusual food," Margery announced as the children wolfed down the meal, which she didn't seem to notice. Ironically if Bethany presented a simple meal Margery accused her of not making an effort. "Oh sausages and mashed potato, that's not hard to cook, anyone can rustle up a meal like that."

Bill did not have much to say about anything, he didn't have to because Margery generally spoke for him before he had a chance to offer an opinion or an idea. Bethany supposed that Bill had given up years ago and now he did not bother trying. It was a very unrewarding relationship for Bethany and the children, Skye and Sam, who were spoken down to by their grandmother who never listened to a word they said. Sam tried to climb onto her knee for a story but she pushed him off saying she didn't like reading children's books. Bethany asked Joe if his mother had always been so disagreeable and he replied angrily that she was okay and had always been a strong determined woman and not disagreeable at all.

"Well," said Bethany, "That's a subject I'll try not to bring up again."

Bill had to fly to New Zealand to finalise some business arrangements and would be away for ten days. Margery informed Joe that she would be staying with them while Bill was away and Joe told Bethany of the fact. Bethany wasn't looking forward to the ten days, she was actually dreading having Margery under her roof for so long. By the time the ten days were up Bethany had a permanent headache and couldn't sleep. Margery didn't help at all, she just sat and read or watched television, occasionally giving unwanted advice or criticism. One afternoon Sam was tired after kindergarten and needed a nap. He was still asleep when it was time for Bethany to pick up Skye from school.

"Margery I'm going a bit early so I can call into the butcher shop to pick up something to cook for our dinner before I get Skye from school, if Sam wakes before I return can you get him up and give him a drink please?"Bethany said as she pulled on her coat.

Margery, who was sitting in the living room reading one of Bethany's magazines, looked up and replied. "I won't be picking him up if he wakes, he will have to wait until you get back."

"Really? You won't just get him up and let him sit with you? I'll be an extra fifteen minutes at the most."

"No Bethany, I told you I will not do any child minding."

Bethany went to the children's bedroom, woke Sam and carried him crying to the car. She was fuming. She could not believe her mother-in-law was so mean and from that day she began to really dislike the woman. Later she told Joe, who was not at all sympathetic. He defended his mother, saying, "That's just the way she is."

Under her breath Bethany said, "Yeah mean and nasty. That's the way she is."

Bethany felt sorry for Bill because he was dominated by his wife so sometimes she asked him for an opinion about current affairs or memories about Joe as a child. If Margery was present she always butted in and took over the conversation.

"Thank you Margery but I was interested in what Bill had to say about Joe playing football," Bethany said louder than usual which annoyed her mother-in-law and she answered rudely, "Bill can't remember the football matches he was always working anyway."

"Really Bill? Didn't you go to see Joe play football?"

"Yes of course I went, I went many times."

Margery replied, "I don't think so, I don't remember you being there."

Later Bill said to Bethany, "Thank you for trying but it's no good trying to outsmart Margery, she is a know-all."

Following this little exchange Bethany and Bill became friendly and had their own conversations away from Margery. Bethany felt good about this because after all, he was Joe's father and her father-in-law and they should get on even if friendship with Margery was not possible.

Bill began visiting on his own sometimes and he and Joe would sit outside and enjoy a beer together and if Bethany was able she would sit with them. One day after Bill had gone Bethany said,

"I feel sorry for your father."

"Why? He's okay."

"It's your mother; she dominates him and won't let him speak."

"That's the way they have always been he's used to it I don't think he cares. Why are you always criticising my mother?" Joe asked angrily.

"I'm not, I just feel a bit sorry for your father that's all."

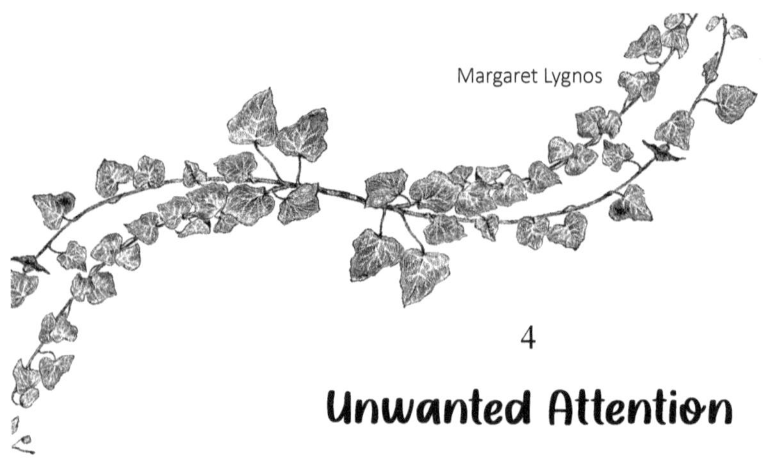

4

Unwanted Attention

Joe continued to go away at weekends and Bill started calling in to see Bethany on those weekends, always saying, "I forgot Joe was away." At first Bethany thought nothing of it but when it happened several times in a row she knew he was well aware that Joe was away. She imagined he was lonely and as he had not made any friends since moving to Australia he probably just wanted company other than that of his wife. So she always made him welcome and provided him with cups of tea and lunch if she was making lunch for herself and the children. He didn't say much but he seemed to enjoy watching Bethany interacting with the children.

"You are a good woman and good mother, very kind and patient with the children," he told her.

"Isn't that the way mothers are meant to be?" she asked.

"Yes," he replied. "Margery was never like that."

"Hmm," Bethany murmured to herself. This did not surprise her.

Several weeks went by and she began to wish he would stop calling in to see her so often. If she went out mid-morning in the hope he would leave her alone he just waited outside until she came home. On one of these occasions she told him she had to go out again to which he replied "Okay, I'll come back later."

"Oh for goodness sake," she muttered, "can't he see that I'm busy with my children and my life."

But Bill didn't get the message whatever she did, so she spoke to Joe about it.

"Joe when you are away, your father comes to see me just a bit too often, I know I befriended him but it's beginning to get on my nerves. He comes too often and If I go out he waits for me to come home and he stays for ages just watching me. It's overkill, it's too much."

"Bethany for god's sake, he's an old man, he just wants company other than with my mother. Haven't we been through this before?"

"Yes but it's beginning to annoy me. I want to be with the children or have friends over to visit and he is making that difficult. I felt sorry for him but now I'm wishing I had kept out of it. Can you speak to him and ask him not to come so often?"

"No Bethany I will not; first you complain about my mother and now you're having a go at my father, what's wrong with you?"

"Joe it's my home and I should have a say in who comes and goes in my home, I just wish he wouldn't come so often, I'm beginning to wish I had never been friendly towards him. It's too much and I don't like it."

"It's your problem. If you are so inconvenienced you speak to him," Joe said angrily.

The next weekend that Joe was away Bethany parked the car inside the garage and locked it. Going inside she closed the blinds and put on a movie for the children to watch and bunkered down for a quiet day. She heard Bill's car pull up in the driveway, and he rang the door bell. "Shush," Bethany told the children, "Keep very quiet," which they did and eventually Bill's car drove away.

"Okay, we can go outside when the movie has finished," she told the children. An hour later they were in the back garden playing and who should open the side gate? Bill.

"Jesus," Bethany said to herself. "What am I going to do?"

"Were you out earlier?" asked Bill and before Bethany could say anything Skye said at the top of her voice, "no we were hiding inside!"

Bill gave her a strange look. Bethany said nothing, thinking this might have been enough to give him a hint, but no, he just stayed as if nothing had been said.

The afternoon became evening and Bethany began to prepare a meal for herself and the children and as Bill seemed to be going nowhere she felt that she had to offer him dinner. After dinner she bathed the children and put them to bed and still Bill stayed.

"I am really tired Bill, I'm going to have an early night," she said in as light and friendly way as she could manage.

Bill didn't reply.

"I need to go to bed Bill, I'm very tired," she said again.

Bill looked at her and said "Can I come with you?"

"I beg your pardon?"

"Can I come to bed with you?"

"What are you saying, what do you mean?"

"You're a beautiful woman Bethany, and I would like to go to bed with you. I know you like me, don't you?"

"Bill, I can't believe what you are saying to me; I am your son's wife."

"He doesn't have to know, I won't tell him."

Bethany stood up and walked towards the front door expecting Bill to follow her but he didn't, he stayed where he was.

"I want you to leave now Bill, at once, go."

Bill walked towards her and she moved to open the front door but he grabbed her and pushed her against the wall.

"Leave me alone," she yelled at the top of her voice.

"Come on, just once," he urged. "I know you like me."

"No, leave me alone and get out!" She yelled even louder this time. "Go away!"

The noise woke Skye and Sam and they both came out of their room rubbing their sleepy eyes, wondering what all the noise was about. Both of them ran to their mother's side and threw their arms around her.

"Mummy what's wrong," asked Skye?

"Nothing darling, say goodnight to your grandfather, he's leaving now."

She opened the door and as he stepped through she whispered to him, "You disgust me, don't ever come here again."

Holding back tears she settled the children back in their beds then pouring herself a glass of wine she sat on the couch and let the tears fall. Leaving the wine on the table she sobbed and sobbed until she got all the shock and disgust out of her system. Downing the wine in one movement she picked up her phone to ring Joe. He didn't answer so she left a message asking him to ring her as soon as possible. He rang about an hour later. "What's wrong? Is one of the children sick?"

"No Joe, it's your father — he assaulted me this evening and I want you to come home."

"What happened? Surely you must be mistaken."

"I'm not mistaken. He assaulted me and I need you to come home, I'm very upset." She began to cry again.

"Assaulted, what exactly did he do?"

"He grabbed me, he told me I was beautiful and that he wanted to go to bed with me. Joe just come home, please, I need you here."

"I'm sure there is some mistake, you must have misunderstood him."

"There is no mistake and I didn't misunderstand him. He is disgusting. That's what he said to me."

"Look Bethany I can't come home now, I will be home in the morning as planned. We can sort this out then."

"Thanks Joe, thanks for putting me first, thanks for taking me seriously, thanks for nothing!" She slammed the phone down and drank another glass of wine. Although she went to bed she was unable to sleep so was up again at 2am. Staring at Cary Grant in an old movie on television, not taking it in, she thought about Joe's parents, both awful people, both difficult to understand, and nothing like Joe or anyone she had ever met before. She wished the two of them had never come to Australia and she did not want either of them in the house again. If Joe wants to see his parents he will have to go to their place, she decided.

5

Unbelievable

Joe arrived home the next day not any earlier but at the time he had indicated before Bethany had rung him. Entering the house he looked upset and as soon as he began to speak it was clear he had already been to see his parents and was unhappy with Bethany.

"Bethany I don't know what has got into you. You have totally misjudged my father's offer of help and insulted him and my mother by making this awful accusation."

"What do you mean offer of help?"

"He was just offering to help you put the children to bed."

"No he was not offering help, he was asking to get into bed with me. The children were already asleep in bed."

"I don't believe you. My father would never do that. For some reason you have really taken a dislike to my parents and you are trying to put a rift between us and them."

"I am not trying anything of the sort, Joe. I'm trying to make my husband believe that I was assaulted by his father."

"Well I'm sorry Bethany but I just cannot believe my father would behave in that way towards you. We'll sort this out with them, they're coming over tomorrow for dinner so we can put things right."

"I'm not cooking for either of your parents, I don't want them here ever again."

Standing over her Joe raised his voice. "Well they are coming whether you like it or not and that's that." He walked off to have a shower leaving Bethany hurt and angrier than she had ever felt. Retuning two saucepans to a cupboard she banged them several times on the kitchen bench, repeating, "I will not change my mind. I will not change my mind," feeling even more determined to stick to what she had said — that she would not cook for them and she did not want them in the house.

The following day Bethany arranged to meet her friend Sally at the school gate at 3.30 when she picked up Skye.

"Do you have time to go to the park for an hour?" she asked Sally. "I need to talk to you."

Her friend agreed and they walked to the nearby park, stopping at a shop to buy ice-cream for the children. Reaching the park the children ran to the play equipment squealing happily, enabling the two women to talk openly at last. Sally listened as Bethany revealed the awful events that had occurred over the last two days.

"I'm surprised that Joe didn't believe you. That's really awful," Sally remarked.

"Odd, and very hurtful on my part; I always support him in anything and everything he does yet this one huge thing that's happened to me and he doesn't believe me. He is bringing his parents over tonight and expects me to be there cooking for them but I won't be there and I mean it."

"What are you planning to do?"

"I'll take the children out for dinner, waste time somewhere then go home later after his parents have gone home."

"You're welcome at my place for dinner and you can stay as late as you like afterwards," Sally reassured her. "Colin or I will drive you home."

"Really, won't that be a bit of an imposition?"

"No, not at all, you have been a good friend to me and I feel I owe you anyway."

Bethany had helped Sally many times when she had her second baby, and afterwards, because she, like Bethany, had no family living nearby. They called the children who became very excited to hear they would be having dinner together that night. Dinner was a noisy happy time and after they had eaten the four children had a bath, Sally lent clean pyjamas to Skye and Sam then they sat on the couch where Bethany read a few stories to them. The children became sleepy and Sally's husband Colin offered to drive Bethany and the children home. By the time they arrived at Bethany's home the children were both asleep so Colin carried Skye and Bethany carried Sam into the house and put them into bed.

Joe barely spoke to Colin as he lowered Skye into her bed and was glowering at him as he left the house. Turning on Bethany he berated her: "You embarrassed me by not being here to provide dinner for my parents. They were very disappointed and were expecting an apology from you."

Bethany looked at Joe's angry red face thinking he was about to burst a blood vessel. Nervously she replied, "Well I'm not going to apologise because I told you not to bring them here and I don't want them in the house again."

"But they are my parents!" he yelled at her, "Grandparents to Skye and Sam."

"Well they are not good parents or good grandparents and I don't want anything to do with them. I wish they would go back to New Zealand. If you want to see them you will have to make other arrangements that do not include me."

Walking into the kitchen she was annoyed to find cooking paraphernalia and dirty dishes all over the benches. Banging dishes in the sink she yelled, "Even between the three of you, you couldn't clean up."

Joe took a doona and spare pillow out of the linen cupboard and went to his study to spend the night. For the first time since they had been married Bethany and Joe slept apart in separate rooms.

The next few days were very strained between them although Bethany tried multiple times to discuss the situation with Joe.

"There is nothing to discuss, you have made a dreadful accusation against my father and both my parents are naturally really upset with you," he responded.

It did not matter what Bethany said, Joe just would not believe her and would not budge; he was adamant that Bethany should apologise and life would continue as before. Without informing Bethany, Joe brought his parents to the house early one evening. Bethany was shocked to see their car pull up in the driveway, making her nervous and dreading what was about to happen. As Margery entered the house she immediately began to rebuke Bethany for accusing Bill of assaulting her. Bethany stood still not interrupting just watching the angry woman's wide mouth open and close rapidly as she demanded an apology.

"I don't know what you are trying to achieve Bethany, but you have ruined any chance of a relationship between us. We can never forgive you for your slanderous accusations. I hope you realise what you have done. You are a family wrecker."

Bethany stood still and silent, allowing her mother-in-law to finish what she had to say and when she was sure the tirade was over, she pulled her shoulders back, took a deep breath, and in a clear unwavering voice said, "Margery you were not here so you do not know what happened or what Bill said to me so I don't know how you can defend him."

She glanced at Bill who wouldn't look her in the eye, then raising her voice: "Look, he won't even look at me — that's because he is guilty."

The argument continued mainly between Bethany and Margery and as it was going nowhere Bethany took the children and walked out.

"Why is Grandma always nasty?" Skye enquired.

"I'm not sure, it seems that is her nature; she is just a nasty woman," Bethany answered.

They walked to the park and then back home again and by this time Bethany was not sure what would happen next and felt sick with anxiety.

After that day nothing improved. In fact it was the beginning of the end of the marriage between Bethany and Joe. As Bethany realised what was happening to them she was amazed at how differently she and Joe had felt about each other. She had loved Joe and would have done anything for him but it was obvious that was not the way Joe felt about her. Another thing she realised was that he, like his father, was dominated by his mother and probably too scared to question her. Her word was law and it probably had always been that way. Joe made it very obvious that Bethany would have to make amends with his parents or their marriage could not continue. Knowing that Joe expected her to give in made her more determined to do what she felt was right for herself and the children. Once she acknowledged that living with Joe had become almost impossible, she realised she had two choices and neither of them were easy; she could apologise to Margery and Bill and forget about his disgusting proposition in order to preserve her marriage; or she would have to separate from Joe and manage on her own. There was no way she would apologise to her in-laws and after the way Joe and his parents had treated her she knew she had to take the latter path. Bethany had one last attempt to talk to Joe, hoping to get him to believe her, but he refused to budge.

"There is no way my father would have done what you have accused him of. If you don't want to end our marriage you have to apologise to him and my mother."

Although she felt incredibly sad that her life was about to change and knowing it would not be easy, she was none the less determined to go through with her separation from Joe and began to make plans. Once again she spoke to her friend Sally about what choices she had and how on earth she would support herself.

"I'm sure Joe will have to support you and the children," Sally assured her.

"I hope so because it's not going to be easy."

"I'm sure he'll have to pay you maintenance for the children and you will probably be entitled to some government assistance."

Bethany decided to make the necessary inquiries the next day and after dropping the children at school and kindergarten she began walking towards home. As she crossed the road at a pedestrian crossing she was suddenly aware of a white car approaching her on her left. She sensed the car was going too fast and it was not going to stop so she attempted to run ahead to avoid being hit but she was not fast enough. The car hit her, throwing her on to the kerb where she hit her head and fell like a rag doll, unconscious, on the side of the road. The car continued down the road not even slowing down at all.

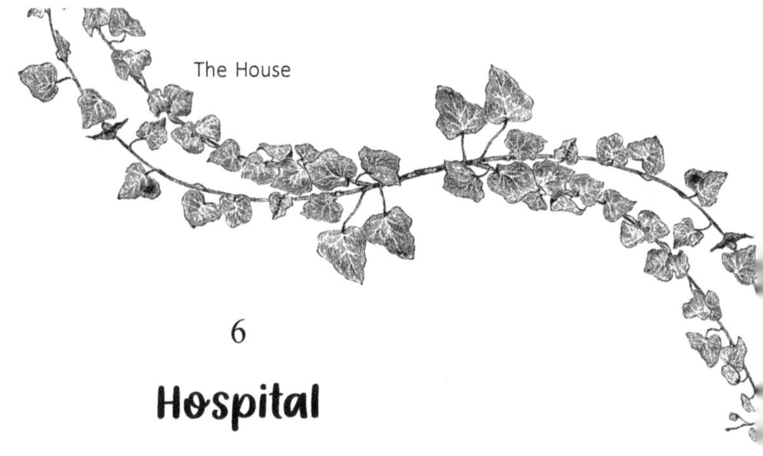

6

Hospital

When Bethany woke in the emergency department she knew she was in hospital, she did not have to open her eyes to see where she was, being so familiar with the sounds of the machine beeping beside her. She was drowsy, her head was pounding and her left leg hurt. Gradually she remembered the car coming towards her on the pedestrian crossing and attempted to sit up. A nurse who was working nearby noticed Bethany stirring and came over to her bedside. Bethany removed the oxygen mask which had been over her mouth and nose.

"Do I really need this?"

"You can remove it while I'm here with you and I'll watch your colour and breathing, but I would like you to continue with the oxygen for a while longer. How is your head?"

"Very sore and so is my leg."

"Yes it must be hurting you, it's quite badly broken. We have already X-rayed your leg and it's your tibia and fibula which have been fractured in two places. You also have a nasty gash on your head and left shoulder. You will be going to theatre this evening to have the bone pinned if you are well enough to have the anaesthetic."

"What do you mean if I am well enough?"

"There was concern about your conscious state because of the big bump on your head. You have been very drowsy but now that you are waking up and talking I'm sure you will be okay. We will be checking anyway."

Feeling apprehensive Bethany asked, "Can I speak to a doctor please?"

"Certainly. She said she would be back to see you as soon as you were properly awake. I'll let her know."

The doctor spoke kindly to Bethany, telling her she would be admitted to a ward after the operation and that she could expect to be in hospital for a few days at least. Bethany thanked the doctor and as she began to walk away Bethany called out, "My children, did someone pick my children up from kinder and school?" The nurse who was nearby rushed over and assured her that the children had been picked up by their father.

7

Post-Op

Following surgery to pin the fractured bones, Bethany slept off and on for twenty-four hours aided by a morphine infusion dripping into her arm. As the morphine was weaned off, it became obvious that Bethany was not quite right. Her head ached, her vision was blurred and she was not able to answer coherently all the questions asked of her. Because of this she was seen by a neurologist who was sure that as soon as the swelling was resolved she would return to normal. In the mean time she would stay in hospital under observation. Joe came to visit her only once but he did not bring the children with him although Bethany had asked him to.

"No, my mother says they will be upset if they see you in such a state and because you bumped your head you're not back to normal yet. I agree it's better that they don't see you for the moment."

This made Bethany very angry and tears welled up in her swollen eyes as she thought of her children and how much she longed to see them.

"Okay but will you can bring them in a day or two please?"

Joe did not answer.

Bethany remained in hospital for a week but Joe made no arrangements to bring the children or take her home, so she had to call on Sally to let her know what was going on at home. Sally had been to see her several times and at first was reluctant to tell her that Joe's parents appeared to be at Bethany's place all the time. Bethany rang Joe who played at being surprised that she was expecting to go home with him.

"You said that you wouldn't apologise to my parents and that we would have to separate, have you changed your mind? You only have to tell my parents that you misunderstood my father's offer to help put the children to bed."

"No, I have not changed my mind and I didn't misunderstand him. I want to go home to my own house and my own bed so that I can recover. Surely the circumstances have changed somewhat?"

"I'm sorry Bethany but that isn't going to happen unless you do as I have asked."

"It's my home and I want to see the children!" They must be missing me."

"The children are fine; my parents have moved in and are taking care of them. Everything is okay."

"Why have your parents moved in?"

"I didn't want to take time off work."

"Your mother said she wouldn't care for the children."

"Well she has changed her mind now that you are not at home."

"But I will be there, I want to be there, I want to be in my own home with my children."

"I want you to be here, but that will only happen if you apologise to my parents."

Joe ended the call and Bethany was left stunned. She had somehow imagined that Joe would move out and let her stay in the house with the children. 'What am I going to do?' she thought.

Sally visited that afternoon, and upon hearing the predicament Bethany was in, she offered to have her stay with her until she was able to work out her situation.

The following day Detective Inspector Marcus West, who was investigating the hit-run incident which had put Bethany in hospital, visited. He introduced himself and told her that there was one witness who had seen what happened and was sure the driver had accelerated instead of slowing down just before she was hit. The witness had been watering her garden, not really looking directly at the road until she heard a car bumping noisily over the traffic speed humps which were on the road leading to the pedestrian crossing. The noise caused her to turn and look at the car, which she saw hit Bethany. It was this woman who rang an ambulance and the police. Detective West also told Bethany he was going door-to-door hoping to find CCTV from at least one of the nearby houses.

Bethany took in all that he said. "Why do you think the driver didn't stop?"

"Probably under the influence of drugs or alcohol and wasn't aware of the collision," he surmised.

"Surely they must have felt the bump."

"Yes, but likely only if he or she was in a normal state of mind, not drugged or drunk," he said.

"Thank goodness that woman was there to see the incident," Bethany murmured.

"I'll be in touch," Detective West said.

Bethany was discharged and went to stay with Sally and Colin, who were very kind and sympathetic to her and went out of their way to help. Colin decided to go and see Joe, hoping to talk some sense into him.

He was not well received. "It's none of your business, it's between Bethany and me," Joe said, refusing to let him in the house. "I'm not going to discuss my marital problems with you. Get out and don't come again."

"Well, that was a waste of time," Colin said to himself as he walked away.

Bethany had not seen her children since the morning of the accident, and, feeling desperate, she went to the school with Sally when she was picking up her children. Hobbling on her crutches to the school gate, she waited anxiously for Skye to emerge from the building. Unfortunately, before she had a chance to see Skye, she saw Margery approaching from another direction pulling Skye towards a gate on the other side of the school ground. Bethany cried with frustration and disappointment.

Sally drove Bethany to her home hoping to see the children there. Walking with difficulty to the front door thinking she could open it and walk in, Bethany was shocked to find that the lock had been changed and her key did not work. Banging on the door brought the children to the window and when they saw their mother, naturally they became very upset. Bethany, already in a frail state of mind, was even more distressed to see her children so troubled. The hurt displayed on their innocent faces caused her to break down crying at the door, pleading with Margery to let her in.

"Margery, please open the door so that I can speak to Skye and Sam, I haven't seen them now for weeks," she begged.

Margery did not reply to Bethany and the children were dragged away from the window; the blinds were pulled down and the door remained shut. Eventually Sally managed to persuade her to leave and they went back to her place.

Bethany rang Joe who repeated once again. "You just have to apologise and all will be returned to normal."

"Normal," she yelled, "I don't think it was normal before!"

Bethany knew that even if she did apologise, nothing would be the same; too much had happened and she had seen a side to Joe that she could never forgive. The next step was to go to the police and report what had been done to her. Following her report, two officers went to see Joe but whatever he told them, it made no difference to Bethany's situation. The officers treated it as if they had just had a minor squabble and the advice they gave her was, "Go home and make up with your husband," which she received with angry tears.

Because of the injury to her leg Bethany was not able to work for some time and had only a small amount of her own money. She knew she could not stay with Sally for much longer but she did not know what on earth to do. All she wanted was to have her children with her, to be away from Joe and his parents and to be independent. Not much to ask, but at the moment it seemed impossible.

Sally made some enquiries and heard of an organisation called Assisting Women In Crisis which was primarily there to help homeless women or women in distress. She made an appointment for Bethany and dropped her at the office two days later.

8

Marcia Takes Over

Marcia listened to everything Bethany had to say and was saddened to be reminded of how cruel a man could be towards a woman he claimed to love. She advised Bethany not to do anything illegal, like breaking into her house or attempting to take the children, until they had been to the family law court and worked out a custody arrangement. Bethany was relieved to hear that she should have shared custody of the children but it could depend on what her accommodation was like. Marcia assured Bethany she would find somewhere for her to live as soon as possible but because she was not living on the street but at a friend's place, she was not on top of the list.

"There are homeless women who are even more vulnerable than you so you might have to wait a while, but don't lose hope," Marcia added regretfully. "I will do my best."

For Bethany it was a very difficult situation considering what her life had been like prior to her father-in-law's assault and her husband basically abandoning her. She had few choices and was determined to be strong so decided to put her faith in Marcia.

Eventually she was well enough to resume work and because she job shared she was able to work alternate days which helped take the pressure off her newly healed leg. Now that she had an income, albeit a small one, she consulted Marcia about having the children with her in the future. The case had been heard by the family court and it had decreed that she and her husband should have shared custody of the children, so Bethany was desperate to find somewhere of her own to live.

Marcia constantly lost sleep worrying about Bethany and other women who were coming to see her for assistance. One night she woke with a start from a dream about her childhood home saying to herself, 'It's staring me in the face — my family house. It's the perfect solution.'

The following morning she rang Bethany, "I might have found a suitable place for you. I've got something in the pipeline, it's not luxurious but it is a house, which could become available very soon. We'll organise a time for you to see it."

9

The House

Marcia had not been to the house for ages and was keen to see what condition it was in. It certainly needed a good clean, and gas and electricity had to be reconnected, but the roof did not leak and it had a large back yard where there was an old garage full of stuff. Most of the rooms had a few pieces of old furniture left over from when Marcia's parents had lived there. There were bed frames, wardrobes and an old kitchen table and chairs among other bits and pieces. The bathroom needed a good scrub to remove the mould from the shower recess but it was all possible, and it would be okay for the time being.

"It's an old run-down house but when it's cleaned up it will be fit for habitation," Marcia told Bethany over the phone later that day. "I want you to come and have a look at it with me and see what you think."

Bethany, having lived only in new modern houses, was shocked at the appearance of the house from the outside but inside she could see it was more promising.

"Well what do you think Bethany, could you live here?"

"Will it be expensive?"

"No, not at all."

"What is the rent?"

"Bethany if you want to live here and can pay for gas and electricity and any other outgoings, you can have it rent free. It belongs to me and I didn't know what to do with it until now. I would expect you to look after the house and garden I will pay the insurance, and I will eventually fix all the things that need attention. You can choose one of the large rooms for the time being because when the house is cleaned up I'll need the other rooms for other women. Also, anything in the house or the shed you think you can use, use it. You will be the caretaker in lieu of rent. It will be the same for any other women who move in with you. What do you think?"

"I think definitely yes," Bethany answered with enthusiasm. "I can picture myself living here with my children, the bedrooms are huge and so is the living room." Walking into the kitchen she looked at the old stove and wood burning oven. "Do they both work?"

"Yes I think so, it's old but still functions I'm sure. Anyway I will have everything checked."

Smiling broadly Bethany said, "It's great. It will be terrific, thank you Marcia, thank you so much."

10

The Car

Marcus, the detective who was handling the hit and run, contacted Bethany telling her they had located CCTV footage of the car from a nearby house.

"It was a white car but the number plates were obscured by plastic so we have been unable to identify the owner," he told her. "Do you know anyone who would want to harm you and if so, does that person own a white car?"

Bethany was shocked to think that someone may have hit her deliberately. Up to that point she had assumed it was a careless drunk or drugged driver who had driven off hoping not to get caught.

"Well the first person I can think of who drives a white car is my husband, our family car is a white sedan. The car is with my husband but I don't think he would be trying to kill me. He is still asking me to apologise and go home."

"There are plenty of white cars around and we haven't finished looking for CCTV in nearby streets," Marcus added.

"Could you see the face of the driver?" Bethany asked.

"It looked like a woman with shoulder length black hair, and she appeared to be wearing large dark glasses."

"Long black hair, that doesn't sound like anyone I know," Bethany replied.

"Okay. I won't give up, I'll be in touch with you as soon as I have anything to report."

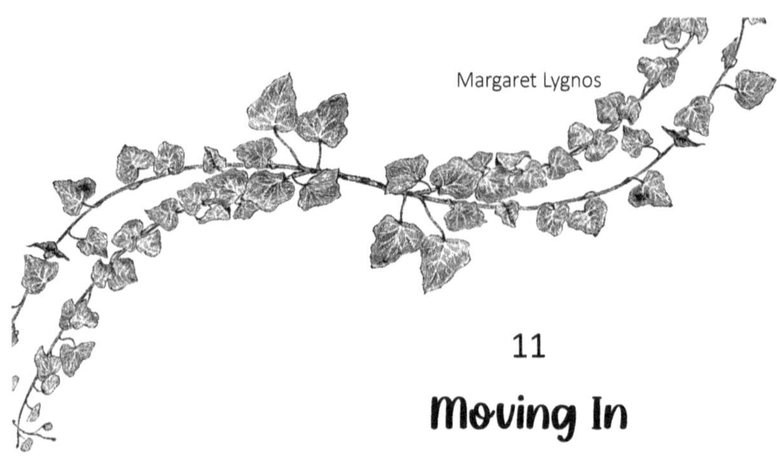

11

Moving In

Bethany was so keen to move into the house that she began to clean the room she had decided to occupy before the industrial cleaners started. She chose a large double bed, a single bed, a large old wardrobe and chest of drawers and pushed and pulled them into the room she had selected. 'Where there is a will there is a way,' she murmured to herself with her back against the chest of drawers as she pushed it along the floor. There was an old piano in the room but as it was a very large room she did not mind it being there. Her daughter Skye had recently begun piano lessons so she might want to play it. At the local opportunity shop she found bed linen and her friend Sally bought new pillows and a doona for her. She picked a bunch of flowers, put them in an old vase found in the kitchen and popped them on top of the chest of drawers.

'That looks very nice,'' she said to herself. 'Inviting and homey.'

While the interior of the house was being cleaned, Bethany spent her time in the front garden weeding and pruning. Finding a hammer and nails in the shed she repaired the broken steps and some loose planks on the front veranda, making it tidier but, more importantly, safer. Next she removed the cobwebs and hosed and cleaned the windows, making them sparkle. Pulling an old rusty garden table and chairs from the shed she brushed and washed them, enhancing their rustic appearance. After placing the furniture on the veranda she filled an old terracotta pot with soil, cut pieces of succulent from the garden and watered them in. Placing the pot on the table she stood back and admired the transformation. "It gives the house a lovely, inviting appearance," she said to no one. "Just one more thing to do." With screwdriver in hand she secured the swinging letterbox and banged the lid shut. Stepping through the front gate to the footpath, she turned to view her handiwork. The shiny windows sparkled like two bright eyes, giving her the impression the house was happy.

"It looks good enough to move in now," she said aloud, as she noticed Colin pulling up in the driveway. He brought her few possessions and a casserole which Sally had cooked for her to eat that night.

"It's quite a nice house," said Colin. "I'd be happy to renovate it and live here."

"Me too," said Bethany, "but that's not likely to happen."

As Bethany farewelled Colin, a large tabby cat strolled in ahead of her and sat itself down in the sun-drenched garden. The cat began to wash behind its ears and a voice from over the fence called, "puss, puss."

The cat totally ignored the voice and proceeded to wash its nether regions.

"You are no lady," said the voice.

Bethany stood still, wondering who would speak to her like that. Turning, she saw an elderly woman peeping over the paling fence.

"A lady wouldn't wash her private parts in public," said the woman.

Realising the cat was the object of the criticism, Bethany smiled and asked, "What is her name?"

"Queenie, and she certainly has the attitude of a high and mighty queen."

"I am about to move in here so I will probably see more of Queenie," Bethany answered, stooping to pat the cat.

"Glad to hear that; it's been empty too long. I'm Elsa, who are you?"

"Bethany," she replied walking to the fence for a chat.

The day after Bethany moved in, Marcia had arranged for a refrigerator, a microwave and a television to be delivered and after work she called in to see how Bethany was getting on in the old house.

"You can have the children to live with you now that you have a roof over your head," Marcia announced. "There is nothing to prevent them from coming. I have asked your social worker to get in touch with you and arrange the first visit. They should be with you once she has spoken to your husband. I think it's better if she makes the first approach, then he will know it's all above board and as the court decreed."

"He won't like that, I hope he doesn't make it difficult," Bethany replied. "He has become quite silly since this whole episode began. It's almost as if his parents moving to Australia changed him and they have become more important to him than me; actually it's his mother who seems to influence him more than his father. Whatever it is that caused him to change, it has changed my life too."

The court had directed that Bethany's children should be with her once she had suitable accommodation, and could visit their father every second weekend and one week night each week, to be decided on by the parents. Naturally Joe was not happy about letting the children go to their mother and tried all sorts of excuses to keep them with him but in the end he was forced to comply with the court's ruling or he would be found in contempt of court. Dropping them off at the old house on a Sunday afternoon he said very little to Bethany as he handed her a suitcase and two large plastic bags before driving away in a blue car. Bethany hugged the children for a long time then she asked, "Where's the white car?"

"I don't know, I haven't seen it, maybe Dad sold it," replied Skye, skipping off to explore the house.

Running up and down the long hallway squealing with delight, the children made it quite clear how happy they were to be with their mother again. They each took off their shoes and, wearing only socks, were able to slide on the polished boards in the hallway.

The situation was now very different but the children quickly adapted to the change. They liked the old house with the long, wide hallway and tall ceilings, and were entranced by the pretty coloured glass that surrounded the front door, lighting up like magic when the afternoon sun cast strong beams of light through the glass and all the way down the shiny floor of the hall. Whooping, they ran around excitedly in the back garden when they saw the spaciousness available to them. Skye noticed a cat disappearing over the fence and began to climb up to look for it next door. "Is that cat ours? Does it live here?

"No she lives next door and her name is Queenie, I think she comes in here so you might be able to make friends with her," Bethany told the children.

"Hope so, I'd like a pet."

Bethany did not ask the children about their grandparents but they had plenty to say about them anyway.

"I don't like Grandma," said Sam.

"I don't like her either," said Skye. "She is only nice to us when Daddy is there."

"She growls at us all the time and even smacks us," Sam added.

"Hm," said Bethany, "does she just? I'll have to speak to your father about that."

"Yes, and Grandpa is not nice either," Skye added.

"Okay that's enough about them, you will be with me most of the time now so let's get you two used to living here."

Bethany planned to let the children take it in turns to sleep with her in the double bed which made them very happy.

Life returned to a sort of normal for Bethany and her children, the only problem being she did not own a car. She was able to walk or catch a bus to school or to work, but when the weather was bad it was pretty awful struggling through the wind and rain. She decided to ask Joe next time she saw him if he had sold the white car and if not, perhaps he would give it to her; after all it was for the benefit of their children.

Sorting out the children's clothing and toys that Joe had brought when he dropped them off, Bethany was surprised to find that many of the clothes did not fit the children. She could see they were growing fast and wondered what they had been wearing.

"You don't have many clothes, where are they all?" she said to Skye.

"Daddy wouldn't let us bring them," Skye replied.

"Really? Where are they?"

"Still in the wardrobe at Daddy's place."

"Oh that's just silly," Bethany muttered. But she decided not to ask Joe for the clothes, thinking he probably wanted to make a big issue out of it. 'I don't suppose I'll get anywhere with the car then,' she thought to herself. Along with the toys there was a bag of dress-up clothes which Bethany put into the bottom of her wardrobe. The teddy bears were placed on the beds and the box of Lego and a few books were taken into the living room.

When Bethany wasn't working and the children were at school, she spent as much time as possible tidying the garden, often observed by Queenie sitting on top of the fence. Finding an old push lawnmower she oiled it and did her best to sharpen the blades so she could roughly cut the grass of the front garden. The back yard was another thing all together. It was overgrown with weeds, rambling vines and old roses. With tools found in the shed she hacked at some of the bushes and long grass which was too long to cut with the lawnmower. Raking the garden refuse into a large pile behind the shed she discovered a chicken coop there which Queenie the cat had made her own morning sun trap for sleeping undisturbed. Adjoining the chicken coop was an old vegetable plot both fenced and gated and also in full sun.

'That will be my next job' she thought to herself. 'I can grow vegies here. Maybe the children would like to help.' After picking up the children from school Bethany told them about her idea and they agreed, so they called into the local plant nursery and bought lettuce, silver beet and parsley seedlings. On Saturday morning between the three of them they weeded and dug over the garden in readiness for planting. The afternoon was spent planting the seedlings and watering everything thoroughly.

"We are like farmers," said Skye.

"Can we have some farm animals?" asked Sam.

"No," laughed Bethany, then she added "Maybe we could have a couple of chickens."

"Can we really?" Sam asked.

"Perhaps, I will see where I can get some from," Bethany replied wondering if she was going to regret having mentioned chickens.

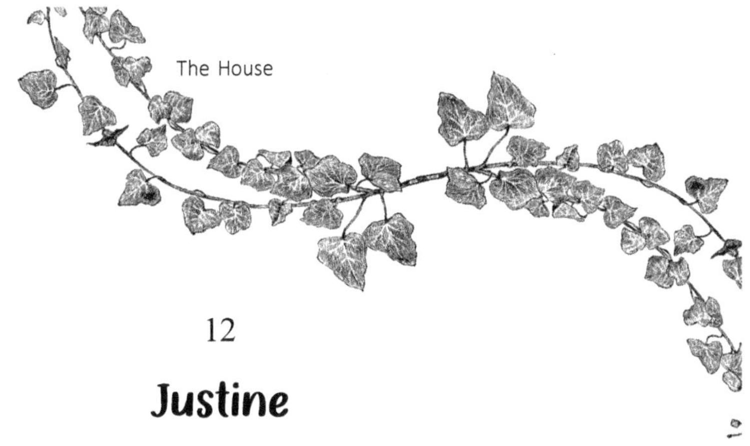

12

Justine

A few weeks after Bethany had moved in she received a phone call from Marcia informing her that another woman would be moving into the house soon.

"She has a fourteen-year-old daughter who will be with her all the time, no visits to her father at all. I will be bringing them early next Monday morning," Marcia said. "Will you be at home?"

"Yes I'll be here, I hope we get on together; it's been very quiet for the past few weeks," Bethany added. "What is her name?"

"Justine. She's a very nice woman as far as I can see, so I have every confidence the pair of you will get on very well."

At nine-thirty on the following Monday morning there was a knock on the door, and opening it Bethany was greeted by Marcia struggling with a large suitcase and her companion carrying two slightly smaller bags. They left the baggage inside the front door and went back to the car to pick up two large boxes which were hauled inside and slid down the polished timber floor to the bedroom that Bethany had prepared for her new house mate.

Justine looked around the large, light-filled room, taking in the polished antique furniture, the crisp white curtains and a vase of flowers sitting on the dressing table. Turning to Bethany she asked, "This is lovely, did you prepare the room for me?"

"Yes, I hope it's okay. The beds and the other furniture are clean and I have washed the curtains," she replied as she pulled the curtains open revealing a pleasant view of the back garden. Justine walked to the window and commented, "What a big garden, is that a vegetable patch I see?"

"Yes, the children and I have started growing a few things and are thinking about getting some chickens."

Marcia beamed at Bethany and said, "You've done wonders with both the front and back gardens, the old house looks and feels loved again. I couldn't be more pleased." Stopping at the kitchen door she added, "I remember my mother cooking at that stove and washing dishes at the kitchen sink. My brother and I would take it in turns to dry up." Sighing she added, "It brings back memories of my childhood."

Moving into the simple, old-fashioned kitchen, the three women sat at the table and shared a pot of tea and a slice of cake which Bethany had made on the weekend. Marcia then left and Justine went to her room to begin unpacking the bags and boxes she had brought. At two-thirty she found Bethany in the garden and asked about catching a bus to pick up her daughter from school.

"I'm just about to go, so we can go together and on the way we can talk about how we will share the use of the bathroom and the kitchen." They set off and by the time they arrived at the appropriate stop it was decided they would take it in turns to cook dinner and the children could use the bathroom for their showers or baths at night before bed and the two women in the morning.

When Bethany returned home with Skye and Sam, Justine was already waiting for them with her daughter Lulu. The children all smiled at each other shyly before going off to do their own things. Lulu was a quiet, polite girl with long fair hair and large brown eyes. She sat on the couch after dinner and read a book so Skye, who really wanted to be friends with the older girl, decided to do the same. They were soon chatting about books that Skye had read and books that Lulu thought she would like to read. The two mothers looked at each other and exchanged a smile.

In a hushed voice Justine said to Bethany, "This is so quiet and peaceful. I hope it stays that way, we have a lot of emotional baggage to deal with and I think this could be just what we need."

And so began the companionship of these two fractured families. The three children became friends and so did their mothers. The two women helped each other with taking the children to school and picking them up and shared the housework and gardening. They did get four chickens, and between them they made the coop fox-proof. The eggs were collected each day by little Sam who was fascinated to learn that the eggs came out of the hens' bottoms. Eggs became a favourite for his breakfast.

Justine was in the house for about a month before either of the women mentioned why they had become homeless. It was Bethany who raised the subject of her own separation and mistreatment by her husband and Justine's story flowed from there.

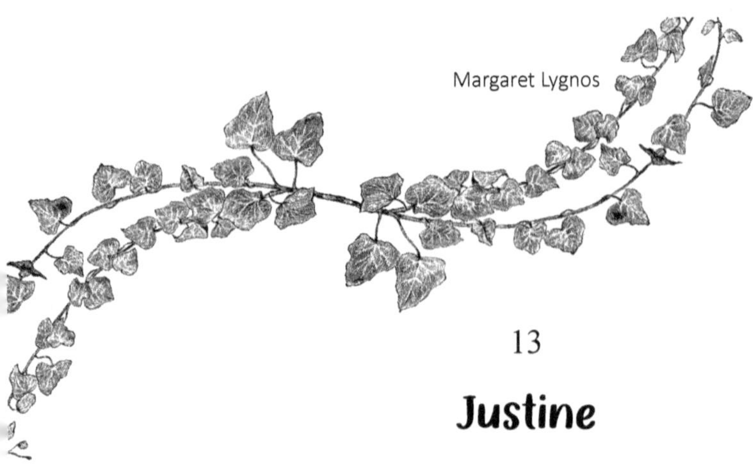

13

Justine

Seated opposite Bethany in the sun-lit kitchen, Justine looked far from comfortable. Arms across her chest, a frown on her pretty face, upright on the chair and in a quieter voice than usual she began.

"Well I suppose I was a so-called happily married woman with a devoted husband and two lovely daughters. What happened to us is the last thing any mother wants to happen to one of her girls." Justine cleared her throat and continued.

"My other daughter, Nadine, who is twenty-two, left home at eighteen to go to university. She shared a house with other students and had a part-time job at weekends. We saw her once a week at first and then hardly at all. She didn't like us visiting her so I usually rang and made arrangements to meet her for dinner or lunch near where she lived. However one day, when I had an appointment in the area where she lived, I thought I would call in hoping she would be home and we could have a catch-up. I hadn't seen her for at least two weeks so I thought I was justified in looking her up in this way. When I knocked on the door it was opened by a young man who told me that she hadn't lived there for more than a month and that he was now renting her room. He wasn't sure where she had moved to but thought she had moved into a townhouse of her own in East Melbourne. This was all news to me and when I queried it, he replied that she seemed well able to afford it as she always had plenty of money.

"I had noticed that the last few times I had seen her that she had been wearing some very expensive clothes and nice jewellery. She had also mentioned in an offhand way that she was thinking about buying a car but I hadn't taken her seriously, thinking she was a poor student."

Justine got up from her chair and walked to the kitchen sink to fill the kettle. Waiting for it to boil she looked at the sunny back garden through the sparkling clean window above the sink. Queenie the cat from next door was sitting on top of the fence watching the chickens stepping and scratching in the soil. The kettle boiled and she made a pot of tea for the two of them. Pouring the tea into two cups, she added milk and carried biscuits and the cups on a tray to the table where she resumed her story.

''Naturally I told my husband at once and he was concerned and angry. He went to the university and hung around for a few days and eventually he saw her. We were pleased that she was still studying at least. He cornered her and insisted that she came home for a visit to explain what she was doing and how she could afford to move; after all, we had been helping her financially with just a little towards her rent. She did come home for a visit and after a lot of questioning she told us she had a wealthy boyfriend who was paying for her to live in the townhouse. She insisted they were not living together but that he was extremely generous to her.

"We believed her but were amazed when we went outside to say goodbye to her and saw that she got into a car that must have cost over fifty thousand dollars. She drove away before we could ask her anything. We hadn't even talked about a car so we assumed it belonged to her boyfriend. After that she kept in touch with us as before and life returned to normal until we had the most dreadful shock."

Justine got to her feet again, walking to the window giving herself time to become composed. Leaning on the window sill and gazing out to the garden she noticed Queenie had moved nearer the chicken coop and with her front feet up on the wire was intently watching their every move.

Turning to face Bethany Justine continued, "We found out that she was dancing at a club in the city. You know the places that are called gentlemen's clubs but are anything but. A business associate of my husband said he had been to a venue in the city and saw a girl who looked like our daughter dancing almost naked around a pole on a stage and other things like that. I never saw her so I'm not sure what she did, but whatever it was, she was earning heaps of money. When my husband told me I didn't believe him, I refused to believe him but he assured me it was true because he'd gone there to see for himself. When I look back I'm not sure if it was a business associate who saw her or if it was actually my husband who went there and got the shock of his life, however it happened and it was the beginning of the end of my marriage."

14

Lulu and Nadine

Lulu had been twelve years old when it was discovered that her adored big sister Nadine was doing something which her parents were not happy about. Although she asked both her parents what it was that was so dreadful, they would not tell her exactly what it was.

"Is she having sex with her boyfriend?" Lulu blurted out one day.

"What do you know about sex?" her mother replied. "You are too young to even talk about sex."

"Mum, everyone knows about sex; even people my age have sex."

This shocked Justine because without actually discussing it she and her husband Tom had decided not to talk to their children about 'the facts of life'. Neither of them were comfortable talking about sex and stupidly, thought if they kept quiet it could be avoided. Their sex life was infrequent and not enjoyable at all for Justine, who never managed to climax, and Tom had enormous feelings of guilt about doing 'it'. Tom had been brought up in an overzealous religious family where anything to do with sex was considered dirty. When Tom was about fourteen his mother became aware that he had been masturbating and she told her husband. Tom's father sent him straight to his room where he was thrashed with a leather belt and confined for a whole weekend as punishment. He was unable to stop masturbating, but after that whenever he did he felt guilty and hated himself.

Justine's problem was not due to religion or ignorance but caused by abuse by an older cousin who had boarded with her family for a year when she was still in primary school. She remembered the events clearly and since then had hated anyone touching the parts of her body that she considered private. Justine had wanted to be a mother, so that was what she thought of when she had to submit to Tom. Once she had given birth to their two daughters she did everything she could to avoid any more sex with Tom and did not want to know what he did with his 'needs' as he liked to call his libido.

Lulu loved her big sister Nadine and they always shared a bedroom even though their parents assured them they could have a room each. Nadine was more insistent that they should leave things as they were because she thought they were less vulnerable in a room together, so she used the excuse that they still liked to talk at night when they went to bed. The girls were very different. Nadine was a girl who as a young child had loved Barbie dolls and My Little Pony toys and had spent hours practising her dance moves. She had attended gymnastics and dance lessons each week and had learned ballet. She wore feminine clothes, loved shoes and makeup and was proud of her long legs and beautifully kept long blonde hair.

Lulu, who was just as attractive as her big sister, was the opposite in the way she dressed and was often called a tomboy. She liked reading but her greatest love was playing soccer and anything to do with soccer, and she was usually dressed in a soccer T-shirt and shorts. When she was not playing soccer with her team she was outside practising kicking the ball into a net in the back garden or reading. In spite of their differences the sisters got on very well and Nadine was someone Lulu could always talk to.

Lulu was surprised and very pleased when Nadine suddenly began accompanying her to her weekend soccer match.

"Why have you changed your mind about coming to see me play?" she enquired.

"I don't want to stay at home with Dad any more," was all she said.

"He is a bit boring, isn't he," Lulu answered.

Averting her eyes from Lulu, Nadine replied, "Yes, he's boring and annoying among other things."

Nadine finished school and left home to live closer to the university, which upset Lulu although she made an effort to keep her feelings to herself as she knew that Nadine had been looking forward to her freedom. Whenever their mother met up with Nadine, Lulu gladly went along to spend time with her sister.

On the night that Nadine came home and told her parents about her wealthy boyfriend, the sisters had very little time alone but Lulu managed to ask Nadine, "Why are Mum and Dad so upset with you? What have you done that is so bad?"

Nadine looked at Lulu and replied, "I have been dancing and getting paid for it, that's all, no big deal. Don't tell them that or they will really go mad."

Lulu accepted her sister's answer and left it at that; what was wrong with dancing anyway?

15

Nadine

Nadine did not like her father and had mixed feelings about her mother who seemed pretty gutless and unsupportive of her daughters. Her father insisted that her mother Justine stay home during the week to look after the family and on the weekend she worked two twelve-hour shifts as a ward clerk in a city hospital. With the penalty rates she was paid it was almost as much money as working a full week. Whenever Justine complained about always working all weekend, Tom persuaded her that it would only be until the girls finished school then they would not need the money. For this reason and also because Tom liked her to be at home during the week, she continued, but often wished she could be there to take Lulu to her soccer matches and maybe take the girls shopping, or the whole family could do some weekend activities together.

Justine worked from eight in the morning to eight at night so it was a long day, up at six-thirty and home just before nine at night. The girls were still asleep when she left and ready for bed — just as she was — when she returned home.

Tom usually drove Lulu to a teammate's home for a lift to matches with her team and he rarely went to watch her play. Nadine was at home with her father and he always asked her to put on her dance costume and dance for him. This had been going on for ages and he applauded and gave her a hug because she danced so well. As she got older, not only did he give her a hug but it became a bit more of a grope. It was not long before he began putting his fingers places he had no business putting them. Nadine did not like what he did to her but he persuaded her that it was okay for a father to touch his little girl in that way. Following the perverted touching he would go to his bedroom and close the door where he stayed for a short time.

She told her mother. "When I dance for daddy he gets a bit excited and touches me too much."

Justine told Tom what Nadine had said and of course he laughed and said, "She dances so well and I am so proud of her that I give her a big cuddle, that's all."

Justine accepted what he said and thought no more about it despite her own abuse at the hands of her cousin. She was very naive and refused to take her daughter's complaint seriously; after all he was her father.

Nadine's friend Ruby had a big sister who was already going out with boys on her own on the weekend. Sometimes Nadine and Ruby would secretly listen in to the older girl and her girl friends talking about sex and what they got up to with boys. It was through these eavesdropping episodes that Nadine realised how serious her father's unwanted touching and strange behaviour was. Following the realisation that it should not be happening, she decided to make sure she was never alone with her father, and never to dance for him again. She did not to tell her mother again, thinking she would not take any notice of her complaint anyway. It was at this point that on weekends she went with her sister to watch her play soccer and once they returned home they kept each other company. The weekends continued like this until Nadine left home the year after finishing school.

Leaving home, and the feeling of independence that came with it, was like opening a floodgate of fun and silliness. At first she worked as a waitress in a Carlton cafe where she earned a meagre wage but got quite good tips from admiring male customers. She enjoyed the attention, and because she had attended an all-girls' school, she was a bit naive where males were concerned. She flirted and laughed and took part in what she believed was harmless banter—much to the annoyance of some of her female colleagues—but that did not stop her. Two men who were regular customers often engaged her in conversation and gleaned from her that she was living away from home and working to support herself.

"It's barely enough money but Mum and Dad help out with my rent," she offered. "I could do with more money but so could all the staff working here so I don't get many extra shifts."

"Would you be interested in a job that pays extremely well and you would only have to work a few hours several nights a week?" Nick, one of the men enquired.

"Naturally I would; how many hours are you talking about and what type of work is it?"

"It's glamorous work, can you dance?"

"Yes I am a trained dancer," Nadine replied excitedly.

"If you are really interested we will introduce you to Calypso and she will instruct you."

He got out his phone and rang Calypso to arrange a meeting with Nadine that evening at six.

16

Calypso

Calypso flicked her dark hair away from her beautiful face as she quickly looked over the striking young girl standing before her. Liking what she saw, she said, "You are stunning: long legs, long blonde hair and a curvy body— everything I am looking for in a dancer."

"Thank you," Nadine replied.

Calypso took her to a large building in the city where she had a small dance studio with mirrored walls and several metal poles secured between floor and ceiling. Giving Nadine a skimpy outfit to wear she put on music and asked her to dance.

"Try using the pole," she called out to Nadine, who was not quite sure how to dance with a pole but she gave it a try.

"I'll show you," said Calypso who took off her outer clothes to reveal a gold leotard which accentuated her light olive skin and beautiful body. She then danced in a very provocative manner around the pole. Nadine watched for a short time then began to easily dance in the same manner.

"You're a very good dancer and will do very well here, you just need a bit more coaching. By next week I think you could be ready to start performing," Calypso announced. They made arrangements for Nadine to attend over the next week for coaching and discussed the money Nadine could expect to earn and the hours of work. When she was told the amount of money she would be paid she made up her mind on the spot and told Calypso that she wanted the job no matter what.

"You will be paid from the beginning of your coaching and your pay will be put directly into a bank account. It might be an idea to open a new account: some of the girls have found it's better to have an account that family members are not aware of."

So began Nadine's career as an exotic dancer in a 'gentleman's club', where she learned to be a woman in a way her parents would never approve of. She loved dancing in front of an audience and because no one was allowed to touch her, she felt safe and disconnected from the patrons. The lights on the stage were very bright and the room in front of her was dark so the audience was basically unseen from up on the stage. Taking her clothes off took a bit of getting used to, but once she had done it few times and received so much applause, she loved doing it; it gave her a frisson of sexual pleasure. She made friends with some of the other girls and one who was studying commerce gave her some financial advice.

"Don't waste the money you earn here," she advised. "You might get sick of this dancing life and if you leave you will find it hard to manage on less money."

"What do you suggest?" Nadine asked with genuine interest.

"Save enough money to put a deposit on a property to live in. You'll get a loan easily, and don't go mad buying everything you see. Also sometimes one of the girls will sell a car and advertise it on our noticeboard in the dressing room. You will probably pick up a good second-hand car right here, so keep an eye out. And lastly, try not to get involved with any of the customers here, they can become very annoying."

"Thank you very much," Nadine said." That all sounds like good advice."

Nadine continued to attend her lectures at university and dance several nights a week with little or no trouble. Mostly she received compliments and applause but occasionally she heard an unsavoury remark directed at her from the audience, so she concentrated on the amount of money she was earning and was able ignore any insults. She continued to live in the share house until she had saved a deposit on a townhouse in East Melbourne. Leaving her share house she gave her friends her new address but told them only that she was moving, not that she had bought the property. She left the secondhand bed and wardrobe behind as she intended to buy all new furniture. Not having many belongings it was easy for her to move.

It was at this time that she began going out with Nick, the man who had introduced her to Calypso and her lucrative new career. He was a good ten years older than her and treated her very well, taking her out to places she had never heard of where he spent large amounts of money. He tutored her on wines and the different cuisines that were available in abundance in the plethora of Melbourne restaurants. At dinner one night in one of Melbourne's best Italian restaurants she was surprised to see that the waiters were actually ironing the table cloths onto newly laid cushioned tables. Before she could comment on this, Nick took her hand and asked her a very personal question.

"Are you still a virgin, Nadine?"

Nadine blushed and with a little coyness added "Yes, I am."

"I thought so; it shows in your dancing. You could be an even better dancer once you have begun to enjoy sex."

"Really? Are you sure?"

"Yes I think so." He smiled at her.

"I've never had a serious boyfriend. When I was at school I was hardly allowed out and since being at uni I haven't met anyone I really like that much."

To herself she thought 'until now.' She did like Nick, and tonight they had flirted over dinner again and once he had started asking her about her sex life it made her feel sexually excited.

"Perhaps you should go to see a doctor and discuss contraception; you never know when you might need it."

Nadine was well aware of the implications of unprotected sex and the thought of an unwanted pregnancy or an STD were frightening. She agreed and said she would give it some serious consideration. After dinner Nick drove her home they stayed in the car for a long time kissing. Eventually he opened the car and escorted her to her front door.

Kissing her again he said "One night soon I'd like to come inside with you."

Entering the townhouse Nadine wished that it had been tonight.

Nadine made an appointment with her doctor and was advised to take the pill and, unless she was in a monogamous relationship, she should insist on her partner using a condom. The doctor also told her of the importance of frequent testing for STDs and put more emphasis on condoms and safe sex. Nadine was happy with this advice and thanked the doctor as she walked with her to the lift lobby where she pushed the down button and they waited together for the lift to arrive. Travelling in the elevator of the thirty-storey building down to the ground floor she looked at herself in the mirrored wall and said to herself, 'Well that's taken care of all; now all I need to do is find a good used car.'

17

nick

Looking at Nick it was obvious he was from a Mediterranean background. Thirty-two-years old, dark haired, handsome, and always dressed in expensive, well-cut clothes and polished shoes. Taking great care of himself his hands were clean, nails manicured and his hair always neat and well cut. He loved women and liked nothing more than to be seen with a beautiful woman at his side. Nick and Nadine made a stunning couple and heads turned when they were out together. They continued to go out to shows or for dinner several times a week to the best restaurants in Melbourne, places that Nadine had never heard of, let alone dined in. Following one such night out and after some prolonged kissing and touching in the car, Nick said, "Tonight is the night I would like to come inside with you, is that okay, would you like me to?"

It had been on the tip of Nadine's tongue to ask him in but now she just kissed him and nodded in agreement and they went into Nadine's townhouse. Nick removed his jacket and as he pulled her towards him she was aware of his strength and his arousal pushing against her abdomen.

Hearing the unzipping of her dress she was conscious of his warm hands moving over her body as her dress fell to the floor. Unsure what to do she just allowed Nick to guide her and tease her until she was desperate to take off her remaining clothes and lie on the bed with him. Nadine was so aroused that she climaxed easily for the first time in her life and was overwhelmed with the way she felt. Lying back, one hand softly caressing the hair on Nick's chest she said, "Oh my god, I had no idea it would be like that."

Nick smiled at her and said "Nature is very clever if we didn't have such strong desire and love-making was not so good, humans would have died out years ago."

Turning towards Nick she asked, "Can we do it again?"

Nick laughed out loud. Pulling her close he kissed her and said. "Not straight away, let's sleep for a few hours and then you never know what might come up."

Nick left Nadine sleeping the sleep of the satisfied, leaving without waking her well after midnight. Waking late the next morning, Nadine was disappointed he was not in her bed and every time she thought of him she felt a surge of desire flash through her body.

The relationship continued for months and Nadine was happier than she ever imagined she could be. She loved Nick and he said he loved her. Occasionally she prepared a meal for him instead of going out to eat and he was impressed by her cooking. Sometimes they were so desperate to make love there was no food consumed at all.

There was no talk of their future together, they were just satisfied as things were and happy in the moment. Nadine became aware that she was feeling love for the first time in her life. She had not realised how unloved she had felt before meeting Nick. At home her life had been more about rules and expectations and keeping a profile that would impress family and friends. She could hear her mother saying on many occasions, "What would people say?" Well, now Nadine did not care what people would say, she was too caught up in her love for Nick and her new life and she did not give a flying fuck.

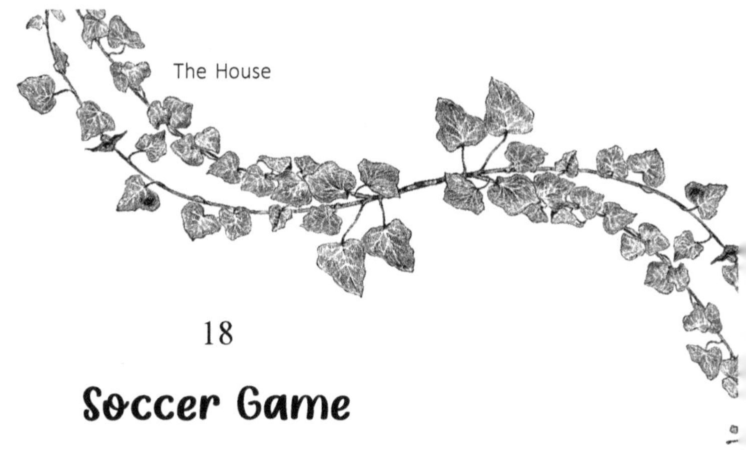

18

Soccer Game

Content with her life, Nadine passed blissfully from day to day, attending lectures and tutorials as required, handing in assignments, dancing at night and spending time with Nick usually three or four times a week. Keeping in touch with her mother and Lulu, she usually met them once a week after Lulu had finished school for the day. On one such afternoon Nadine took her sister to a sports shop and bought her a pair of the newest, most expensive, bright red soccer shoes which were the latest fashion. Lulu was thrilled and mentioned that her soccer team was in the Victorian finals and pleaded with Nadine to come and watch her play as she would be wearing the new shoes so could very well score a goal.

"Yes I'll come, it's been a while since I've seen you play."

Lulu gave her the details and when they parted she said "Thank you Nadine, I really think these shoes will help me kick a goal — maybe the winning goal."

"I hope they do," laughed Nadine. She said a quick goodbye to her mother and sister and hurried off, impatient to get ready for a night with Nick.

Lulu's next game was at eleven on a Saturday morning at a soccer ground in the eastern suburbs of Melbourne. Nadine arrived at ten-thirty and looked around for Lulu and her teammates. Unable to locate anyone that she recognised, she sat down to wait at the top of a sloping grass area where seats were provided for spectators. There was another game being played on the soccer ground so she watched the little boys running up and down sometimes passing the ball but usually trying to kick a goal whenever it was at their feet. The children were very young and they all followed the ball wherever it went, reminding Nadine of a swarm of bees following the queen bee to a new hive.

Standing on the fenceline, the amused families of the little boys cheered and encouraged them in loud voices. She noticed a well-dressed man who looked like Nick standing with the crowd — taking a second look she realised it was Nick. He had mentioned his nephew played soccer so she assumed he was there watching and supporting him.

'That's nice, I'll go over and join him, he'll be surprised to see me and I can meet his sister and the little boy he is so fond of,' she thought to herself.

Approaching Nick she noticed a woman carrying a baby walking ahead of her. The woman stopped beside Nick looked up into his eyes and they kissed on the lips. Smiling down at her, he put his arm around her shoulder and pulled her closer to him. The woman continued to look up at him and as she spoke he bent down, kissed the baby then, turning his attention back to the woman, they kissed again. Nadine was shocked and sickened by what she saw. Suddenly a huge penny dropped, smashing her dreams and answering some unpleasant lingering questions. Taking a few steps backwards she clumsily plopped onto the grassy slope, her heart beating rapidly.

'Oh my god he is married. That's why he never stays overnight, that's why we never see each other on the weekend. I'm a fool and he has been dishonest with me and used me, how could I have been so stupid, oh no Nadine, how could you have been so gullible?'

Beginning to feel sick and shaking with the shock and realisation of what she had just witnessed and what it meant to her future, she was not sure what to do. Should she confront him? Should she go and stand near him so that he could see her, should she just keep out of his sight or perhaps go home? Nadine wanted to flee but did not want to disappoint her sister, so she walked away from the soccer field hoping to disappear into the large crowd of people.

As she started to walk away Lulu's team, which had been warming up on another field, began to sprint down towards where she had been standing. The whistle blew indicating the end of the little boys' game and parents crowded around their children. Nadine felt that she was well hidden but Lulu was looking out for her and saw her in the crowd of people.

"Nadine, Nadine, come down here," called Lulu, waving madly at her big sister.

Nadine shrank back but not quickly enough. Nick, at the sound of the familiar name, looked up to where Lulu was waving and then to the person she was waving at and his eyes met Nadine's. The look on his face said it all: surprise, guilt and dread. Nadine returned an expressionless face to him then turned away, refusing to even glance at him again.

Lulu played well and she did score the winning goal in extra time, so she was thrilled that someone from her family had seen her play. Nadine wanted to get out of the place as soon as she could. She needed to go somewhere and let go of the awful feelings that were welling up inside her and about to spill over. She was hurt and betrayed, she wanted to cry and kick something. Most of all she wanted to be alone. She told Lulu she was tired and feeling unwell but Lulu begged her to stay for the presentation, which she did, but that was all she could manage and when she finally left she was feeling light-headed and nauseated. Driving away from the soccer ground her tears began to fall. Pulling over to the side of the road she put her head on the steering wheel and howled.

For the first time since she had been dancing she wanted to take a night off. Thinking it over she knew it would get back to Nick so she decided to push herself and go to work, hoping it would show him she was strong and wouldn't let his betrayal get under her skin.

Nick did not get in touch with her for a few days, and when he did she met his request to see her with a flat refusal. He continued to ring her and even called to see her at home but she refused to let him in. He sent flowers and chocolates and even a beautiful gold bangle. Nadine put the flowers in a vase, ate the chocolates and wore the bangle but she would not budge, refusing to even discuss their relationship with him.

Eventually he met her at uni, having waited for her in the car park. Nadine was about to open the car door when he approached and quietly whispered her name. The sound of his soft voice sent shivers through her body and it reminded her of the way she felt when he caressed her. Turning to face him she said, "Persistent aren't you."

"Yes. I need to talk to you Nadine, I miss you terribly, why won't you answer my calls?"

"You know very well why."

He moved closer to her, gently pushing her against the car and making her even more aware of how his firm, tanned body could affect her. Bending down he began to kiss her. She was so tempted to respond but remembering seeing him kiss his wife at the soccer ground, she put her hands on his chest and pushed him away.

"No Nick, it's over between us," she said. "You tricked me, you were dishonest with me, and you have treated me like a plaything not a serious partner. I know dancing is not the most respectable career but I have feelings and I don't want to be second best in anyone's life. It's all or nothing."

He stood looking at her and said, "Nadine, I love you."

"What about your wife, don't you love her?"

"Yes, I love her and I love you; it's possible to love more than one person at a time."

"Not me, I can't and I won't, I do not want to be in that kind of triangle. Please Nick, leave me alone and let me get on with my life."

Nadine turned and stepped into her car, quickly locking the doors and driving out of the car park, tears cascading down her cheeks again.

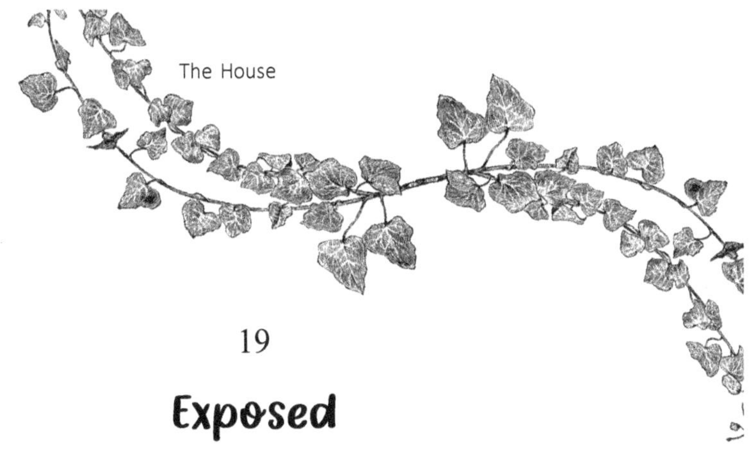

19

Exposed

Nadine was approaching the end of her studies and would soon be graduating. Also her twenty-first birthday was in two months' time. She started to think about her future knowing she could not continue her present way of life for much longer. She knew she had to make a plan and stick to it. The following week something happened which caused Nadine to quickly put her partly-thought-out plan into action.

She was on the stage for a second time that night and it was getting late, as she tossed her blonde hair over her right shoulder and hummed the tune of the song that was playing. It was one of her favourites, 'You Can Leave Your Hat On'. After midnight the venue always became busier and often the men were noisier and more intoxicated. Although the lights made it difficult to really see who was in the audience, sometimes a face would become illuminated for a brief moment as she turned and moved about on the stage. On this night a familiar face appeared to her right but only for a moment, then about five minutes later another familiar face came up close to the stage and she recognised a man who was a colleague of her father. He grinned at her then moved away to where two other men were standing. She was not sure but she thought the third man could have been her father.

'That's not good, that's really not good,' she said to herself, 'still, it was bound to happen sooner or later.'

That night at home she thought over what would probably happen next, knowing that the proverbial shit would hit the fan or all hell would break loose, one thing being much the same as the other.

It was her mother who contacted her first and demanded that Nadine meet her that day no matter what she had planned. Nadine invited her mother to her townhouse, where she had never been before as Nadine had always kept her address a secret.

Approaching the heavy ornate security gate at the entrance to the unit, Justine was amazed at the opulence of the building. Hedging and a manicured garden led to the heavy front door. Admiringly she noted that at least her daughter was living in a secure building. Before Justine had a chance to ring the bell, the door was opened and Nadine stood back allowing her mother to enter. Without saying a word she walked back into her home ushering her mother to a seat in the lounge room. Sitting opposite her daughter she blurted out in a strangled voice, "Why Nadine, why have you been doing something so awful? What is the matter with you, why have you done this? What will people say?"

"Because I've made a lot of money, lots of money very quickly and I will be able to do things with that money," Nadine answered testily. "Things I would never be able to do otherwise."

"But it's so disgusting; all those men looking at your body."

"It's not only men, women come too."

"I can't believe, after the type of upbringing you've had, that you would do such a thing. You have brought disgrace to the whole family. Your father is so ashamed of you, and to think that his friends saw you."

"I think he was there also."

"Your father? I don't think so. He was told by his friends that you were dancing in the all-together."

"Well I'm not certain but I thought I saw him too."

"No. He would never ever go to a place like that."

"Don't be so sure Mum; he is no angel — he's just as perverted as any other man."

"What do you mean?"

Nadine was so upset she decided it was time to show her mother what she thought of her lily-livered attitude and get a few things off her chest.

"Remember when I was young and I told you I didn't want to dance for him because he was doing things I didn't like when I danced? He touched me in places he shouldn't have, do you remember me telling you about that?" she taunted.

"Yes, but he said you were exaggerating, anyway what has that to do with this?"

"Mum, you might not equate one with the other but I do. You won't like me telling you this but he would go into the bedroom and close the door. One day I went in after him and I saw that he was standing in front of the mirror playing with himself and he asked me to stay and watch him. He put his arm out and started to move closer to me and I was scared because of the way he looked at me and that's when I decided never to be alone with him again. That's why I started going with Lulu to her soccer games."

"Are you trying to tell me that your father was—was--- well, I don't know what you are telling me, what are you saying?"

"I'm telling you that I think if I hadn't taken matters into my own hands it could have escalated and then who knows what would happen."

Nadine's mother walked around the townhouse crying on and off for the next hour or so until her husband arrived, when she immediately asked him about what Nadine had accused him of. He flatly denied it until Nadine stood up in front of him and related the episodes of his creepy behaviour and what followed.

"I was just an innocent girl then but now I'm much more aware of what some men are like and how they feel about sex. I know for sure sex should be between adults, not with naive children."

Her father, looking stunned, said, "What have you been up to? I suppose you have been having sex. Are you still a virgin?"

"No I'm not a virgin but that's none of your business. I'm an adult now."

"You should have been keeping yourself for your husband."

"Oh for god's sake Dad, sex is normal human behaviour and not unpleasant and dirty as you and Mum always implied. Being a virgin is just the way the body is before it begins to have sex. It's a stupid word anyway; we are built to have sex, it's all perfectly normal and healthy."

Nadine was angry and she wanted to hurt and shock her parents even more, so she continued in a taunting, aggressive way, not her usual manner of speaking. "What word do we use to describe a person before they have their first meal, or their first breath, or first haircut, or their first shit for that matter?"

"Nadine! Stop using such vulgar language, that's enough," said her mother, raising her voice and turning to look at her husband. "Is what Nadine says true? Did you do those inappropriate things to her?"

"I can't remember doing such things," he replied sheepishly.

"Mum, who do you believe, me or him?" Nadine demanded.

"I don't know what to believe," she answered sadly and began to cry again.

Nadine stood up and pointed towards the door, "I want you both to leave now. I have to work tonight and I like to rest for a few hours before I go."

They left, her mother still crying and her father looking awkward. Nadine was glad to see the back of them.

The following week she received a phone call from her mother who said, "Nadine, I do believe you. I have asked Lulu if she had anything to tell me about your father and she did."

"Oh no! What did he do to her?"

"Fortunately nothing too serious, but he had started frequently walking into the bathroom when she was showering and sitting on the edge of her bed watching her when she was dressing for soccer when I'm not there. She asked him to leave the room but he kept doing it and it made her feel very uncomfortable."

"Who knows what he was planning," Nadine said. "What are you going to do Mum?"

"I've left him. I'm not with him any more," her mother replied in a voice Nadine had never heard before. "I don't like him. I hate him. I'm staying with a friend at the moment and I want a divorce as soon as it can be arranged."

"What about the house, can you go back and live there?"

"No, it will have to be sold and we will divide the money so that I can buy a small place of my own."

Nadine was really surprised that her mother had made such a radical move but relieved that her mother had believed her. At the same time she felt some responsibility for the explosive events and destruction that had befallen her family.

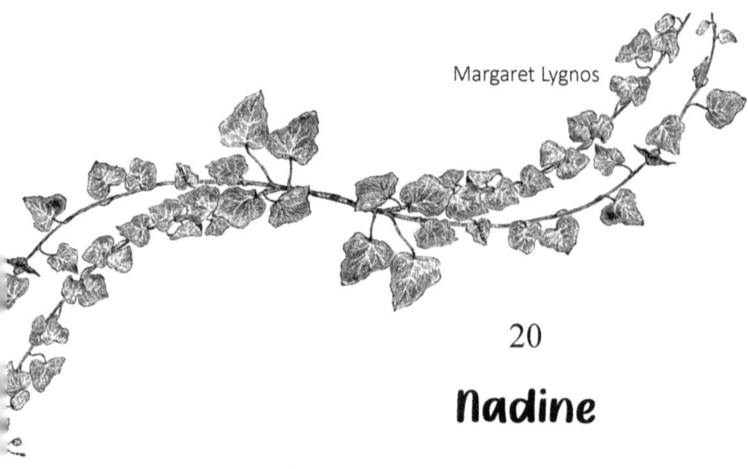

20

Nadine

Nadine knew it was time for her to continue with her plan: a plan not written down but a plan that had been circulating in her head for some time. She had graduated and her twenty-first birthday had been and gone. She had refused to celebrate her 'coming of age' with her family, feeling it would be too difficult after all the recent upheaval. Her townhouse was put in the hands of an agent and was let almost at once, so she purchased a one-way ticket to the UK. On the day she was to fly overseas she met her mother and Lulu for lunch. They were both upset that she was leaving but her mother was relieved she had given up dancing.

"What type of work will you do?" her mother wanted to know, scared it might be more dancing.

"I have a job with an international consultaning firm that provides professional assistance for businesses all over the world, but I'm having a month off first to do a bit of sightseeing around London," Nadine replied. "I might go to Scotland and Ireland as well and I might even go to France and Italy if I have time." Her mother looked relieved. During lunch Nadine gave Lulu a gift card and told her, "This is so you can always buy the best soccer shoes you want."

Then she handed her mother her car keys saying, "You can have my car, the insurance is paid and I have listed you as a driver, it's about time you had a decent car." Her mother up until now had driven an old bomb. Justine had tears in her eyes as Nadine kissed them both and quickly left the restaurant. A taxi was waiting for her at the kerbside. She hopped in and was off on her new adventure.

21

Lulu

My sister Nadine has gone away and I miss her so much. She is beautiful and so kind to me. She always listens to me and I can talk to her about anything. She had lunch with Mum and me before leaving for the airport to fly to London. Mum and I are both sad that she has gone away. She gave me a card with money to buy soccer shoes when I need them.

Dad didn't come to lunch — we don't see him any more and Mum doesn't mention him. I'm not sure what has happened because Mum won't tell me.

There is a boy at school who says he loves me but I don't know what to say to him. If Nadine was here I could talk to her about him because she has had a boyfriend. I want to talk to Mum but I know she won't like me asking about boys. I miss Nadine. I wish she hadn't gone away.

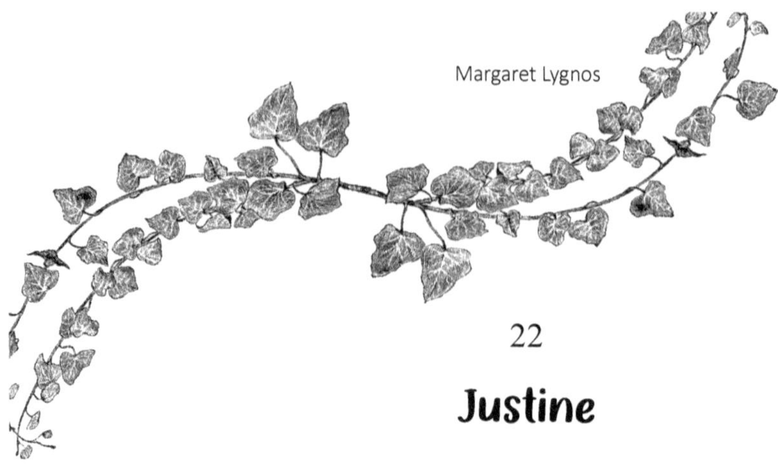

22

Justine

Unfortunately things did not go as planned for Justine, who found the shocking revelation about her husband extremely traumatic, causing her to fall into a pit of depression which made her unfit for work for some time. Waiting for the house to be sold she tried to devote her time to Lulu and finding a place to rent. The sale of the house went through but there was no money left over because they still had a huge mortgage. Tom had borrowed on the value of the house to prop up his business and the house was basically owned by the bank. Justine became even more depressed when this was revealed and although she needed to work, she was not in a fit state to do so, which meant she lost her lucrative weekend job.

Unable to stay indefinitely with her friend who needed the room for her sick mother, Justine and Lulu spent a few nights in the car. Realising that they were now homeless she was more than grateful when a local government employee found her in the car early one morning and directed her to Assisting Women In Crisis, where she was interviewed by Marcia.

23

Bethany and Justine

The two women got on well together from the very beginning and quickly worked out how they could support each other. Along with the school drop off and pick up, the cooking and housework, they found they were able to share almost everything. They tended the vegetable garden and maintained the cottage garden at the front. At weekends they often caught public transport to watch Lulu play soccer. Neither of them had a car and they could not afford to buy one. Justine's husband Tom had taken Nadine's car and sold it along with his own, and was now driving the old bomb that Justine had driven for years. The only money Justine had was a fortnightly payment from the government but pressure was being put on her to start looking for work.

As Bethany had been a nurse and Justine had been a ward clerk, they wondered if they could find a job to share, maybe in a clinic or medical centre because they were both familiar with medical terminology and could both use computers. That was their goal, so each of them began to get in touch with various people from the past who they thought might be able to help them. By sheer chance the receptionist at the nursing home where Bethany job shared had taken another job. Bethany immediately approached the manager and asked if she would consider her for the position.

"Part time or full time?" asked the manager.

"I would like to continue to job share if possible, and the woman I would share with is very experienced, more than me actually."

"Tell her to ring and make an appointment, I will certainly consider the two of you if she meets my requirements," The manager replied.

Justine had her interview and was given the position so she and Bethany between them worked out a roster that suited them both and suited the nursing home. The two women were very relieved to have secured the position between them, giving each some certainty for the future.

24

The Dress-up

The three children had a lot of fun together and after several days of whispered secrets they surprised their mothers by putting on a play. It was a simple story about a woman who believed in fairies and spent her time searching in her garden hoping to find them. Lulu played the woman and Sam and Skye were an elf and a fairy. The children dressed up appropriately, Sam had a green peaked cap on his head and a green jacket. Skye wore wings and an old pink tutu and Lulu had on an old dress belonging to her mother and a long black wig. Bethany recognised the dress-up clothes as the ones she had been given along with the children's toys. Both mothers laughed as Lulu chased the two younger children under chairs and tables decorated to look like shrubbery. Finally she located them in a pretend cave behind the couch. The three of them sang a funny song they had written together, took a bow, and thanked the audience for attending. The mothers laughed, clapped and hugged the children because it had been so much fun and had made them all happy.

"Is that your wig?" Bethany asked Justine.

"No I've never seen it before. I assumed it was yours," she replied.

When the children were getting ready for bed Bethany asked the children about the black wig.

"It was in the bag with all the other dress-up clothes," Skye told her mother.

Bethany took the bag out of the wardrobe and tipped the contents onto the floor. Picking up each piece of clothing she replaced them one by one back into the bag, all except the wig and a pair of over-large sunglasses.

25

Nadine in London

Arriving at Heathrow airport, Nadine checked into the Hilton hotel for a few nights to give herself a chance to adjust to the new time zone, get over her jet lag and search for a place to live. She perused the rental apartments available in London via the internet and after two nights she took the train to Earls Court to view two places which appealed to her. The first one, which was in a street opposite the train station, was ideal so she took it and did not bother to view any other. It was a small cottage which had been part of a stable attached to a large house and was now converted into a small, comfortable dwelling of high quality. Being close to transport was important as Nadine didn't intend to buy a car, and had been told the underground and the buses were frequent and used by most Londoners. The following day she checked out of the hotel, caught the train to Earls Court, dumped her few belongings in the cottage and hopped on a bus heading to the city for sight-seeing and the beginning of her new life.

The bus stopped close to the Victoria and Albert Museum so she hopped off and went in to spend most of the day wandering the halls and galleries of the magnificent building. Finding herself at last in the hugely decorative Victorian cafeteria, she ordered a pot of tea and scones, thinking wistfully that her mother would probably have loved to be there with her. 'Maybe I can bring her here one day,' she said to herself.

26

The Garage

Sam and Skye wanted to ride their bikes in the nearby safe riding track frequented by local children.

"Where are our bikes Mum?" Sam asked.

"Well if they're not here they must be still at your father's place."

"No our bikes aren't in the bike rack."

"Maybe they have been put somewhere else; have you looked in the garage?"

"The garage is locked and we can't get in," Sam answered.

"Well next time you're there have a look through the window. That's the only place I can think they could be."

The two children went to their father's place the following weekend and when they returned they told their mother that they had looked in the garage and both of their bikes had been hung on the wall opposite the window and could just be seen behind the old white car.

"Oh, so the car is still there, I could have had it all this time. My goodness your father is a selfish, thoughtless man sometimes."

Instead of waiting to see Joe when he next had the children, she rang him that night. "Hello Joe. I have a few questions to ask you."

"Okay go ahead, what do you want?" he said gruffly.

"One thing, the children would like their bikes."

"Okay, that's not a problem," he said.

"Secondly, why is the white car locked in the garage? I could have been driving it all this time instead of catching buses on cold winter mornings in the rain."

"My mother was driving it when she was here and when she left I just put it in the garage."

"Where has your mother gone?"

"My parents have both gone back to New Zealand. They decided they didn't like Australia after all."

"Don't you mean after all the trouble they caused?" How selfish and careless they both are."

"They might still return; I don't know what they are doing," he replied.

"So now you have the house to yourself, perhaps we can sell it and divide the money between us, plus I would like the white car," Bethany said.

"I'm not selling the house, but you can come home now, can't you?" Joe asked.

"No. Not ever. We've separated Joe and I want a divorce and my share of the house," Bethany answered calmly, not wanting to argue with him.

"Won't you consider coming home Bethany?" he pleaded.

"I said no and I'm not going to change my mind. You behaved very badly towards me when your parents were here and it showed me what type of man you really are. I thought I knew you but I was wrong. I certainly know you now and I don't want to be with you any more. I can never forgive you."

"I think you'll change your mind in time; you'll find it hard living on your own, you'll need me sooner or later."

"I'm going to hang up now Joe. Please bring the children's bikes so we can go for rides together."

"How? Do you have a bike?"

"Yes, I found an old bike here and it's the only means of transport I have, otherwise I catch the bus, which is okay if it's not raining. I'd still like the white car." She ended the phone call and wondered how long she would have to wait for the bikes to arrive and if he even cared about them walking in the rain.

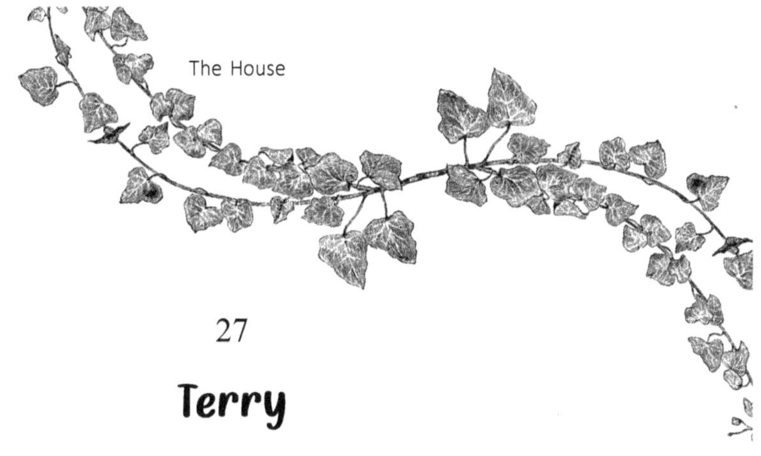

27

Terry

Marcia rang Bethany to tell her there was a third woman who would be joining them soon.

"She is older than you two and her circumstances are quite different, but she is in great need of a place to live and some female company. I will bring her tomorrow night at about five."

"When you come, would you like to stay for dinner with us?" Bethany asked.

"Yes, that would be lovely," Marcia replied.

Marcia arrived with Terry just before five pm the next day. She had very little luggage but she did have a little white fluffy dog with her called Pippy.

"I forgot to mention the dog when I spoke to you," said Marcia apologetically.

"I don't think any of us would mind having a dog, would we?" Bethany said looking at the children.

"Yay!" Sam yelled, "We love dogs don't we Skye?" Skye agreed and the three children began to fuss over the dog, throwing a ball and waiting for her to retrieve it. Unused to children, the little dog hid behind Terry, looking uncertainly at the noisy children.

Taking Terry by the hand, Marcia drew her into the house and with an arm around her shoulders she introduced her. "This is Terry."

The women greeted each other and Bethany and Justine, who had prepared a room, carried her luggage and the dog's bed into the bedroom for her. Terry looked around and said she liked the front garden which she could see from her bedroom window. Sitting heavily on the bed she slumped forward and said quietly. "This will do very nicely. I don't need much, just the simple things."

She straightened up, making an obvious attempt to appear okay, then changing her demeanour she quickly stood up looking at the other women and said, "What can I do to help you?"

"Nothing tonight, just get yourself settled and we'll have dinner at six," Bethany answered. "We want you to feel relaxed and comfortable with us."

Marcia had brought two bottles of wine to drink with dinner so the mood was light and friendly. Terry refused the wine saying that it didn't agree with her, and eventually Bethany related the conversation she'd had with her husband Joe regarding the sale of their house.

"He says he won't sell it and has asked me to return home to live with him because his parents have gone back to Auckland. I don't even have to think about what he's suggesting, I'm never going back to him."

Looking at Marcia she asked, "Can he refuse to sell, or can I make him sell?"

Marcia said she would look into the details of the house and get back to her as soon as possible.

The following morning when Justine was working Bethany showed Terry around, pointing out all that they had done to the place since living there. Terry was surprised to see the chickens and so was the dog, which had never seen a live chicken before. The timid little dog quickly realised that there was some fun to be had in their new home and poked the tip of his nose through the wire fence, fascinated by the chickens. Terry was impressed with the vegetable garden and the vegies that were growing successfully.

"We share everything but if there is anything you are particularly good at or love doing, you are welcome to do it."

"I love baking and cooking in general and I can even make bread if you would like me to," she replied happily.

Terry fitted in really well and as she was retired and liked to be at home, she offered her child minding services. As well as baking she was good at sewing and said she would be happy to share her dressmaking and mending skills with the other women.

One night when the children were all in bed, Terry began to share her story with the other two women. The subject had come up but Bethany and Justine did not want to intrude, knowing she would probably tell them when she felt comfortable with them. Now that she was feeling at ease with her house mates she felt she could tell them why she had ended up in the house with them.

Sitting on the couch opposite Justine and Bethany, clasping her hands in her lap, Terry took a deep breath and began to tell her long, sad story.

"I was born in Tasmania and came to Melbourne before I was twenty after my fiance jilted me a week before our wedding. Luckily I found a position with a government department as a filing clerk. That was the best job I could get as I had only worked in a supermarket in Tasmania. It was very expensive to rent in Melbourne so I had to find a second job on the weekends to help make ends meet. I worked in a cafe for eight hours each Saturday and Sunday."

Filled with emotion, Terry's voice became dry and croaky so she got up and went to the kitchen sink to get a drink of water. Sitting down again, she looked at the two women whom she happily realised had become supportive friends already.

"We don't want you to upset yourself Terry. If it's too traumatic we will understand," said Bethany.

"It's okay, it's okay, I want to tell you."

Continuing, she explained that because she wanted a better job, she attended night school to learn some professional office skills. During the time when she was studying at night, working as a filing clerk and serving coffee in the cafe, she met a man called Eric. He was a customer at the cafe who bothered her until she agreed to go out with him. They began dating regularly and she really fell for him. He was older than her and quite experienced with life in general and particularly in bed.

Eventually she finished her night school studies, was promoted to a receptionist position then private secretary, all in the same department. As she was earning better money she was able to give up the weekend work. After knowing each other for two years, she and Eric were married and then things began to change. Eric was very jealous and wouldn't allow Terry to go anywhere without him except to work. He bought a house for them without even telling her and furnished it with his choice of furniture. He even insisted on going shopping with her to buy her clothes and, unbelievably, he would not consent to her cutting her long hair. They were both pleased when she became pregnant but Eric seemed to be spending a lot of time away from her and sometimes stayed out all night. When she asked him where he had been he refused to tell her. She asked him if he had been with another woman, he hit her across the face causing a black eye and a blood nose. She had never expected to be treated like that and cried in despair as she realised the awful life she was leading. Although he apologised, it happened again several times.

Terry gave birth to a baby girl called Irene and they were both over the moon for a short time. Without consulting Terry, Eric bought a mixed business in the northern suburbs of Melbourne and informed Terry she would be working in the shop with him. Terry had intended going back to her job once the baby was old enough but Eric said she would not be going back to work.

It wasn't easy looking after a baby and serving in a shop, and most of the time she was there on her own. Eric opened the shop in the morning and once Terry had fed the baby he disappeared for the day, sometimes coming home for dinner, sometimes not. She never knew when he would turn up.

"I had to shut the shop occasionally if the baby needed attention and as she got older she was awake longer and I couldn't just leave her in the pram. One day Eric came home when I had to close the shop to attend to Irene. He was very angry with me and we had a big argument about it and he hit me again.

A few days after that incident, a woman came to the shop looking for him; she had been given the address by someone who knew Eric. She asked me if I could give her his contact number because she was pregnant with his child and wanted him to take responsibility and marry her.

"I almost fainted but I didn't let on that Eric was my husband," Terry said. "I was really upset but I somehow managed to keep my cool although I was on the verge of breaking down."

"What did he say when you told him?" asked Justine.

"He denied it, naturally, and said it was a mixup and that one of his friends who was married had been seeing the woman and had called himself Eric so his wife wouldn't know. I knew he was lying because it was the stupidest, most childish, thing he had ever said to me. I couldn't argue with him, there was no point, but I knew then that I had ruined my life by marrying him and I had to get away."

"Did you get away from him?" asked Bethany.

"It wasn't easy because I didn't have any close friends, he had made sure of that, and the only person I could go to was my mother in Tasmania. I didn't have any of my own money so I kept back a little money every week from the shop; it took months and months before I had enough to pay my fare. I went by taxi to the airport and with a sigh of relief boarded the plane."

"You must have felt liberated when the plane took off," said Justine.

"I did, and as soon as I reached Tasmania I rang my mother from the airport. She came to collect me and I went home to my village where I had grown up. After I told her the story she cried and said it was like history being repeated only that my father had been worse than Eric. I had never met my father, Mum had always refused to talk about him."

Suddenly Terry stopped talking and got up to make a pot of tea for the three of them. Waiting for the kettle to boil she gazed out into the garden where she could see the hens doing their stepping and scratching routine as they looked for something tasty to eat in the soil. Smiling to herself she removed a cake tin from the cupboard and took out a raspberry slice that she had baked the day before. Carrying a tray to the other women she sat and poured the tea.

The women drank their tea and complimented Terry on her cooking before she resumed the story. Terry said she and the baby were happy with her mother and that she was able to look for a job because her mother offered to babysit. Terry went for an interview and was told on the spot that the position was hers and that she could start as soon as possible. Thrilled, she rushed home to her mother who met her at the garden gate with a look of fear on her face.

In a troubled voice she uttered, "He's here, your husband is here, he tracked you down but he is being very pleasant."

Terry felt her stomach drop and her heart began to beat rapidly.

"Oh no, why couldn't he leave me alone?"

Eric was at the door holding baby Irene. "Hello Terry dear, have you had a nice break?" he said sarcastically.

Terry stared at him with disbelief but didn't answer.

"It's time to go home now. We're booked on a plane to Melbourne in the morning."

She thought to herself 'I'm not going anywhere with you' and turned to follow her mother inside but Eric grabbed her arm and pulled her towards him. He was still holding Irene in his arms as he said to her, "you will come with me tomorrow and if you refuse I will take Irene with me and you will never see her again." His words made her stop dead in her effort to get away from him. Then he added "and I will burn your mother's house down with you both inside."

Terry had to stop telling her story there because Bethany's little boy Sam called out from the bedroom for his mother. Bethany went to him and didn't return to the living room, so Terry said she would continue with her awful story another time.

28

Nick

The next Saturday when Lulu was playing soccer they all went to the game except Terry, who stayed home to bake pies for dinner. Before Lulu began her game she was approached by a handsome young man who addressed her by her name.

"Hello Lulu, are you playing today?"

"Yes that's why I'm here, to play."

"How is your sister Nadine?" he enquired.

"She's fine, how do you know my sister?"

"She is a friend of mine and we have lost contact. Where is she living these days?" he asked.

"She has gone to England to live, we don't know when she will be back. She does ring us every week."

"Would you be able to give me her phone number?"

"No, I don't think I should give her phone number to you because I don't know who you are."

Lulu was toying with the idea of giving him the number when she heard the coach calling the team onto the ground so she left him standing. Nick watched the beautiful young girl as she sprinted over to her teammates to begin their warmup. "So beautiful, so like Nadine," he said to himself.

After the game when they were going home, Justine asked Lulu "Who was that man I saw you talking to before the game?"

"He said he was a friend of Nadine and he wanted her phone number in England."

"You didn't give it to him, did you?" her mother asked anxiously.

"No, I was not sure that I should."

"Good," said her mother, "you did the right thing. We don't know him and if he is from her recent workplace we don't want to know him. If he ever approaches you again, tell him to speak to me."

29

Terry Continues Her Story

Several nights later when the children were in bed Terry resumed her story about her husband Eric.

"Naturally I had to return to Melbourne with him, I couldn't risk being separated from Irene or anything happening to my mother," she bagan. "As we sat in the plane he told me he had a buyer for our shop and that I would be going back to work. I was completely surprised about the sale of the business but at the same time I was pleased I wouldn't be stuck there any more. I was able to get a job through contacts with the people who I had worked with previously and Irene went to childcare.

"Eric started a little business repairing washing machines, fridges, vacuum cleaners and anything else he was asked to do. I earned good money and paid for everything, including the rent on an old house in North Melbourne. The house we had previously owned had been sold to buy the shop apparently — all news to me."

Justine leant forward and said "You were frightened of him weren't you Terry?"

"Frightened and reduced to a pathetic, depressed, sad individual. My work colleagues knew I was in trouble but I never told them the truth about my situation at home. Every morning Eric would drive me to work and we dropped Irene at childcare on the way. What he did during the day I didn't know, but I'm sure it was mostly gambling. Sometimes if he had a big win we would go somewhere really expensive for dinner and he would spend up big and pretend to be a millionaire. On Saturday I cleaned the house while he did our shopping with my money. On

Sunday I cooked food for the following week and drank wine which he encouraged me to drink. He bought me a cask of white wine every Saturday and by Sunday evening I was sloshed."

"Is that why you don't drink now?" asked Bethany.

"Yes. I won't touch alcohol again. It's very addictive, better I don't indulge."

"You've had a really awful time, haven't you?" Justine added sympathetically."

"Yes and it didn't improve. Poor little Irene saw and heard some dreadful things and she was scared of her father. He never hit her but he often roared at both of us and she would run to me for comfort, and if she couldn't get to me she hid under her bed right over next to the wall.

One morning when I went to work following a beating and I was sporting a black eye and bruising on my arms, the boss called me into his office and offered to help me. I thanked him but I lied saying that I was okay and I'd had an accident. Always at the back of my mind was Eric saying he would take Irene from me and burn my mother's house down."

"What made him hurt you like that?"

"That time it was quite serious because he discovered that I was taking the Pill. I didn't want to bring another child into our awful family but he wanted another child, preferably a son. He threw the pills down the toilet and belted me. Irene was hiding under the bed and he raped me as she lay quivering underneath us. He was a cruel bastard and I hated him. I just didn't have the strength to stand up to him and certainly couldn't leave him. I wished he would die and I even wondered if I could kill him without being found out. I considered Ratsak, oleander leaves, ground-up glass, a knife, all sorts of things, but I didn't have the courage to do anything. I would have been found out and what would have happened to my baby girl? We bought another house — well, he did. I had nothing to do with buying the house, I didn't even see it until the day we moved in. It had a nice garden and some beautiful trees. He bought a swing set for Irene and an outdoor table and chairs where we ate dinner on summer evenings. That was all okay at first but then he became obsessed with the idea of another child and I was repeatedly raped. I call it rape because I never consented and always said no. He said that because I was his wife he could do whatever he wanted. Fortunately I didn't get pregnant and that made him angry. He forced me to consult a doctor who diagnosed stress and anxiety as a possible reason. He thought that was rubbish and continued to have sex with me against my will. He often woke me overnight, making it difficult to go back to sleep and I had to get up at six am on work days."

Terry stopped talking and looked over at the shocked faces of Justine and Bethany. She thought to herself 'they probably don't believe me or they think I'm stupid because I didn't leave him, maybe both.'

Getting to her feet she sighed and announced. "I think I'll call it a night, as they say, I'm finding it quite draining talking about Eric tonight, it brings a lot of the pain and trauma back."

"Terry, did he really treat you so badly, could any man be so awful to a woman and yet want her to stay with him?" Justine asked, not disbelieving but incredulous at such behaviour.

"Oh yes, but at least he didn't kill me, and I did think he would sometimes. If it was not for Irene I think I would have killed myself," she answered sadly.

The three women went to bed. Terry went to sleep easily because although she was upset, she was free of Eric; the other two women not able to settle wondering about what Terry had told them. Could it all be true? Why did she stay? Surely she could have left him somehow?

The next time the three women were together Terry told them more of her story.

It had become possible for her to retire early and she was entitled to quite a large amount of money. Eric wanted her to retire because she would get a large payout. So Terry retired, Eric bought an expensive new car with her money and after a month decided to go to Ireland to see his elderly parents whom he had not seen for years. Terry was alone at last and if she had been sensible this would have been her chance to get free of Eric, but she did not. When Eric returned he had changed and become a born-again Catholic. Because they had been married in the Registry Office he declared they were not married in the eyes of God. A priest in Ireland had told him they should very quickly marry in a Catholic church.

When Terry reminded Eric that she was not a Catholic and couldn't be married in the church, he went off to consult a local priest. The priest announced that she could convert and all she had to do was visit him and he would tutor her. Terry refused, so the priest began visiting her and tried to persuade her to convert because, he said, they were living in sin.

"I don't care. I have endured an awful existence with Eric and I will not do what he is demanding this time, it's silly."

"He wants to marry you properly," the priest argued.

"I would be lying if I did and said those things you are asking me to do," Terry said, thinking that the priest was starting to bully her just like Eric.

"It's very relevant for Eric and his faith."

"It's not relevant to me, you are not relevant to me and your church is not relevant to me, and god has never aided me."

When Eric heard from the priest he was so angry he was about to hit Terry when she said to him, "So your religion allows you to bash your wife does it?" Surprisingly he dropped his lifted hand.

Terry regretted leaving work and Eric, she discovered, was involved in illegal gambling in which he took bets and was visited by men putting on bets or picking up winnings every day. She worried about her money and wondered how much they still had. Her life was filled with constant anxiety caused by his unpredictable selfish behaviour and demands.

30

Bethany's House

Marcia rang Bethany a few days later with some bad news about the family house where she had lived with her husband Joe and their two children Sam and Skye.

"The house was never in your name, it is owned outright by Joe's parents. It seems they put the deposit on the house and they have contributed to the mortgage and now they want to sell it because your marriage has failed," Marcia said regretfully. "If the house is sold I might be able to get some money for you because it was the family home and you did contribute to mortgage payments and the upkeep etc."

"Yes I'm sure when I was working my money was paid towards the mortgage. I never checked where it was going because I trusted Joe and we never went without any necessities. Bloody hell, I didn't expect this. It looks like I'll be here much longer than I first thought."

Although Bethany was working part-time she was not able to save much at all. Whenever she managed to put away a few hundred dollars it was swallowed up by a utility bill, new shoes or clothes for the children (and they were expensive) or other requirements. Money was not wasted but between the women they existed happily most of the time although they lived a frugal life.

Bethany had a dream one night from which she awoke and couldn't get back to sleep. Going to the kitchen she prepared a warm drink of milk and honey which she took back to bed to sip and ruminate on the meaning of her dream and the awful suggestion it threw up.

She had dreamt she was driving somewhere when a car being driven by a fearsome creature jumped out of nowhere, waved a black wig in her face, laughed and flew off into the distance.

'What am I seeing, what does this mean, could it mean what I think it does?' she thought to herself. It kept her awake for ages, the milk did not help but she did eventually drift off into a semisleep just before the alarm shrieked at six am.

31

Terry

When Bethany returned from taking the three children to school she found the cat Queenie sitting on the fence watching Terry and her dog Pippy outside talking to the chickens as she scattered seeds for their breakfast. Terry had made a bench with four bricks at each end and a plank between in order to sit and observe the chickens as they scratched and played each day.

"They are so entertaining, I love watching them," said Terry. "Some of them are very bossy and then they settle down next to the one they have just bossed and sleep together in the sun."

"Just like families I suppose," Bethany replied.

"Not mine though," Terry answered sardonically.

"No, yours wasn't like that. I don't know how you put up with it."

"Bethany, I was browbeaten and scared. I think if it had not been for my job and Irene I wouldn't have coped. I existed, that's all, I lived day to day hoping things would improve."

"Did things ever improve?"

"Yes and no. When Irene finished school she went to a rural university to get away from Melbourne and her father. He was angry and I was heartbroken, but at the same time I understood why she did it. I hardly saw her after that and when she graduated she went to New Zealand with friends and worked over there. I missed her so much but I will never blame her for escaping. She asked me to join her but Eric was aware of this and prevented me from getting a passport. Eventually she went to the UK and is still there. I haven't seen her for years."

"You must miss her though."

"I miss her terribly and I would have been visiting her now but I'm broke."

"What happened after the priest and the marriage business? Did you go ahead with it?"

"No. Eric lost interest quite suddenly and I think the priest lost interest too. Eric got sick and became depressed and I hoped he would get sicker and die but he rallied and things continued as before. Then we had the disappointment of Irene leaving home and he began gambling heavily, his little business had ceased; he started to get very tired in the afternoons and often had a snooze in his lounge chair. He drank cans of beer one after another and smoked cigarettes continuously — the house always smelt awful — then he would fall asleep. Often he fell asleep with a can in his hand and it would spill on the carpet along with an ash tray full of butts."

"So you looked after him I suppose?"

"Yes I did, but he organised his medication and kept it locked in a cupboard, I think he imagined I might have tampered with it."

"Is he still alive?"

"No, he died in his lounge chair one afternoon after he was in too much pain to get up and get the medication to put under his tongue. Not that it would have saved him though. He had a massive heart attack and called for me to help him. I was just outside the back door putting beer cans in the bin and I heard him calling. I entered the kitchen but I did nothing because I could see that he was dying and at last I would be free. My heart was beating rapidly because I knew I was being cruel but I pretended not to see him and I went back outside to water the garden and let him die. I didn't ring an ambulance until I was sure he was dead. I had always told myself that I had to outlive him and I have. Awful aren't I?" she gulped.

Bethany stared at Terry as she digested what she had just heard, wondering if she would have been able to do something which seemed so inhuman. Then considering Eric and his cruel treatment of Terry she answered, "Not really, I can understand why you wouldn't help him and it sounds like a massive heart attack; who knows he may not have survived anyway."

The two women returned to the house carrying the brown eggs laid that day and sat down sharing a pot of tea. Bethany told Terry about her dream and what was worrying her about the wig and also the fact that her house was in her in-laws names.

"Before you ask Joe about your house I think you should casually ask about the wig and where it came from. If you argue about the house he might not talk to you about anything else," Terry suggested.

"Yes, I'll try to ask him nicely without him thinking it's an interrogation," Bethany replied.

As it happened, Joe called in that evening bringing Sam and Skye's two bicycles. The children were so happy to have their bikes they took them outside and rode around and around the house from the front garden to the back yard over and over again. The chickens, which had been let out, squawked and scattered in four directions as the dog ran after them barking with excitement.

"They'll sleep well tonight," said Joe as he stood with Bethany at the kitchen window, watching Terry pick up Pippy to prevent a slaughter. "While they are busy can I speak to you in private?"

"Yes, come into my room," said Bethany. "Actually I want to ask you something." Once in the room Bethany took a bag from the cupboard and tipped the contents onto the floor at Joe's feet. "Joe this bag of dress-up clothes you brought here for the children had a black wig inside, do you know where it came from?"

Joe looked down at the pile of clothes but did not answer straight away. He seemed to be thinking deeply before he answered, "I found it in the children's bedroom. Why?"

"I was just wondering, it doesn't belong to me, I had never seen it until the children dressed up for a concert they did one night."

"Well it doesn't really matter where it came from, they can have it," he said.

"Okay that's all I wanted to ask you. What was it you wanted to say to me?"

Joe moved towards Bethany as if to take her in his arms, but not wanting him to touch her she stepped backwards, causing her to fall onto the bed.

"Bethany," he said, "I really want you to move back in with me, I miss you and I think we should try to fix our relationship."

Bethany rolled onto her side and hurried awkwardly off the bed, not wanting him to misunderstand her in any way.

"Joe it's not going to happen, you made it very obvious how you really feel about me when your mother was ruling your life and when you refused to listen to me regarding your father."

"I'm sorry about that. Can't we put it behind us?"

"Why? Do you believe me now? Do you believe what I told you about your father?"

"I didn't say that, just come home will you?"

"You must be joking. You even left me in the hospital when I was ready to be discharged and you didn't bring the children to see me, you changed the locks; you were cruel and I can't forget that."

"Surely you would rather be in our home than in this shabby old house living with a bunch of losers?"

"They are certainly not losers but good women who have been mistreated by men who professed to love them. Which brings me to the next item on the agenda — the house."

"What about the house?"

"Who does it actually belong to?"

"Us, of course."

"Us meaning you and your parents?"

"And you."

"The solicitor informed me last week that the house is in the names of your parents, not you or me."

"I'm sure that's a mistake that can be fixed," he lied, his face turning bright red.

Bethany moved quickly to the door, opened it and called to Sam and Skye, "Your father is going home, come and say goodbye."

Then she walked with him to the front door and closed it after him. The two children ran back to the living room and Bethany leaned against the closed front door and shook her head from side to side. To no-one she said, "He's not going to like the next thing that's about to happen."

32

The Garage

During the school holidays when it was raining the three children asked if they could play in the garage in the back yard. The old building was quite large and had double wooden doors at the front and a door with windows on one side. The double doors were locked with a padlock but the side door was unlocked. This was where Justine had found the gardening tools and garden furniture that she had used to decorate the front veranda. There was an old car parked right up against the locked double doors and behind the car there was plenty of space. One side held shelving from floor to ceiling and on the opposite wall there was a work bench with a peg board containing all types of small tools hanging and carefully outlined in black paint. A huge old wardrobe with locked doors was on the back wall.

Lulu and Skye began opening the boxes that filled the shelves while Sam tried the car doors, hoping to sit in the car and pretend to drive it. When he found he could not get into it he joined the girls and began rummaging in the boxes looking for a car key.

"Look at this," said Lulu holding up a box, "It's full of old keys."

"This one has some really old coins in it," said Skye holding out another.

"Are there any car keys?" Sam asked.

Lulu sifted through the keys and produced two on a key ring which appeared to be old car keys.

"Do you think these would open the car door? Let's give it a go."

She inserted the first key into the lock.

"Hey presto, it's open!" she yelled. The three of them climbed in and Lulu, because she was the oldest, sat in the driver's seat and put the key into the ignition.

"It fits." She turned the key: nothing. "The car is probably too old to work," she announced.

"I bet someone could make it work," said Skye.

"Yeah when I grow up I'll make it work," said Sam.

"'I hope it's sooner than that," Lulu replied, laughing.

Over the kitchen table at dinner time the children told their mothers about the things they had discovered in the garage.

"There are so many old and unusual things in there, all kept in boxes and drawers. There are even old coins and medals," Lulu announced.

"Well everything belongs to Marcia, so we should tell her if you find anything valuable," Justine told them.

"Will you come and have a look Mum?" asked Lulu.

After dinner they all went to the garage to have a look at what the children had discovered.

"Some of these coins and medals are very old and two of the medals are from the Crimean and Boer wars so are probably quite valuable."

"Mum, look at this car, it's really cool but it doesn't work any more."

"That's an old Holden," said Justine, then added, "It appears to be in good condition, it could probably be started with a bit of work. It might just need some petrol. I'll speak to Marcia next time she contacts me."

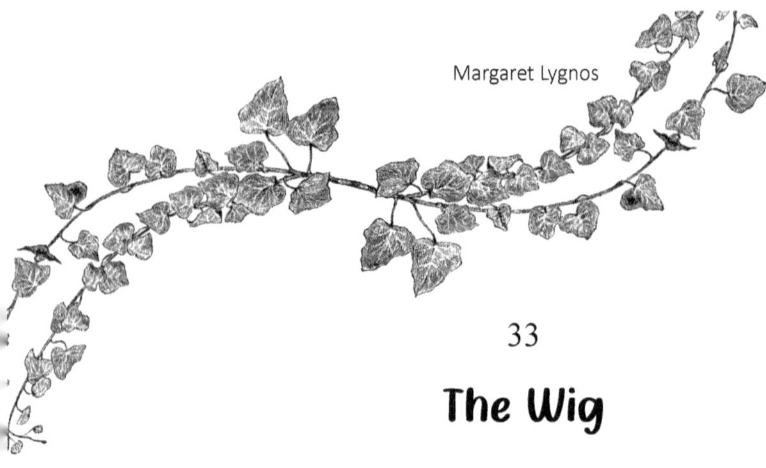

33

The Wig

Bethany contacted Marcus, the policeman who was investigating her hit and run. After listening to what she had to say about the wig and the driver of the car that had hit her, he made an appointment to visit her at home.

"This is the wig I found in with the children's dress-up clothes," Bethany said as she turned the bag upside down allowing the contents to drop to the floor. Each piece of clothing fell out along with the wig and the pair of overly large sunglasses.

"That *is* interesting" said Marcus.

"What is?"

"The big glasses — remember I told you the person driving the car had long black hair and sunglasses?"

"Yes I remember."

"Well I'm not sure if I told you, they were big sunglasses."

"No, just sunglasses?"

"I'll take these and compare them to the photos I have from the CCTV cameras in the nearby streets on the day of the hit and run," Marcus said as he put the two articles into a bag.

Bethany experienced a sinking feeling in her gut as she realised the seriousness of what was being suggested by the two items. Taking a big breath she uttered, "It's very likely to have been someone from my household driving the car isn't it, and that's very worrying. Someone wanted to cause me harm or kill me, but which one I wonder? I'm guessing it's probably my mother-in-law."

"Maybe, but don't jump to conclusions," Marcus said. "We need more evidence than we have."

"Well, the car is locked in the garage at my husband's address I hope you can have a good look at it. If it's damaged on the front left panel and we have the wig and glasses, then at least we will know it was probably that white car that hit me."

"When and if I have established that it is the same car, I will get you to view the CCTV footage with me and try to find anything that will give us a lead. Because you know the three people you think could be involved, you may see something that will identify one of them."

"Not very nice is it?" Bethany said sadly.

"No it's not nice at all, it's horrible, but I'm determined to get to the bottom of it, then you can put it behind you and get on with your life again."

"Thank you Marcus, I'm sure it will be my mother-in-law," Bethany replied, holding back tears. "From the moment she set foot in Melbourne she made it clear she didn't like me."

Marcus liked Bethany and as he drove away he felt sympathy for her situation and also a little protective towards her. He felt she was a woman who deserved justice for the hit and run, the injury and the abuse by the awful man she had married. He really wanted to solve the mystery of the driver who had struck and injured her and fled the scene.

34

Lulu

On Wednesdays after school Lulu went home with her friend Amy who was also in her soccer team. Amy's mother drove the two girls to soccer training then later drove Lulu home. Lulu was looking a bit downcast when she entered the living room.

"What's wrong, darling?" asked Justine.

"There is a trip to New South Wales with the soccer team next month and I had to tell the coach I wouldn't be able to go," Lulu uttered quietly.

"Why can't you go?" her mother asked.

"Because it will cost $400 each and I know we don't have money to spare."

"Oh I see," her mother replied sadly.

"We have to pay for a bus, accommodation, food and a special jacket," Lulu told her mother. "Some of the parents are going too. I wish you and I could go."

"Let me think about it and we'll talk tomorrow," Justine answered, feeling she was letting her daughter down and wondering how on earth she could find the money. She had just under $400 saved at the moment but there were bills coming up and she had to contribute to them equally. In the past money had not been a problem, she would have just handed over the $400 without a second thought. Presently the best she would have was $100 to contribute to the trip, not nearly enough. It worried her and kept her awake that night.

In the morning she asked Lulu how much money was on the gift card her sister Nadine had given her. She imagined there was something still outstanding although stupidly they had never checked the initial amount.

"Give me the card, Lulu, and I will find out today what money is still there for you to spend," Justine said hopefully.

Not sure how to proceed, Justine took the card to the bank and a teller showed her how to check the amount.

"Oh my god I had no idea there was that much money there," she told the teller. There was an amount of $1750 and they had only bought soccer shoes twice. Justine was shocked to think that Nadine had been able to give Lulu such a large amount of money, while she and Lulu were living a hand-to-mouth existence in one bedroom in an old, rundown house. Then she reminded herself that she had never told Nadine the finer details of their situation or that they were having money troubles so she should just be thankful her daughter had been so generous. The car Justine had given her had been generous too but Tom had taken that and sold it, the selfish bastard, she thought to herself. Oh well, let's just get on with it. At least I've got good news for Lulu. She will be able to go away with the team.

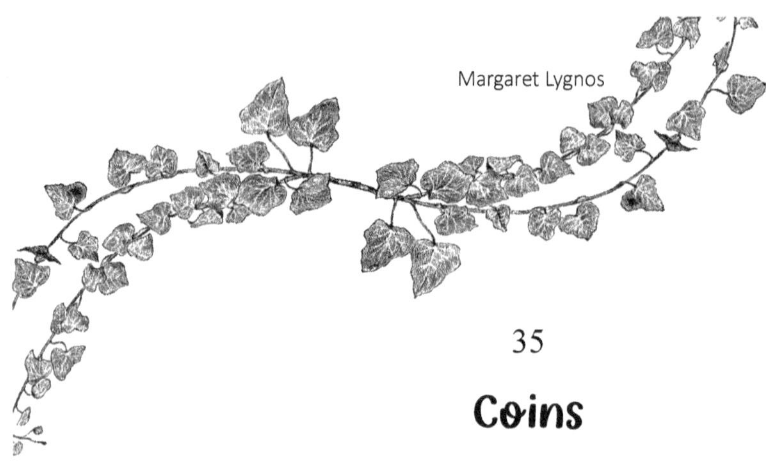

35

Coins

Marcia rang Justine to let her know she was bringing a man called Jeff to give her a quote to paint the exterior of the house. Jeff arrived at five o'clock and Marcia not long after. When she had finished negotiating with Jeff, Marcia entered the kitchen where Justine and Terry were preparing the evening meal.

"Will you stay and have dinner with us again Marcia?" Justine asked.

"Yes I would love to, thank you," Marcia replied.

At the dinner table Marcia finished her meal and, putting down her cutlery, announced there was another woman who would be moving in with them soon.

"Oh okay, who is she?" Bethany asked.

"Her name is Crystal and she is very young, just eighteen, and has recently given birth to a baby. Her background is very sad and troubled and I thought her being here with the three of you would be beneficial and supportive in so many ways."

"That is young," said Terry. "She could be my granddaughter."

"That's what I thought," Marcia replied. "If she fits in with you it could be like an extended family, something she lacks. I am giving you a little bit of say in this because with her being so young and having a baby, it is a different dynamic. What do you all think?"

"Where would she go if not here?"

"There is a place where she has been living but there are no other young mothers and no good role models for her there," Marcia said.

The three women looked at each other and between them quickly agreed that Crystal would be welcome with them. "If we are able to make her life easier why wouldn't we," Terry said. "And a baby — that would be wonderful."

"I had a feeling you would be okay with her," said Marcia, smiling at the group. "Someone will deliver her belongings tomorrow and probably she will be discharged from hospital the following day then come home to you."

"Oh, so it's a newborn baby. Will you let us know when she is arriving for sure, just so we have her room ready; and what about a cot for the baby?"

"That's all taken care of cot, pram, nappies and newborn clothes," Marcia added. Standing up she prepared to leave, "Oh and the painting of the house will begin next week."

"Marcia, don't go yet, we have something to ask you," Bethany interrupted. "The children have found some valuable coins in the shed and we thought you should have them. Have you got time to look at them now?"

"Sure, let's have a look. They were probably my father's — he collected all sorts of things."

They all went to the garage where Lulu handed the box to Marcia and watched as she opened it.

"Oh wow! These are interesting and yes, probably worth quite a bit of money. I'll take them and have them valued; the money will be useful," she said.

"We thought so," Justine said.

Marcia turned and looked at the old Holden which faced the locked garage door. "That belonged to my brother, it was his pride and joy. It was the car he drove until he became sick and died."

"So it's in good condition, I suppose" Bethany added.

"Yes it would be in good condition," Marcia replied thoughtfully.

Driving away from the house Marcia thought of some other things her father had collected, stamps, paintings, war memorabilia among them.

'I wonder where all that stuff is?' she said to herself.

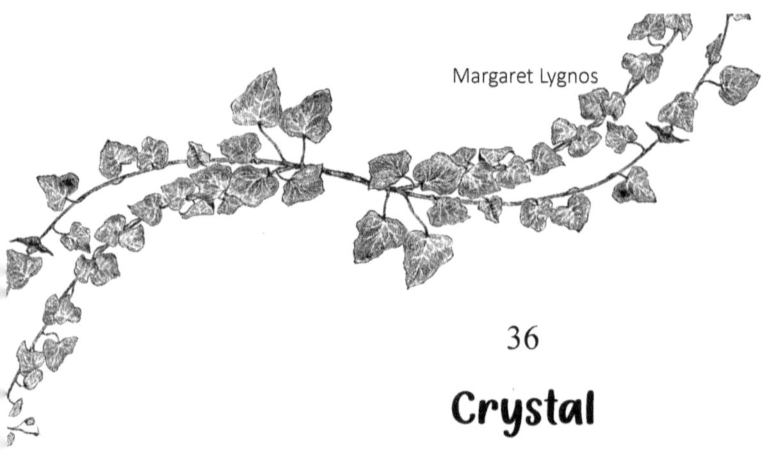

36

Crystal

Crystal arrived two days later just before lunchtime. She was accompanied by a social worker who carried Crystal's bags and Crystal carried the baby. Terry and Bethany were at home and smiled warmly at the young girl, wanting to make her feel welcome.

"We have prepared this room for you," Terry told her, standing at the door to the room they had organised for her and the baby.

The curtains were open and sunlight filled the spotlessly clean room. Between the three women they had made the room as friendly and homey as possible. New bedlinen and several colourful cushions had been used to make the room appear inviting and a few simple toys had been placed in the cot. An old tea trolley was pushed up against a wall and covered with a soft white towel and the nappies and other clothes were placed on the shelf underneath. The cot was on one side of the bed and a small table and a comfortable chair were on the other side. Directly opposite the window stood an old wooden wardrobe with a large full-length mirror on the central door. Crystal stood and took it all in, turning to the women she asked in a surprised voice, "Is this beautiful room all for me? It's wonderful."

"Yes this is your room. We are just about to have lunch so when you are ready come into the kitchen and join us," Terry replied.

Crystal came to the kitchen almost at once, stating that she would like to eat while the baby was sleeping.

"Tell us about the baby," said Terry.

"He is so beautiful and so tiny. His name is Finn, I like the name; it's short and sweet and he won't have trouble spelling it. I fell in love with him as soon as I saw him. I wasn't sure how I would feel but as soon as he was born and placed on my tummy, I felt enormous love for him."

"That's the maternal instinct kicking in," said Bethany. "Now you will understand why mothers protect their children and stand up for them against all odds."

"Some mothers don't," Crystal answered sadly.

Suddenly the cry of the newborn baby alerted Crystal, who jumped to her feet and ran to the bedroom to pick him up. Returning to the kitchen with the tiny bundle in her arms she rocked him from side to side and cooed to him but he continued to cry.

"He must be hungry again, babies need a lot of feeding don't they," Crystal said, looking at Terry and Bethany.

"Yes they do, especially when they are newborn."

"Do I have to go into my room to feed Finn?"

"No not at all, this is your home; you sit wherever you are comfortable." Terry replied. "Justine, Bethany and I have all had babies and all breast fed so we know a thing or two between us. If you need us we are here to help you."

Crystal sat and put the baby to her breast where he began to suck hungrily. "The nurses told me that the more I let the baby suck the more milk I will make, that's strange isn't it?" Crystal commented.

"I suppose it seems strange but it's the truth, that's how the body knows to produce more milk for your baby. So don't worry if he needs lot of feeds, he is just making more milk for tomorrow and the next day. Nature is wonderful isn't it?"

"Yes it's all wonderful and being here is wonderful, so peaceful. Are there children living here too?" asked Crystal, looking at the Lego and children's books.

"Yes" said Bethany, "I have a boy and a girl and Justine, who is at work, has a girl. Terry has a daughter who is overseas and we have a dog and four hens."

"What, in the back garden?" Crystal asked with surprise.

"Yes, and we are attempting to grow a few vegetables and herbs."

"Mum and I could never do that because we lived in a high-rise flat, plus mum was not the type to be growing something she could buy at the shops."

Sitting on the back veranda the autumn afternoon passed pleasantly for Crystal, Terry and Bethany. When the hungry children arrived home from school and sat to eat their after-school snack, the cry of the baby startled them as each had forgotten about the new woman who was coming to live with them. They jumped up and rushed in to see the tiny baby who was lying on a soft white towel having his nappy changed by Crystal.

"Oh it's a boy," said Sam. "That's good."

The children were fascinated by the tiny baby and the strange noises he made. They were amazed that he fell asleep so often and slept on and off, making a lot of noise when he woke up. More than anything they were intrigued with him getting milk from Crystal's breasts.

"When will he be able to play with us?" asked Sam.

"Not for a long time" his mother replied.

"Oh," Sam said obviously disappointed that he wouldn't have a little boy to play with for ages.

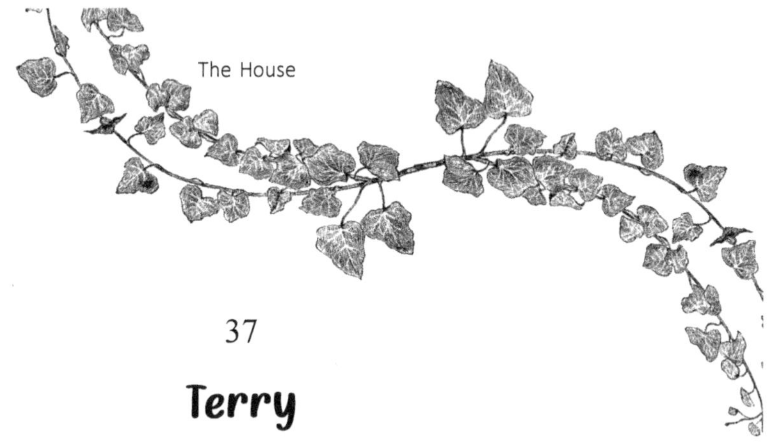

37

Terry

Over the next few weeks Terry continued telling the other women about her dreadful marriage to Eric.

"Have you noticed my little dog has a limp?" she asked one day.

"Yes I had wondered about that," answered Justine.

"Well the poor little thing was kicked into the air by Eric because she got in his way when he had lost a lot of money gambling. She had the leg in plaster for weeks and even after the plaster was removed she walked on three legs. After that she always kept out of Eric's way."

"Was it the gambling that caused you to end up without any money?"

"Yes and no. After Eric died and I thought I would be able to live my life in comfort, I was informed that the house was mortgaged up to the limit and I had very little money of my own. When Eric went to Ireland to see his parents he had pretended that we were rich. He took his parents, his sister and her husband on a trip to England and Scotland and as they all enjoyed it so much they went to France and Italy as well. They flew business class, stayed in the best hotels and resorts and he spent about two hundred thousand dollars of my superannuation."

"Jeez Terry! How did he get access to your super?"

"By force — I was so intimidated by him that to keep the peace I did whatever he wanted, otherwise he abused me."

"Did you ever report him to the police?"

"Yes and that backfired. After a visit from two policemen I was left with a black eye and a sore back and he threatened to kill me if I reported him again. I was a shell of a woman, surviving one day at a time and

I had lost my sense of identity. I was much less than the woman I am today."

"How do you know he spent your money on tripping around Europe with his family; he could have put it somewhere else that you are not aware of."

"No his sister rang me to thank me for my generosity, having been told by Eric that he was spending the money on them with my blessing. She told me all about the holiday they had together." Pausing she added, "He never took me anywhere. When I realised what had happened to my money I was very depressed because I had always thought that if I could just outlive him that money would keep me going. When he came home from Ireland he just continued as if nothing had changed."

"What happened when you told him you knew about the money being spent?"

"He denied it, said his sister was exaggerating and flatly refused to talk about it."

Taking a long look at Terry, at her deeply furrowed forehead, sad eyes and nervousness, Bethany realised that with the knowledge of her terrible life with Eric she now understood the reasons for her unhappy demeanour. She understood why Terry often appeared distracted and uncertain, she had been browbeaten and belittled by her captor. Her spirit had been broken.

Putting her arm around Terry's shoulder quietly, sympathetically she asked, "What have you been doing since Eric died, where have you been living?"

"In an institution for part of the time, then in shared housing which was not really to my liking. Then I was referred to Marcia through a social worker and here I am, thank goodness, and very happy to be here."

Bethany looked at Justine and said, "The three of us have a lot in common besides the husbands who have let us down. We have all had houses which we partly paid for and yet here we are with nothing to show for it."

38

Painting

The following week the house painter, Jeff, arrived with his son Jason to begin painting the house. Telling the women the first week would involve preparation of the old timber for repainting, he advised them to keep the windows closed to avoid getting dust into the house.

"Better not put your washing on the line while we are here either," he said.

At ten am on the first day, Terry asked the two men to join them for a cup of tea on the back veranda.

"You're welcome to sit here to eat your lunch each day," she told them.

Jeff introduced his son Jason to Terry and Justine who were sitting in the shade with the sleeping baby in his pram. Crystal emerged from the house obviously fresh from the shower. Holding a towel she was rubbing vigorously at her long, rich, pink-gold hair. Jason was surprised to see this young girl in the house, having been told it was a refuge. He assumed Crystal was the daughter of one of the older women. When the baby began to cry he was shocked to see Crystal lift the baby from the pram and cuddle him.

"Oh you are awake, my darling boy, come with Mummy and I'll feed you."

Crystal went into the house and Jason asked Terry, "Is that her baby?"

"Yes, it's her baby; she is a young mother and coping very well here with us."

"Oh, I see," he said surprise written all over his face.

Jason had been struck by the young girl called Crystal. He thought he had never seen a more beautiful sight when the sun had been shining on her rose-gold hair, illuminating her clear skin and sparkling blue eyes.

How could such a young girl already be a mother, was there a man in her life? he wondered and later asked his father. His father replied that he did not know anything about the women living in the house, only that they were all in need of a place to live.

"You will have to ask those questions yourself if that's what you want to find out," he told his son kindly.

39

Jason

Jason had finished school and was studying landscaping and garden design at a tertiary institution. When he was able he helped his father, earning himself a small income, otherwise he spent time with friends or listening to music. His last girlfriend had left him to travel in Europe and he had toyed with the idea of following her when he completed his study, but as time went by the idea had lost its urgency and his feelings for her had faded. Seeing Crystal this morning had put all those plans well and truly out of his mind.

40

Marcus

Marcus continued to work on investigating the hit and run which had injured Bethany. Several CCTV images of that day were now in his possession. Although they were not very clear images of the driver, they were something to go on so he contacted Bethany to make a time for her to view the films.

Before his meeting with Bethany he rang Joe and asked what had happened to the white car he'd previously owned, and was told by Joe that he no longer owned it. Marcus was not convinced by Joe's answer so he went to the house when there was no one at home and by climbing over a side fence could see through the garage window. The white car was there, still inside the locked garage. Following this discovery, Marcus went to the house when Joe was at home and asked to see the car in the garage. Joe lied and said there was no car in his garage and that if Marcus wanted to view the interior of the garage he needed a search warrant to come onto the property. Marcus returned the next day with the warrant and was led to the garage. Joe opened the door, revealing an empty space.

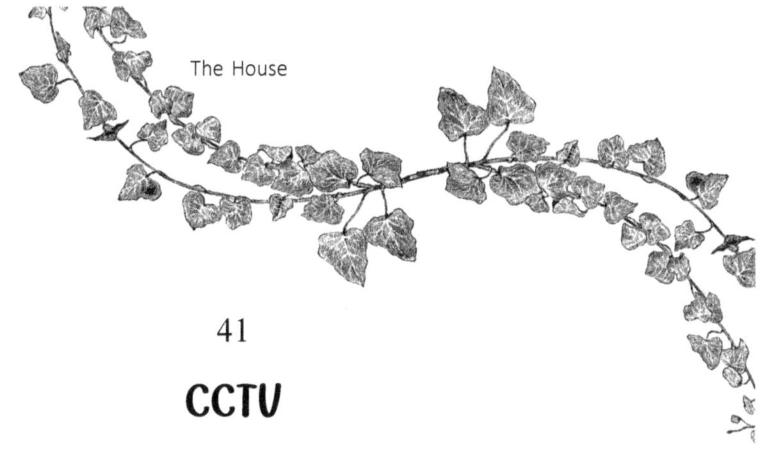

41

CCTV

Sitting in the office waiting to see Marcus, Bethany realised that she was actually looking forward to seeing him again. From their first meeting he had demonstrated how keen he was to help her and they had become friends. Her mind wandered a little and she wondered if there was a chance they could become more than friends. She hoped so. Bethany was jolted out of her fantasy as Marcus emerged from his office and, smiling broadly, invited her inside. Shutting the door he moved a chair close to his to enable them to view the CCTV together.

"There are three short films to look at," he told her.

He played them each twice then stopped and enlarged the best picture of the driver.

"Who's that?" he asked.

"It's really hard to say," she replied.

"We can see the driver is obviously wearing a wig which hides his or her cheeks and the glasses are so big they conceal most of the face," Marcus commented. "Also the driver is tall because their head is right up near the roof."

"Well, they are all fairly tall, and whoever it is could be sitting on a cushion to appear even taller," Bethany noted.

"Yes, so let's look at other things. The clothes, the hands, anything else we can see."

"I honestly can't recognise that person," said Bethany. "It could be anyone."

"That's a pity," said Marcus, "But I'm not giving up yet, I've got a few more houses in the area to door-knock and ask about their CCTV."

They said goodbye and Marcus promised to keep in touch with her. Feeling a little letdown by the CCTV and wishing she could spend a bit more time sitting close to him, Bethany continued home to her children and friends in the house which she now happily called home.

42

Crystal's Mother

Crystal announced one morning that her mother had been in touch with her and was going to visit that day to meet her grandson.

"Are you okay with her visiting here?" asked Terry.

"Yes, as long as someone else is in the house I will feel comfortable," she replied.

"Well I will definitely be here with you, whatever time she comes," Terry reassured her. "I'll be home all day."

"Thank you Terry, that's good to know."

Crystal's mother arrived mid-morning and knocked loudly at the front door. Terry let her in and introduced herself.

"I'm Jade, Crystal's mother," she announced.

Jade was very like her daughter; short, slight build with blue eyes, but her hair was dyed bright pink.

"Hello Mum," said Crystal, walking down the hall towards the front door. "My goodness, you have pink hair, that's nice, it suits you."

"Hello my darling, how are you? You don't look too bad for someone who has just had a baby."

"Yes I'm very well, and my friends here are really looking after me. I'm getting plenty of rest and lots of good food and fresh air."

"Where is my grandson, can I see him?"

"Yes but he's just gone to sleep so we have to be quiet."

The three women crept into Crystal's bedroom and leaned over the cot.

"Oh, he is a beauty," said Jade loudly, pushing the cot and waking the baby. "Oh he must have heard his grandmother's voice and he wants to meet her."

"You woke him, Mum," Crystal said, annoyed, but she picked up her crying baby and carried him to the living room. Her mother sat beside her and put out her arms to take the baby.

"Can I hold him?"

"Yes but I'll just give him a little feed to settle him again."

Crystal put the baby to her breast and her mother tut tutted, "You're not breast feeding are you? Why not give him the bottle? It's much easier."

"Breast feeding isn't hard for me, it's easy. All I have to do is offer him my breast and he feeds. It couldn't be easier and it's the best food for a baby."

"I could never do it," her mother said. "Anyway formula is just as good as breast milk isn't it?"

"No Mum, it's processed cow's milk with additives, milk that's really for calves, not human babies."

"Oh, well whatever you think, if you can do it good on you."

"I'm getting plenty of rest and help from my house mates and that makes it easier for me.'

"Still, I'd put him on the bottle if I were you then you can leave him and go out."

"I don't want to leave him and go out," said Crystal. "I want to be here for him whenever he needs me."

The baby settled and was almost asleep again so Crystal gently passed him to her mother.

"Here, give him a cuddle then I will put him back to bed."

Jade gazed at the baby and asked, "What have you decided to call him?"

"His name is Finn."

"Finn! What sort of silly name is that?"

"It's not a silly name. It's an Irish name I think. It's short for Finigan or Finius."

"How about you call him Jet, then his name will be more in line with our names — you know, Crystal and Jade are earthy, organic names and he should have an earthy name too. If he'd been a girl you could have called her Ruby."

"No, he is Finn and I'm not changing my mind," Crystal retorted firmly, wishing her mother would leave, but she was giving no indication that she was in a hurry to go.

Terry had made minestrone soup and toasted sandwiches for lunch and invited Jade to join them. As they were seating themselves at the kitchen table Jade announced, "I have heard from your father and he wants to meet you. When I told him you had a baby he was thrilled to hear that he is a grandfather and can't wait to meet the baby as well."

Crystal, gulping a mouthful of soup, almost choked. "What? I thought I didn't have a father?"

"Everyone has a father," Jade replied.

"Yes but you always told me you didn't know where he was. How did he track you down?"

"He's been away for a long time and when he returned he found me through other people who know both of us."

"Well I'm not sure about meeting him. Where has he been all of my eighteen years. We could have used a bit of help from him in the past. It's a bit strange for him to reappear out of nowhere. No, I don't think I want to meet him."

"Think about it Crystal, he is your father after all."

"Mum you told me some awful things about him and the reasons you left him. Surely you haven't forgotten those things, because I certainly haven't."

"I don't know what I told you."

'Shall I remind you of the time he punched you and threw you out of the house?"

"Alright, alright; that's enough. I'm going."

Standing up suddenly she accidentally knocked over a chair which crashed to the floor, then she rushed to the front door and let herself out.

Terry looked at Crystal who was on the verge of tears. Reaching her hand towards her she said, "You don't have to see him if you don't want to."

"I'm not going to see him — my mother can't have forgotten what he did. According to her he was brutal sometimes."

"Perhaps she chooses to forget, it's easier that way sometimes," Terry said knowingly.

43

Jade

Jade was annoyed with herself for losing her cool and running out of the house the way she had. She really wanted to fix her relationship with Crystal and wanted to be involved in Finn's life. She knew she had not been a good mother to Crystal and hoped she could somehow make up for her failures. All she had ever wanted was a few children and a nice man to take care of her. Now she knew it was better that she had not had other children because her life had been a disaster. So many men had been in her life, so many that she had lost count. She had been badly treated by most of them and had had several miscarriages along the way.

Now at forty five she was beginning to tire of the aimless existence she was living. She was just starting to think she might be able to put men out of her life all together and then Crystal's father Sean had reappeared, expecting her to be happy to see him. Well she really was not happy to see him, and wished he would disappear again. She had been living with Bob for a year or two but he ran like hell when Sean threatened him the night he came knocking on Jade's door. She did not expect to see Bob again but he wasn't much company anyway, all he did when he was at home was smoke and drink beer while watching television, her television, and now Sean had hinted that he would like to move in with her.

'Oh god, I go from one mess to another,' she thought as the bus approached. Finding a seat by the window, as the journey progressed Jade had to admit Crystal was right, she should not have anything to do with Sean. He was awful then and for sure he would be just as awful now. He would probably mistreat them and take advantage of them. At that point she decided she wouldn't tell him where Crystal was living.

'Let her be happy and safe in that big old house with the three women who are mothering her in ways I had never been able to,' she thought. Admitting that to herself produced a cascade of tears down her cheeks, obscuring her view from the bus window.

Alighting from the bus she dropped into a bottle shop and bought a bottle of cheap wine. Hurrying home she pictured herself sitting on the couch that night drowning her sorrows.

44

Jade in Need

It was well after midnight when everyone in the house was woken by someone banging on the front door. Then the distraught voice of a woman was heard sobbing, "Please let me in."

Terry and Bethany were up and moving towards the front door when Crystal emerged from her room saying loudly, "I think that's my mother — oh god what has happened to her now?"

Opening the door they were confronted by a dishevelled Jade, dressed in pyjamas, her feet bare and her pink hair clinging to her wet, tear-streaked face. A man displaying a puzzled expression on his young face stood to the side of her, waiting. Behind them in the driveway the hazard lights of a taxi blinked off and on, causing the dewy grass to sparkle like Christmas tree decorations.

"The fare is twenty five dollars thanks," he announced impatiently.

Terry fetched her purse and paid the taxi driver, who turned quickly as the door was closed. Jade was taken to the living room and the heater was turned on. Soon the room was warm and the kettle was boiling. Terry made tea and toast for everyone. Jade was more composed after drinking her tea and eating a little piece of toast. She began to talk haltingly, describing what had happened to her.

"It's Sean, he came back today — he wanted to know where you ... and the baby are living," she said, looking at her daughter.

"I said I didn't know but he didn't believe me — he pushed me around and threatened me. He said he would throw me down the stairs or over the balcony. He dragged me to the door, opened it, pushed me towards the railing and banged my head on the hard edge."

She indicated a laceration on her forehead. "A man who lives nearby came out of his flat and yelled at Sean to leave me alone. He was a big man and he pushed Sean against the wall and told me to run. When I got to the street there was a taxi dropping a passenger off so I jumped inside and that's how I got here."

She slumped forward, head in her hands, and began to sob again.

"You have to contact the police," said Terry, handing Jade her phone.

"Yes I know, I will — but in the morning because now I need to sleep."

In the morning Crystal was up early with Finn so she made a phone call to the local police station to report the assault on her mother. Later in the day Jade received a phone call informing her that Sean had been found in her flat and because he had violated his parole conditions, he was in custody again. Her demeanour changed with the news and she actually smiled. Crystal gave her mother some clothes to wear and after a long shower she washed her pink hair, blow dried it into an attractive bob and emerged looking like a new woman.

Feeling that she owed these women something for taking her in and showing her such friendship, she offered to make lunch for everyone. Looking in the pantry and the fridge she came up with the ingredients to make a vegetable omelette, accompanied by a fresh salad from the garden.

The children were at school so when they had finished eating she was able to speak freely about her relationship with Sean and to tell them exactly where he had disappeared to for all those years.

"He was a tall, handsome man who always had money to spend and he charmed me with his lovemaking and generous gifts," she said. "We lived together and everything was fine until I became pregnant with Crystal. I was very unwell for most of the pregnancy and had to give up my job earlier than I'd expected, and that caused arguments about money. And then there was my lack of interest in sex which really annoyed him. I was only out of hospital a few days when he insisted on having sex which I didn't want, but he made me. I began to dislike him because he was rough with me and the baby and he got really annoyed when she cried. She cried a lot because he wouldn't let me pick her up. He said it would spoil her. As if he would have known anything about babies."

"Sounds like someone I was married to," said Terry.

Jade continued, "I have never told anyone but the police exactly what he did to me to end our relationship but it was mainly because of his selfish treatment of me and my stupidity in aggravating him. When we had sex he didn't care about my enjoyment and once he had climaxed he got up and left me on the bed. He did this to me so many times and although I asked him to consider my enjoyment and fulfilment he just laughed and said 'maybe next time it will happen.' So one day I decided to get on top of him and this enabled me to climax quickly. I got up off the bed and said to him, 'it's not very nice when it happens to you is it?' He grabbed me, punched me in the stomach and slapped my face repeatedly, then he threw me on the bed and raped me violently. I was almost unconscious when he had finished with me and yet he threw me outside into the corridor where I was found half-naked by a neighbour, who called an ambulance and the police."

Crystal wrapped her arms around her mother. "Mum, that's much worse than you ever told me, he sounds like a monster."

"He is a monster, but from what he told me about his childhood it's no wonder, he was terribly mistreated as a child by multiple people."

"Anyway," Jade continued "When he was arrested and fingerprinted it was discovered that he was wanted over an armed robbery from several years before, so he was charged with armed robbery not domestic abuse, and sent to jail. I was free of him at last but I hadn't leant my lesson where men were concerned, and in the years following I was silly enough to become involved with other awful men, though none as bad as Sean, thank god."

"I have to agree with you there Mum," said Crystal "The first night I met Bob he leered at me and said 'Oh two of you, how delicious.'

That's why I left. I didn't want any more unwanted attention from dirty old men."

"Bob wasn't an old man," Jade objected.

"He was to me Mum. He was just like so many of the others you brought into our home, and I never felt safe with any of them."

Bethany interrupted the conversation, "I'm going to ring Marcia and ask her advice. She might have somewhere you can go to get away from your current home so you can start a new life."

"No, I will be okay going home now that Sean is locked up again. I have a few friends nearby and I have my part-time job on the weekends. Perhaps I can work more hours during the week, I will be okay so long as I can remain friends with all of you and particularly with Crystal and Finn."

Crystal hugged her mother and reassured her that she wanted her in her life and she was welcome to visit her any time, but not with Sean or any strange men.

"I won't be inviting any man to live with me again," Jade said resolutely.

45

Marcia

Marcia visited often and had become good friends with the four women. She loved Finn and showered him with gifts of clothes, toys and books.

"He's a bit too young for books, isn't he?" Crystal asked.

"Oh no," said Marcia, "You can encourage a love of books from a very early age, just read a little to him and he will take notice and enjoy the colours and pictures in the book; that's what I've heard though not from direct experience of course."

"Thanks Marcia, you are very good to us."

"I had the coins valued," Marcia announced, "and I'm using the money to bring a motor mechanic here to look at the car in the garage and hopefully get it running. I like and trust this man, his name is Kosta and he will do a good job for us. When and if it's roadworthy it will be for your use — I assume you all drive, and it can be shared between you."

"Oh Marcia, that's wonderful, you are such a generous person." Bethany gushed.

"Well, I don't need it and you do, so it will be part of the agreement of living in the house, part of the deal. I'll pay the insurance but you will be responsible for the running of the car. It will be good for driving the children to school, doing the shopping, that sort of thing. It's not for one person only but to share between you or anyone else living in the house. I'll leave it to you to work out the way you do it. After all, you have done very well together so far with sharing the bills."

"I'll ask the children to sort through the box of keys to find the padlock key so we can open the double doors of the garage." Bethany said. "Otherwise we will have to resort to bolt cutters."

"There might be other valuable things in the locked cupboards," remarked Marcia. "My father and my brother were great collectors of various things."

"When can we expect the mechanic to come?" Terry asked

"Sometime this week, probably after hours because he is busy at his workshop. He services my car so I know him well and trust him," she reiterated.

46

Marcus

Marcus kept in touch with Bethany by phone, telling her about the white car which was there one day and not the next.

"I'll ask Skye to look in the garage on Wednesday when they are staying overnight with their father," she told him.

"Does that mean you are free that night?" he asked'

"Yes, I will be at home with the others but not my children."

"Would you like to go out for dinner with me?"

"I would love to Marcus, that would be really nice. I haven't done anything like that for ages."

"Okay, I'll pick you up at six pm, is that a good time?"

"Perfect."

Marcus made a booking at a small Italian restaurant in Carlton and when they were seated he asked if she liked red or white wine.

"I prefer white," she said.

"Yes me too, something dry perhaps?"

Between them they chose a bottle of wine and enjoyed a glass as they perused the menu. The restaurant was only half full and quiet, the service was excellent and the food was home-style Italian cuisine. After dinner they strolled hand in hand down the street window-shopping. The wine had relaxed them and they found little things to amuse each other. Marcus bought them a gelato which they ate while gazing into the window of an antique jewellery shop. Bethany admired an old Victorian bangle decorated with pearls and a ruby. "I'm sure my grandmother wore a bangle just like that, I remember it would jangle against her wrist watch when she wore it. I wonder what happened to it?”

Driving home Marcus said he had enjoyed her company and hoped they could make it a regular thing when her children were with their father. Bethany agreed. She had been admiring Marcus all evening; his dark hair and eyes were magnetic and when he smiled at her his whole face lit up which in turn made her feel special. Seated in the car outside Bethany's home, Maurice turned to look at Bethany and repeated to her how glad he was to have met her and hoped she would go out with him again. Bethany smiled at him but said nothing, feeling nervous and very happy with how the evening had gone. She leaned over and kissed him on the lips. Aware of his gasp of pleasure she kissed him again, feeling his full soft lips responding to her. Not wanting to move away from him she moved closer and gently kissed his neck. Her cheek was resting on his chest and she breathed in the scent of his body, a faint smell of soap and a strong aroma of masculinity. It was wonderful and intoxicating. She felt she wanted more and was sure he did too but she felt it was a bit soon, even though they were both mature adults. Anyway if she took him inside, the other women would be awake, there would be a little bit of conversation and by the time they got to her room it might have lost its spontaneity. ‘Plenty of other times,’ she thought to herself.

“Goodnight Marcus, thanks for a lovely night out.” She gave him another quick kiss on the cheek and opened the car door.

“I'll ring you,” he replied, a broad smile on his face. Bethany went straight to her room and flopped onto her bed, still aroused from the kissing and closeness in the car. She wished with all her being that this budding relationship with Marcus would be a forever liaison that would include her two children Skye and Sam.

Driving home, Marcus sang along happily with a favourite CD he always kept in his car. In his mind he could still clearly see Bethany sitting opposite him in the restaurant smiling and laughing at his little attempts at Italian pronunciation of the food on the menu. Her shoulder-length hair freshly washed and dried had framed her pretty face which was only slightly made up. Just a little lipstick and mascara; she didn't need anything to make her anymore appealing. 'I hope this goes well, she is just the type of woman I like,' he said to himself. Then he thought of her children and, continuing to talk to himself, he said 'I will have to meet the children and see if we can get along.'

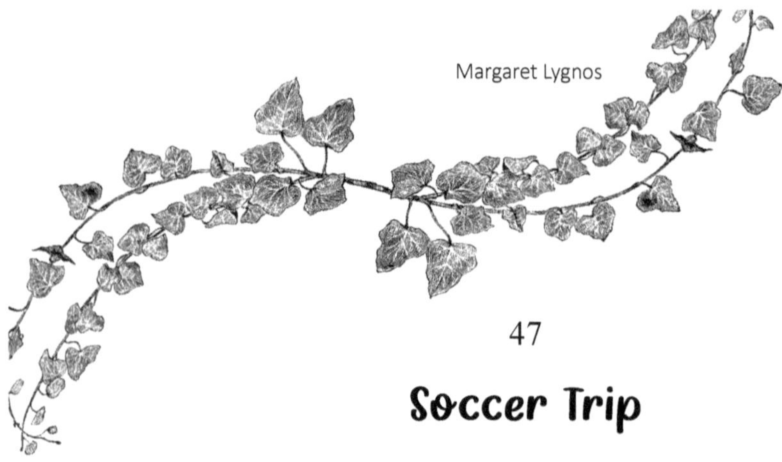

47

Soccer Trip

Once Justine established that they could pay for Lulu to go on the soccer trip, she began to think that maybe she could go as well and act as one of the supervisors. The club had asked for volunteers and when she offered, she was told half her fee would be paid by the club. It was still a lot of money for her to outlay but she thought it would be a positive experience for them both, and Lulu was thrilled that her mother would be accompanying her.

48

Jeff and Jason

The preparation for painting the house was completed and Jeff said there would be less dust now as the painting was about to go ahead. They gathered on the back veranda for morning tea as had become the habit.

"What colour will the house be?" asked Terry.

"Nothing too outrageous, off-white with a pale green trim," Jeff replied.

Jason, as always, was looking forward to Crystal joining them. Sometimes she didn't come outside if she was feeding the baby and then he had to wait until lunchtime to see her and even then she did not always appear.

"How is Crystal?" he asked Terry, who he had got to know better than all the others because she was always at home.

"She's really well, and the baby is putting on weight and sleeping quite well between feeds," she replied. "I think she is putting Finn to bed now so I'll see if she will come outside for a cup of tea with us."

Jason was pleased to hear that and even more pleased when Crystal emerged from the house wearing jeans and a long, pale-pink linen shirt. Whenever Jason saw her he thought she looked more beautiful than the last time. He moved over so that she could join him on the wooden bench. Crystal smiled at Jason and said good morning to Jeff who was grinning knowingly at Terry. In a quiet voice he asked Terry, "Has Crystal noticed Jason?"

"Noticed — what do you mean?"

"He's really smitten with her and can't wait to come and help me when he is available."

"Oh I see, I must admit I haven't been paying attention to them but now that you mention it, I suppose there are a few things that would indicate a little bit of interest on both sides."

"I hope they can get together," Jeff said.

In the afternoon Terry put a leash on her little dog Pippy and accompanied Crystal on a walk, as they had been doing regularly. "Crystal, have you noticed that Jason seems fond of you — or should I say is interested in you?"

"He does always come over to talk to me and I have noticed him staring at me. I have wondered about him but I thought that because I have Finn he probably wouldn't want to be involved with me. I do like him though."

"Well I know for a fact that he really likes you, so it's up to you to let him know if you are keen on him."

"It would be nice, but Finn will always be my first priority no matter how much Jason likes me or I like him. I never want Finn to feel neglected or unimportant like I did."

"Let's stop and have afternoon tea at the local cafe?" Terry suggested.

The sun was shining through the few remaining autumn leaves and a few sparrows flitted under the table looking for crumbs as the two women sat enjoying their coffee. Adjoining the cafe was a small park where young mothers with prams and toddlers were chatting happily in the sun, all the while keeping an eye on their children. Several of the children began to plough through the thick carpet of autumn leaves on the ground laughing as they kicked them into the air. One little boy fell and began to roll in the leaves. Standing up he found the damp leaves had stuck to his hair and clothes which he did not like. He could not brush the leaves off so he ran to his mother crying. The mother reassured the child, brushed off the leaves and gave him a kiss and a cuddle, sending him back to the other children. "That's the type of mother I want to be," Crystal announced.

"I can see you are already a good mother, Crystal."

"I hope so."

Walking home Terry thought about how fond she was of Crystal, who had become like a daughter to her, and Finn who was an adorable baby. At the same time it made her sad to think she had a daughter but had not seen or heard from her for a long time.

49

Alone at Last

It was late Saturday morning and Bethany was having a day on her own. Skye and Sam were with their father, Justine was away on the soccer trip with Lulu and Terry and Crystal had gone to the zoo.

As Bethany stood in the shower shampooing her hair, her thoughts turned to last night when she had been out for dinner again with Marcus. The relationship was getting serious, they really liked each other, and yet they still had not been really alone and intimate, she mused. Last night Marcus had suggested a weekend away in the very near future and Bethany had agreed enthusiastically.

Stepping out of the shower she viewed her slim body and wondered if Marcus would find her attractive; her body was not too bad for a woman who had given birth to two babies, she thought to herself. Turning away from the mirror after drying her hair she walked to her bedroom. The doorbell rang, making her jump. "Oh bother I was going to sit outside with the dog and read today," she said to herself, pulling on a loose cotton dress as she walked to open the front door.

Peeping through the partly opened door she found Marcus smiling at her. Their eyes locked, neither of them spoke as he stepped in and closed the door behind him. Looking at each other an accumulation of desire and craving propelled them together. Marcus pressed her up against the wall each and of them sighed with pleasure as they kissed. He put his hands on her bottom and pulled her closer. Bethany pressed her body towards Marcus indicating her matched longing for him. Taking him by the hand she led him quickly to her bedroom. The bed was unmade and glancing at it Marcus was thrilled at the prospect of being in her bed with all the scents of her body and where he imagined she had been lying dreaming of him. Pulling off her dress and revealing her naked body he heaved a sigh and said, "Oh so you were waiting for me." Pulling him onto the bed she helped him to undress and very soon they were at last able to feel and enjoy each other's bodies.

Bethany rested her head on his chest and whispered "I don't think I have ever wanted anything as much as I have wanted you."

"Yes," he replied "It has been torturous for me too."

"How come you came here today — how did you know I was on my own?"

"Last night you told me that everyone in the house was doing their own thing today so I thought I'd take a chance at finding you alone. I even thought you might have told me on purpose. I'm glad I took the chance."

"So am I," Bethany replied. "No I didn't realise I gave you that information but I'm so glad I did."

They slept a little then she woke him as she moved onto his body and, gazing into each his eyes, they slowly made love again.

Suddenly Marcus looked at his watch and exclaimed "I'm sorry Bethany, I'll have to go. I'm working this afternoon."

"Oh that's a pity, I was thinking I could cook lunch for you."

"Next time we'll plan this better so I don't have to rush off," he answered regretfully. He dressed quickly, then feeling in his jacket pocket he withdrew a square red velvet box and handed it to Bethany.

"I almost forgot about this."

Bethany took the box, opened it and took out the antique bangle they had admired in the shop window in Carlton.

"Marcus that's so special, thank you, I love it!"

"You deserve it," he said, kissing her goodbye.

She heard his car reverse out of the driveway and zoom up the road as she remained in her bed reliving the past two hours of love and lust.

'How delicious was that?' she said to herself, sighing and stretching her long legs towards the foot of the bed; 'Oh so delicious.'

Getting out of bed wearing nothing but the antique bangle she viewed her image.

'Now I know what Sally means about that look. I've got the look at last—that 'just fucked' look and I love it.''

50

The Car

If the car was to be made ready to drive they had to unlock the garage door. The children were asked to try to locate the key to open the large padlock on the garage door; it was Lulu who took over and made it her mission. On that day she had spent ages sorting all the keys into groups according to types and size. She created a line of keys along the bench top. At one end there was a type of key she had never seen before, large black metal items with huge handles, and at the other end of her display were tiny keys which could have been used to open a jewellery box or a locked diary. In the centre, amongst the middle-sized keys, she found the correct key to unlock the heavy garage door.

The mechanic came on a Sunday morning and spent less than a day servicing the car, which was working by mid-afternoon.

"This car was very well looked after by someone," he proclaimed. "It's running like a new car," he added after returning from filling the tank and giving it a test drive.

"Here are the keys," he passed them to Terry who said, "I'm going to have first go at driving, it's not automatic; not everyone can drive a manual car."

Bethany and Justine both said they could but Crystal said she had never learnt to drive at all.

"I'll teach you," Terry offered, "This car is very similar to the one I learnt in."

The three children and Pippy the dog piled into the car with Terry and she drove them to the milk bar to buy them each an ice-cream. Terry was so happy with her life at the moment and wished it had always been like this, happy children chatting and joking, the little dog waiting for a dollop of ice-cream to drop his way and the prospect of a safe, harmonious evening ahead.

51

Sean

Crystal's father Sean sat with his head in his hands. Feeling absolute despair and self-loathing he began to berate himself for his recent behaviour. 'Everyone hates me, I hate myself.'

There was no one to talk to and no one to listen, so, lifting his head, he looked at a face some previous occupant of the cell had drawn on the wall. It was a life-sized face of a woman and beneath the drawing was written 'MOTHER'. The more he stared at the face the more it morphed into his own mother's features as he remembered them. He had not seen his mother's face since he was a very small boy and his father had destroyed or hidden all photographs of her following her sudden death. He had adored his mother and remembered her as a gentle, quietly spoken, loving woman who often kissed and cuddled him for no reason other than that she had loved him. She had read to him every day and taken him by the hand, leading him around the garden to look at the creatures crawling or flying about them as they picked flowers for the house. From her early instructions he had developed an interest in insects and birds and any other little animals living freely in the wild.

"They are all a part of nature's plan and they all have a right to live," were her words.

His mother had gone into hospital for an operation and had never come home. No explanation was given to Sean, his father simply told him "she has gone to heaven so we won't be seeing her again." Sean asked where heaven was and couldn't they go there to try to find her; his father said no. That was all, NO. Sean was heartbroken and when his father, without prior preparation, took him to a boarding school and left him there he thought he would die.

He didn't die but he was unwell for some time until June, the kind woman who cared for the young boys, recognised his depression and comforted him and encouraged him to eat, so he eventually resumed school and sometimes played with the other boys. He rarely saw his father and was one of the unfortunate boys who spent the holidays at the boarding school, where they made the most of what was on offer. He continued his interest in garden animals and insects and more than once cared for a bird with an injured wing or a blue-tongued lizard that had been hurt. Occasionally he picked a bunch of flowers for June, who was always thrilled or seemed to be thrilled. She felt sorry for the little boys in her charge and believed they should all be at home with their mothers, therefore she made every effort to treat them in a way she would have if the boys had been her sons.

When it was time for Sean to begin his secondary education he was moved to another part of the school, the senior school, where some of the boys were almost full grown and looked like men to him. He missed the junior school and in particular he missed June and her kind attention. She had been his lifeline and without her knowing he had pretended she was his mother. She had encouraged him to concentrate on what was expected of him and to just do the best he could. Although he used her advice, he also learned from a young age to go into himself when a situation or a person became difficult. He would concentrate on the one thing in front of him and avoid the periphery. This way of coping worked for him but it bothered others who thought his behaviour strange and unsociable, but it was the only way he could cope. He existed alongside the other boys but never made a close friend. They were just part of the school and his sad empty life.

He managed to finish secondary school and passed his exams with good results and was rewarded with an offer to go to university. Unfortunately, being an institutionalised young man, university — where he was expected to stand on his own feet — did not suit him. He needed direction and constant rules and expectations as he was used to in the boarding school. He stayed for a short time then dropped out and went to see his father, looking for something but he was not sure what. His father, who had never bonded with him, now had a new wife and two young children and he made it very clear Sean was not welcome with them.

His father did provide him with a small allowance but it was not enough to get him very far so he looked for a job. He began work in a garden centre and did landscaping work with a man called Kurt who worked in the business. Through Kurt he was introduced to smoking weed which helped him to cope with his life, and was led into petty crime. First it was small amounts of merchandise then one or two larger items that were not missed. All sold easily down at the pub for a substantially reduced amount of money. The types of crimes increased and he took direction from Kurt, and as the money was easy he continued to live this way.

The armed robbery was a well-planned and executed crime which yielded quite a substantial amount of money. Sean and his co-criminals assumed they had got away with it so Sean was very surprised when, because of his fingerprints, he was subsequently nabbed for the robbery, even though he had been arrested for the assault of Jade.

Sean was a good-looking man and found it easy to attract women and girls. His first experience was with a woman ten years older than him who was extremely experienced with sex and taught him how to give and receive amazing pleasure. Prior to that, his only sexual experience was not lovemaking but had been at the hands of an older boy at school who was known for taking advantage of the young innocent twelve-year-olds new to the secondary school. Sean had been horrified but he refused to think about it and pushed it right to the back of his mind, burying it beneath his mother's death and his father's lack of interest in him.

The violence towards Jade was something he could not understand. It was just that some things caused him to really lose it. He would never hurt an insect or an animal but he hurt Jade. Why he couldn't understand

and he wished he had never laid a hand on her. He really liked her but sometimes she gave him a hard time, or so he thought. She was not there when he wanted her, she burnt a saucepan, there was no beer in the fridge, she wouldn't have sex or any other trivial thing. He just had no control of the red rage that engulfed him and turned him into a ferocious creature. Jade called him a monster and he admitted now that she was right, he was a monster when he behaved like that. "It's not really me though, is it mother?" he said to the drawing on the wall. "I just wanted to see my daughter and my grandson and they won't let me."

In his cell Sean was pleased to find there was a black spider which had spun a thick grey web in a corner. He was fascinated with both the spider and its web. The web was so thick that when it was dark the spider was invisible. Sometimes Sean touched the web gently and the spider jumped out with raised fangs. When it came out at night and hunted for some unsuspecting insect, Sean was mesmerised by its quick action catching prey. He never hurt the spider; he liked it, and occasionally if he found a dead fly or mosquito he gave it to the spider. That was his life, the woman's face drawn on the wall and the spider, and he considered them both his only friends.

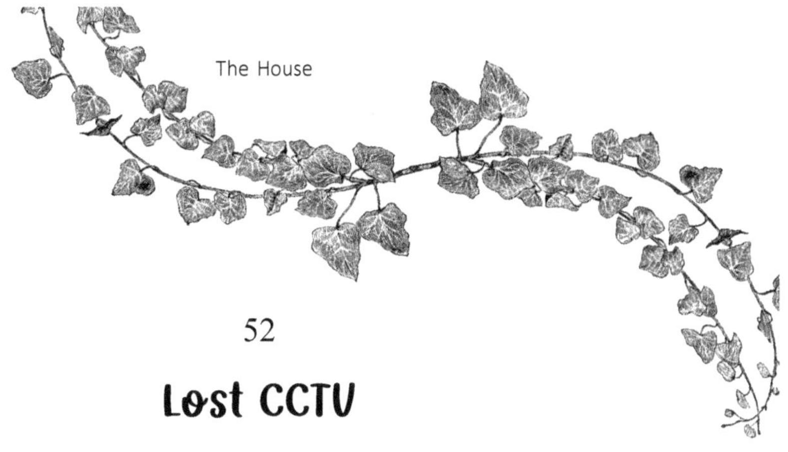

52

Lost CCTV

Marcus and one of his fellow officers had canvassed all the local houses and businesses in the area of Bethany's hit and run and so far nothing useful had been found. It really bothered Marcus that he could not put a line under the case. Time had passed and the likelihood of anyone remembering seeing the car and the disguised person driving it became less and less each day.

Working at his desk one day, he began to discuss the case with another colleague who was unaware of the finer details.

"Have you viewed all the CCTV," she asked.

"Yes twice, most of it," he replied.

"There are some tapes in Jan's desk drawer I saw them the other day when I was looking for a pencil sharpener. Have you seen them?"

Jan was on long service leave and had been assisting Marcus prior to going on a holiday.

"Probably but I'm not sure; I'd better have a look," Marcus said, jumping up and opening the drawer. "I'm not sure that I have seen these — why on earth are they stuck in a drawer?"

He examined the dates and addresses of the two tapes and said angrily, "Damn, no I don't think I have seen them."

Putting the tapes into the machine he began to scrutinise them carefully.

53

Party

Finn was six months old, half a year, and Crystal wanted to celebrate his birth and the fact that she had survived and was enjoying being a mother. Actually now that she was a mother she was keen to have a birthday party because she had never had one, plus it would be an excuse to invite Jason to the house.

"I know I'm being a bit silly but I want to do it anyway. Couldn't we just have an afternoon tea party on the weekend?"

"I don't see why not, he is old enough now and he'll sit up and smile at everyone. He might enjoy it," Terry agreed.

It was decided and plans were made. They invited Marcia, Marcus, Jeff and his wife, Jason, Kosta and his wife. A table was set outside and Terry made a passionfruit sponge and scones and Justine and Bethany made ribbon sandwiches. No alcohol, just tea and coffee or mineral water to drink. Finn enjoyed his party and smiled happily as he was passed around between the visiting women.

Jason had never plucked up the courage to invite Crystal out on a date so he was hoping he would get an opportunity at the party. Crystal had missed him after the painting had finished and wondered if he would still show some interest in her. She was not disappointed. He asked her about the hens and they walked over to the chicken coop, accompanied by Pippy, where they could speak without being overheard. Crystal was relieved when he finally asked her out. Looking up at his smiling, happy face flanked by soft wavy hair, her heart did a little jump.

"Yes I would like that very much," she told him.

"I'll pick you up and we'll go out for dinner, that way we can talk. I'd like to get to know you better," replied Jason.

The party was a success and led to a budding romance.

Eating pasta and enjoying a glass of wine together the shyness quickly disappeared and the two got to discuss some topics which were uppermost in their minds. Jason was reluctant to ask about Finn's father and Crystal knew he would want to know. She was not sure if she wanted to tell him and decided that until the subject came up in general conversation, or unless he asked her outright, she would not offer the information. Besides, they were only having dinner together, nothing more.

He drove her home and they kissed goodnight, agreeing to see each other again on the following weekend.

The relationship blossomed slowly and with caution because Crystal wanted to take her time; she wanted to be sure of Jason's intentions before she went to the next level. She was determined not to have another baby as a single mother and she had to be sure that any man she was with would include Finn in their future.

It was after only three months of going out together that Jason asked Crystal to marry him. She knew he loved her because he was always telling her so and she felt sure she loved him equally. Surprisingly, he had never asked her about Finn's father. Now that she was considering marrying him surely he should know who it was.

"Jason, why have you never asked me about Finn's father?"

"I've been waiting for you to tell me when you felt you wanted to. At the same time it will make no difference to the way I feel about you. I love you and I have loved you from the first time I saw you drying your hair in the sun."

"Jason, you are so special, I can't believe you have chosen me."

"We have chosen each other, haven't we?"

"Yes I suppose we have." Crystal moved over to Jason and, putting her arms around his waist, she pulled him closer and they kissed for a long time. "I owe you an explanation now," she said to him.

54

Finn's Father

When Crystal moved out of her mother's flat she had felt very vulnerable but in the flat she felt both vulnerable and unsafe. Her mother, Jade, was very careless with Crystal and seemed unaware of the behaviour of some of her male friends. More than once Crystal had managed to avoid unwanted sexual attention from her mother's male friends and it caused her anxiety, insomnia and inability to concentrate at school. The last time it happened she felt it was better to just get out of the flat before she was raped.

Crystal knew a girl from school who had walked out of home and was living in a squat in North Melbourne. After asking around at school it took her only a couple of days to locate the girl, Mandy, who was pleased to see her and made her welcome. There were always six or more people living in the house and some stayed for a night or two while others were always there. It was far from luxurious, no electricity or gas, but thankfully the water was still connected. Most food was consumed cold but there was a camp stove fuelled by a gas bottle which was used when someone had the money to have the bottle refilled. The house was old and had fireplaces in most of the rooms, therefore when it was very cold a fire could be lit for warmth and to cook toast on a fork. Baths and showers were cold so if they wanted a hot shower they went to the nearby swimming pool to use the facilities there. A collection of old mattresses, plenty of blankets and shabby old chairs and couches suitable for sleeping on were scattered around the rooms. It was a bit of a mess but it did not seem to worry the occupants. Simon, one of the occupants, was a quiet young man always accompanied by a sketch pad and a little dog called Dot which seemed to never leave his side. Wherever he went Dot went, sleeping with him or sitting beside him at all times. To Crystal both the dog and the young man appeared to be sad and needy and she gravitated towards him without knowing why. Actually he was not a man but a teenage boy who was very tall and needed a shave. He and Crystal, being of a similar age and both very unsure of what they were doing, just seemed to fit together.

Crystal did not go to school because it was too far away and difficult to get to in the morning. She had little money and because of this she thought about going home, but Mandy took her into the city where they could beg for money. Mandy was quite brazen. Crystal was not and she did not like asking people for money. They were criticised and mocked by some people and Crystal hated that.

Simon persuaded her to stick with him and took her for a walk to the local shopping centre to purchase new pencils and paper for his drawing. He used a card to withdraw money from an ATM.

Amazed, Crystal watched. "You have money in the bank," she said.

"Yes my parents put it there for me," he replied. "You can have some but don't tell anyone."

About once a week Simon bought food for everyone, usually it was fish and chips or hamburgers. The others never asked where the money came from, assuming he had begged for it. He and Crystal became a couple and along with Dot were always together. They slept together, actually, clung to each other, with the dog at their feet. Neither of them had any experience with sex and it just happened in a beautiful natural way led by nature's plan for humans to be together and to procreate. They were both happy to have found the other and were not worried about the immediate future. Sean told Crystal he was from Bendigo and had come to Melbourne on the train to see a concert and never gone home again.

"Why don't you go home?" asked Crystal.

"I will when I am ready," he replied. "Why don't you go home?"

"It's not safe," was all she told him.

As time passed Crystal realised that she could be pregnant but did not tell Simon just in case she was wrong. After she had missed two periods she realised she had better tell him but she didn't get the opportunity.

Simon's parents had been extremely worried about him because he had autism and was very immature. They had allowed him to go to the concert with a friend and had assumed he would return home with him. The friend was unable to help locate Simon because as far as he could remember, Simon had gone to the toilet during the concert and not returned to his seat.

The toilets were on the outside of the old venue and as Simon was washing his hands he heard a dog crying. Walking through a cobbled laneway he found himself at the edge of a busy road. Tied up under a tree was the crying dog. She was small, white and fluffy. Just above her tail was a dot of tan which looked like a splash of paint. Beneath her red collar was a note on which was written 'FREE TO A GOOD HOME'. Simon picked up the dog and walked away from the concert thinking only that he had his own dog at last, and that her name had to be Dot.

Simon's parents hired a private investigator who was able to trace him with the assistance of the bank where he had been taking cash from the ATM. He was located and the parents, along with the man they had hired, arrived one morning to take him home. He was pleased to see them and happy to go home with them but he didn't want to leave Crystal. "Can Crystal come with us?" he asked his mother.

"No," she said, "you will have to say goodbye to Crystal."

The parents' arrival and departure with Simon was all over in a matter of minutes. Sean had picked up the dog and followed his mother to the car without a backwards glance. Crystal was left feeling shocked and abandoned. Stunned at the sudden change in her situation she was frightened and did not know what on earth she would do without Simon and what she would do with her baby now that she was alone. To make things worse, with no Simon or Dot the cold, dark house was now exactly that, a cold, dark house with no warmth or comfort. She looked around and saw the cracks in the walls and ceiling, the cardboard in place of glass in the windows and the mouse droppings in the corners. Things she had not noticed so much before. Not wanting to cry because she knew she would not be able to stop, she got up and gathered her meagre belongings in a plastic bag and walked into the city.

Remembering the few times she had begged in the city she had been approached by a woman who informed her of a place where she could go if she needed help.

'I have to find that place,' she told herself.

55

Putting a Line Under It

Marcus was gobsmacked when he realised what he was seeing. He was glad that he had some valid information at last but angry that the two tapes had been stuck in a drawer so close to where he sat each day when he was in the office. He would have to speak to his colleague about that.

The tapes were both from the same address, a garage used by a motor mechanic in a nearby industrial site. One tape was from the front of the premises and the other from the back. He looked at the front view tape first and there was the evidence he had been searching for over the last few months.

He made two phone calls: the first was to Bethany asking her to come to his office as soon as possible, the other to the colleague who had left the tapes in the drawer without them being viewed. He was pleased for Bethany and angry with the other woman.

Bethany was able to meet Marcus that afternoon and as he ushered her into his office she felt very nervous. Marcus had told her she would be required to identify the driver although he was pretty sure he knew who it was now, and that for Bethany he was sure it would not be difficult.

"Sit here and I'll run the tape," he said.

Bethany sat and looked at the blank screen. When it lit up she saw a white car pull up across the road from the garage. The person behind the wheel had long black hair and was wearing large, dark sunglasses. Her insides cramped as the driver removed the wig and threw it into the back seat. Next the sunglasses were removed and followed the wig into the back of the car.

The driver's door opened and out stepped the driver, who walked to the front of the car then to the back, where pieces of plastic were peeled from the registration plates. She gasped as it was revealed to her very clearly who it was at the wheel and who had tried to harm her.

"Oh my god! I never imagined it would have been him, how could he do that to me?"

"I want you to say out loud who it is that you recognise as the driver," Marcus instructed her.

"It's my husband Joe," she replied, beginning to cry.

"I thought it was him although the time I saw him it was night and with the inside light behind him, so I wasn't one hundred percent sure," Marcus said.

"I'll get you a hot coffee." He went out of the room and returned with a mug of coffee for Bethany. By this time she was shaking and crying bitterly.

"A few weeks ago he was asking me to go back to him, to live in the same house with him. He might have tried to kill me again," she sobbed.

"Not now he won't. When you finish your coffee I will take you home and then I'm off to arrest Joe for attempted murder. The smug bastard," he added under his breath.

Bethany told the other women what she had seen today and naturally they were all shocked and sorry for her. It was obvious she was upset so they sat her down with another warm drink and covered her legs with a quilt to keep her warm. To keep her company Crystal sat beside her with Finn, who was chewing on a teething ring and gurgling happily.

"What do you feel like eating?" asked Terry "I'll make anything your heart desires."

"I don't mind what you cook but I would like a large glass of wine, thank you."

Bethany sat and drank her wine and eventually she stopped shaking, but she repeated over and over, "He loved me once and I adored him, what happened?"

56

nadine in London

Nadine had never been happier than when she was living in Earls Court London, catching the underground to the centre of the city each day for work and shopping in the famous London shops. She loved her job and had made some good friends, and had been out for dinner with several very nice Englishmen. Her little flat a stone's throw from the underground station was a picture-perfect cottage which she had furnished with both modern and antique furniture pieces which she felt went well together. Walking down Regent Street the first day in London she had come across Liberty, a wonderful shop where she fell in love with an antique Turkish rug that was now on the floor of her living room. It contrasted well with the blonde Swedish table and chairs and the small English oak dresser. Looking through the small-paned windows of her home she was able to look onto a petite but pretty cottage garden full of lavender, pentstemon and roses. She loved her little home and often wished her mother and sister Lulu could be there to enjoy it with her. 'I suppose I will invite them sometime soon.'

With her new friend Polly she began to take small breaks over the weekend to various parts of the UK and then to Europe. Paris was the first European trip and once she got the bug she went for a trip as often as she was able. Her friend suggested they should take two weeks off work and go to the island of Crete, where she had holidayed in the past and loved.

"It's a big beautiful island with lots to see and do and the food is always fresh and delicious," she told Nadine. "Not to mention the handsome Greek men," she added.

Nadine agreed so they made arrangements to fly there in June. Hiring a car at the airport they drove to a hotel in Hania in the western part of the island.

The weather was warm — actually hot compared to London — and the sky was always clear blue. The hotel where they stayed was in one of the many renovated Venetian buildings which had been built in the thirteenth century. It was a charming township fall of narrow walkways lined by shops selling colourful clothes, art and jewellery. There were many tavernas, and icecream shops, a beautiful old church which rang its bells loudly all day on Sunday. Nadine had never seen anything like it and was totally in love with the vibrant busy place.

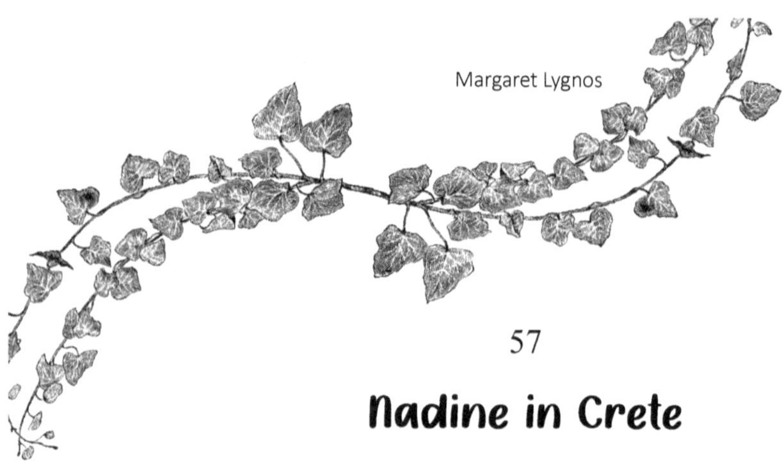

57

Nadine in Crete

Each night In Hania the two friends went out for dinner to one of the many outdoor restaurants along the water's edge. The crowded esplanade was a wide, paved area illuminated by street lights and the bustling restaurants. Large groups of people, both tourists and locals, walked up and down looking for a place to eat or just gazing at the surroundings and enjoying the evening. It was noisy and it was jam-packed with happy people just taking pleasure from the simplicity of life.

Nadine and her friend had been swimming during the afternoon and then, after a sleep, had showered and dressed up for the night out. The restaurant they chose to eat in that night was very popular with Greeks so they assumed if it served the type of food the locals liked, it must be authentic. They were seated at the front of the restaurant close to the esplanade so they were able to see everyone who came in or out.

Nadine had realised since arriving in Crete that the young Greek men were on the whole very attractive and many reminded her of Nick. To her friend she said, "I hadn't realised until we came here that Mediterranean men are the type of men I'm attracted to. I was involved with a man in Australia who is very tall, dark and handsome and now I see why I fell for him. In fact many of the men here remind me of him. His name is Nick," she said wistfully.

Sitting at the table next to the two young women was a noisy group of men and women who spoke in a mixture of English and Greek. Two of the men moved to the end of their table to be close to Nadine and her friend Polly, introducing themselves as Steve and Ari, and began chatting to them. It turned out the group were all from Australia.

"Small world isn't it," said Nadine. "I'm from Australia also — Melbourne — but I'm living and working in London at the moment."

"I'm just here for a holiday," said Ari, "I have to return home to Sydney in a month."

Nadine was attracted to Ari and he made it obvious he felt the same about her. The two women were included in the group and they shared the platters of food and drank the local white wine over the next few hours. Nadine noticed that although it was very late there were still many children up and about, running around playing, squealing, riding their bikes and having fun.

"It's a bit late for those children to be out, isn't it?" Nadine remarked.

"Greeks are smart," he said tapping the side of his head. "That way the children will sleep late tomorrow which means the parents can have a sleep in too," Ari laughed.

Eventually Nadine and Polly admitted they wanted to go as they were tired, so Ari and Steve offered to walk back to their hotel with them.

"Can I see you again tomorrow?" Ari asked.

"Yes," said Nadine, "but we have decided to go to the cemetery at Souda Bay first thing in the morning for a swim. Why don't you come with us?"

It was a short drive from Hania to Souda Bay and the four young people, who had been full of laughter on entering the cemetery, were quickly plunged into silent sorrow when they were confronted by an awful sight. Rows and rows of white crosses as far as their eyes could see. Crosses placed there in remembrance of the thousands of young allied men who had died in Crete during the Second World War when the Germans had occupied the island. Nothing much was said until they were relaxing later on the beach at midday. Swimming and a light lunch eventually lessened the heart-rending sight of the memorial to the wasted lives of so many young men and boys. Ari and Steve both acknowledged that many of the men were younger than they were and wondered just how much of their lives would be affected had they been forced to fight in a war. Realising how fortunate they were had given them all plenty to think about .

Later in the day, after a sleep and a shower, the four met up for dinner. They were now very obviously two couples and Nadine felt a stirring of feelings towards Ari that she remembered having had for Nick. She would never forget Nick, he had awakened her sexuality and enabled her to move from girlhood to womanhood in a very sensual way. She had loved him but now she was over him well and truly; the feelings she had for Ari were proof of that.

58

In the Garage

After Kosta the mechanic had completed work on the car and set it free, Lulu decided to solve the mystery of the other keys. A few were easily identified and opened drawers and boxes in the garage. One drawer contained bullets so she quickly closed that one and locked it. There were old car keys, door keys, school locker keys and others she could not recognise. She asked her mother for help but it was Terry who went with her to the garage and offered to assist her.

Looking at how Lulu had arranged the keys she was amused and interested and able to explain what some of the unusual keys had been used for. "Those big dark keys are for the rooms in our house. All the doors would have had locks once, in fact I think one or two still do. These medium keys are for old wardrobes and display cabinets."

"Okay," said Lulu. "But which key will open this door?" indicating a large wardrobe along the back wall of the garage.

"Well let's try a few and we will probably establish which is the correct key."

The two of them tried numerous keys until they found the right one. The door creaked as it was pulled open and a musty smell wafted towards them. Inside there were a number of boxes, also locked, and on the floor something in a frame which appeared to be a mirror or painting wrapped in thick sailcloth.

"Oh, this looks interesting, I wonder what's in here?" Terry began to unwrap the material, revealing a painting. "It actually looks familiar, at least the style is familiar," she added.

"What do you mean by that?" asked Lulu, who was excited that they had found something in the cupboard.

Terry remembered only a few things from her three years at secondary school, one of which was art classes with her teacher Mrs Barrow who had given her a love of nineteenth century Australian artists.

Smiling at Lulu she began, "There was a group of painters called the Heidelberg School who painted in the nineteenth century. They were impressionists and painted beautiful bush scenes and people at the beach as well as portraits. This looks like it could be one of them. She picked up the painting and carried it to the window where the light was better and read out the name of the artist.

"McCubbin." Terry gasped. "It's painted by Frederick McCubbin and it looks like it's never seen the light of day. My god, this is amazing!" Terry carried the painting into the house, Lulu running ahead yelling, "We've found a treasure!"

Justine and Bethany were as excited as Terry but Crystal could not see what all the fuss was about.

"It just looks like a lot of lanky gum trees," she muttered to Lulu.

"I'm going to ring Marcia, she has to be told. After all it is hers." Terry picked up her phone and made the call.

59

Marcia

Marcia took the painting to the national gallery to have it authenticated and valued. After investigation and consideration, the painting was declared not authentic but probably painted by one of McCubbin's fellow artists or followers. It had some value but not the millions Marcia had hoped. She vaguely remembered it hanging in the house when her grandparents were still alive and had never thought of it until now. Had it been a McCubbin it would have cost a great deal to insure, and she wanted to have it hanging in her own home as it brought happy childhood memories — plus it was a beautiful painting. Really she was pleased it was not by McCubbin because now she could keep it. At dinner the next week she told her friends that she was going to hang the painting in her home but when she died it would go to the Ian Potter Gallery in Melbourne where it would be exhibited with other paintings from the same school of artists if they wanted it. Maybe they could identify the artist.

"You never know what else could be in the garage, it's possible there are other valuables that my brother stashed away."

"What sort of things?" asked Lulu.

"I don't know, but my brother was a Vietnam veteran and when he returned to Australia at the end of the war he was depressed and wanted to be alone. He did tell me he was collecting stamps and old books, and he spent a lot of time in secondhand shops. Whenever I visited him I noticed that the house had less furniture and more stuff all over the place. He said he didn't need all the things in the house so he pushed a lot of things into the rooms he didn't use and the garage, I suppose. He was a damaged man who should never have been forced to become a soldier. He paid dearly for what was asked of him."

"Who forced him?"asked Lulu.

"The government conscripted young men according to their birth date and they were sent to train as soldiers then shipped over to Vietnam to take part in a war that had nothing to do with Australia."

"Why?"

"The prime minister at that time, Harold Holt, was sucking up to the Americans and anything they wanted he would have given them. The phrase he used was 'All the way with LBJ.' J stood for Johnson who was the American president at the time. It was a very divisive time because the men were just boys really, nineteen years old, and most people were against conscription, as it is called. Of course the sons of those two men and other politicians didn't go to Vietnam."

Changing the subject, Marcia said to Lulu, "Keep hunting, you might find something else valuable."

Driving home Marcia thought about her brother — she had tried to reconnect with him after his return to Australia but he had backed himself into an invisible isolation bunker. Their parents, who were still living at the time, tried to help him resume his pre-Vietnam life but he was unable to meet their expectations. He worked off and on but had difficulty holding down a job. Working on his car and motor bike and reading were his pastimes as far as she could remember. Her parents were sad for their son and angry at the government for what had been forced upon their boy and so many other boys. They had always voted for the Liberal Party but after the Vietnam debacle neither of them ever voted Liberal again. Marcia recalled that prior to leaving Australia her brother Carl had been engaged to a young woman called Jenny but when he returned he stubbornly refused to talk about her or even say her name.

"What a sad life some people have," she said to her cat as she walked through her front door. "Not you though puss, you're living the high life up here in the penthouse." The cat answered with a loud purr as she was scooped up into Marcia's arms.

60

Terry

Terry had always thought she would like to keep chickens but had never had the opportunity, so when she had seen the hens in the back yard she had been thrilled. Although they belonged to Bethany's children she somehow took over their care. She researched the best diet and what to put in their water to keep them healthy and was rewarded with delicious eggs. Each day she took food scraps to the coop, topped up the grain, changed their water then sat on a little seat to watch them. They had all been given names which she could never remember and wondered if the children kept changing the names or she was just getting forgetful. There is definitely a pecking order in our little flock, she thought, as a large red hen pecked at a smaller black hen.

As she sat watching the chickens scratching and pecking at the ground she felt a sudden severe pain. Clutching her abdomen she lowered her head to her knees and groaned loudly. She had experienced this pain before but it had always been brief and subsided, so she had ignored it. Today it did not go away but became a severe stabbing pain which did not let up. She struggled inside to take some paracetamol and lie down which made very little difference. Realising it was something serious she called out to Crystal to come to her room. Crystal could see at once that Terry was very unwell and rushed to her side.

"Ring an ambulance please Crystal," she managed to say.

Crystal fetched her phone and returned to Terry's room as she dialled 000. Terry was writhing in pain and vomiting some awful-looking fluid. Trying to keep her cool, Crystal grabbed a nearby towel and held it under

Terry's chin. Holding back tears she watched as her friend suffered.

"What can I do for you?" She pleaded.

"Just stay with me until the ambulance arrives."

A siren could be heard as an ambulance pulled up in the driveway, and Crystal raced to the front door to let the paramedics in. Ushering them to Terry's room she stood at the door, with tears falling down her cheeks as she watched as Terry continued to vomit. One of the paramedics inserted an intravenous line into the back of her hand and injected medication to stop the vomiting and another to deaden the pain. An oxygen mask was put over her nose and mouth and her blood pressure was taken.

"How long has she been like this?"

"Not long, it seems to have just happened."

A plastic bag of clear intravenous fluid was connected and began to run into her arm. One of the women listened to Terry's abdomen with a stethoscope and lifting her head said, "There are no bowel sounds, maybe a bowel obstruction."

Looking at Terry she said, "We'll take you to the hospital at once. You need to have some investigations today."

Crystal was left alone. She had wanted to go with Terry but could not because of the baby. Sobbing, she rang Bethany to tell her what had happened.

61

Fire Sickness

Terry lay in the hospital bed, eyes shut, not asleep but not quite awake. Thoughts were swirling through her head, coming and going from one thing to another. Eventually as her mind began to clear she imagined herself as a child, an unhappy child. Her childhood had been unsettled and disconnected, moving from one place to another at least every year. That meant that her schooling had been disrupted many times and friendships had been hard to sustain. The other children at school were not cruel to her, they were simply indifferent. More than once she'd had a friend who was a loner like her, but sooner or later she or the loner would move on. Her mother had been the only constant person in her life. A shy and uncertain child, she had been unable to look adults in the eyes when spoken to, particularly adult men. Actually she was unaware of her uncertainty and shyness, she just drifted from one thing to the next trying to do what seemed to be expected of her. She did not even recognise she was an unhappy, lonely child; she was just Terry doing what was usual for her. Up in the morning, walking to school alone, returning in the afternoon to an empty house. After school she filled in time playing school with her dolls until it was five pm, when she began preparing dinner for her mother and herself. Each night it was the same meal, mashed potato, peas and carrots and a grilled chop or sausage each. After dinner she and her mother washed up together and watched TV for an hour or two.

She could not remember her father and rarely thought about him, but sometimes she awoke from an awful dream where she had been trying to catch up with him as he flew off into the distance. In the dream she tried to fly after him, flapping and jumping like a fledgling bird, but could only get a little off the ground before she would fall back again, allowing her father to quickly disappear into the distance. When she awoke her heartbeat was fast, noisy and frightening but it would always settle down and so did she. Terry had never told her mother.

As a twelve-year-old she realised that boys liked her, and one or two even asked her to go to the pictures with them. She had said no because it was a step too far into the unknown but at fourteen she thought she was in love for the first time. John, who was a few years older than her, had already left school and was working as an apprentice builder. Without meaning to she began a sexual relationship with John. It just happened one night: they were on a bed and he just moved from one thing to another until Terry realised what they were doing. He had not asked her or told her what was happening, and because it felt so nice she let it go ahead. For the first time in her life she felt what she thought was love and affection. She didn't really like the way John looked — his nose was too big and he was short and thin — but because he made her feel so good she stayed with him, even though he did not always treat her very well. Occasionally he would come to see her and without uttering a word would push her onto her bed have sex with her, then leave. Surprisingly, after a year John up and left her to go to Melbourne for better work prospects and she was left alone. She had depended on John's company and affection and had got used to the pleasure of sex. Now she felt empty and sad. Depressed and struggling to keep going to school, she decided there was no point staying so she left school without telling her mother; she just stopped attending.

Terry answered an advertisement in the local shopping centre to work as a shop assistant and began working as a cashier. She felt moderately happy and her plan was to save enough money to go to Melbourne and find John. As time passed she forgot about John, and for one of the few times in her life she made friends with a girl her own age, whose brother, Phil, fell for her and she for him. Very quickly the relationship became physical and Terry felt a welcome return of the sexual pleasure she had become used to with John. Phil, who seemed to care for her, insisted that she go on the pill which made her wonder about sex with John and how she had not become pregnant. She and Phil were engaged when she turned sixteen and planned to marry a year later. A month before the wedding was to take place, Phil told her the wedding was off and that he had to marry someone else. 'Had to' were the words he used, no further explanation. She had been heartbroken and went to bed for a week without speaking to a soul. During that week her mother, who could see her daughter repeating her own mistakes, suggested they move to another part of Tasmania where she would not have to see Phil. Terry went one better and moved to Melbourne.

Terry realised now that her life between leaving Tasmania so many years ago and moving into the share house she now occupied had been filled with darkness and gloom, much like her childhood. After Eric died and she realised that she owned nothing and had no money, she had almost wanted to give up living. She did not actively hurt herself, she just went to bed and didn't get up. She was found by a neighbour and taken to hospital and later admitted to a psychiatric hospital where she was treated and began to recover. One of the nurses who had cared for her was a Korean woman who told Terry that her condition was called Fire Sickness in her culture. She hung onto that diagnosis and told herself often that she had suffered from Fire Sickness because she liked the unusual name rather than mental or psychiatric illness.

Living in the share house had been the happiest and most fulfilling time of her life because she was able to be herself the way she should always have been, and she was appreciated for it. She loved helping Crystal, minding Finn, picking up Justine and Bethany's children from school and anything else she could do to help her new-found friends. She loved them and they loved her — and her cooking. Though her dishes were simple, they were beautifully cooked and presented therefore everyone was happy to let her cook whatever she liked. It was a simple, happy existence, also tending the garden and caring for the chickens.

Terry enjoyed watching the birds fly down to the table where she spread seeds for them. Almost every day she picked flowers and greenery from the garden to put in the living room. She felt like she was part of a big loving family in which Justine and Bethany were her daughters and Crystal and the other three children were her grandchildren. As for Finn, whom she had grown to love dearly, he was the light in her life and she spent as much time as possible with him. Until the day she became sick Terry had been very content with her new life and now here she was in hospital probably about to die of some dreadful disease.

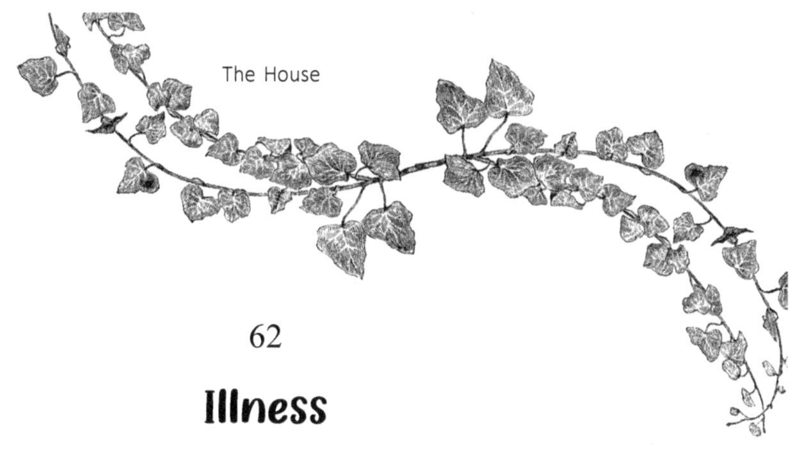

62

Illness

Bethany became the contact person for Terry while she was in hospital and therefore was given an update on Terry's prognosis and treatment. Following all the investigations that were carried out in the hospital, Bethany was requested to sit with Terry when she was to hear the results.

Terry did not know Bethany had been asked to attend so when she saw her she said, "I could be getting some bad news this afternoon, I'm glad you will be with me."

It was bad news, awful news. Terry had terminal cancer which had metastasised from her ovaries to her liver, bowel and lungs. The doctor was amazed that she had not been aware of various symptoms prior to the day she had been admitted with agonising abdominal pain. Had it been just one of her internal organs that was affected they might have been able to treat her successfully, but she was riddled with advanced tumours. To treat one then the other with surgery and chemotherapy would be long and drawn out and may not lengthen her life a great deal. However, the doctor told her that if she wished to try they would make a plan for her and attempt to give her a little more time.

After the doctor ended the consultation she squeezed Terry's hand and said she would be back to see her tomorrow. Bethany looked at Terry, eyes brimming with tears. "Oh Terry, I'm so sorry, I don't know what to say."

"No I don't know what to say either, but you have no need to be sorry. I've had a few symptoms which I've ignored so I only have myself to blame. I'll think about it and talk to the doctor tomorrow then I'll make a decision."

Terry didn't need too much time to think about whether or not she would accept treatment. She wanted to see Irene before she died and there was one other person she needed to communicate with while she had time. The next morning she began to write two letters, one to Irene and the other to a woman named Marie O'Malley, whom she had never met but who had written to her from Ireland after Eric's death.

63

Letter to Irene

My darling Irene,

It's been too long since we have been in touch and I have left you alone knowing you were happy over there away from the memories of your father and all the traumas of your childhood. However I would really like you to come home for a visit as soon as you can because I am very sick and don't have long to live. I would really love to see you again before I die.

I'm sorry that I cannot assist you with money for the fare but you can stay with me when you come.

I hope you can come home soon,

Love Mum xxx

64

Letter to Marie O'Malley

Dear Marie,

I was astonished to receive your letter and I had trouble grasping the information you wrote about. It was a bolt from the blue and such a surprise that I have neglected to answer your letter, not knowing what to say to you. It's not that I don't believe that you have a son fathered by Eric, it's just that the information was so unexpected and quite shocking.

I am prompted to write to you now because I am in ill health and am trying to tie up some loose ends in my life before I die. When you met Eric in Ireland all those years ago, he and I were still married (not happily) so you could have kept him — in fact I wish he had stayed there with you. I know he let people believe he was wealthy but that was not true, the money he spent over there was not his.

I am sorry that you were left with a child from Eric and I am sorry that there is no money for you from Eric. I worked all my life and have been left with nothing because of his selfish, arrogant behaviour.

I wish you and your son the best of health and happiness, something you would not have had with Eric.

Yours sincerely

Terry

65

Treasure

Lulu decided to have a good look at everything in the garage cupboard in the hope of finding some other interesting or valuable items. Standing on a step ladder, she reached the top shelf and with the help of Skye took all the boxes down and placed them on the bench. None of them were locked so they began to open each one. There were lots of documents and letters stored in half the boxes, a large stamp album in another, and bits and pieces of old jewellery in a small brown box. The two girls thought the jewellery looked valuable so they took it inside to show their mothers.

"I think it's mostly costume jewellery," said Bethany.

"Yes but some very old costume jewellery can be valuable, it's very collectable," Justine responded.

"What's in that little brown box?" asked Bethany, picking up the box and opening it. "Looks like an engagement ring," she added, putting the ring on her lefthand ring finger and extending her arm to show the others. It was a gold ring set with three equal-sized diamonds in a row and a smaller one at each end.

"What beautiful diamonds," Justine said admiring the ring. "I think we had better tell Marcia about this."

Lulu and Skye went back to the garage followed by their mothers, who now helped the girls look through the papers and letters.

"Here are the original plans for this house and the accompanying letter is addressed to Mr. Jack Weatherly, who it seems had the house built."

"So we are living in the house that Jack built!" said Lulu. She began to recite the nursery rhyme, *"This is the rat that ate the cheese that sat in the house that Jack built."* etc.

They spent the afternoon going through the letters and found a collection from a woman called Jenny which had been written to Carl, Marcia's brother. Each letter was folded and enclosed in a large, torn brown envelope held together by a large metal clip.

"These are letters written to Carl after he was conscripted and sent to Vietnam," Bethany said. "There are a few of them and they are all in chronological order." She sat on the top step of the step ladder and began to read them.

"This woman was very fond of Bill; she swears her love and assures him she will be waiting for him when he returns. I feel a bit like a peeping Tom — should I even be reading these letters?"

"Well, they are old letters and some people would say they are historical."

"Yes, that's true" said Bethany as she skipped to the last letter in the bunch, and her face changed as she read the contents out loud.

Dear Carl,
I have something important to tell you. I am so sorry but I am
going to break off our engagement because I have met someone
else who I wish to marry. I did love you once but not now.
Jenny

"Oh the poor man, no wonder he became a recluse, not only was he forced to become a soldier and kill people but his fiancée didn't wait for him," Bethany said sadly.

Justine picked up the ring and squinted trying to read an engraving on the inside. "Yes this was her engagement ring; it says 'J&C Together Forever'."

The women looked at each other, both thinking they had another reason to ring Marcia and invite her for dinner again. Not that they needed an excuse to speak to Marcia as she enjoyed their company as much as they enjoyed hers.

Marcia looked at the letters and after reading a few she picked up the ring and uttered, "This was a very expensive ring, I remember my parents telling Carl it was far too much money to spend on an engagement ring when he was so young and had very little money."

"Well at least she gave it back to him, so he could have sold it."

"I don't think he would have even considered selling it. He was a broken, heartsick man when he returned, poor Carl. It's silly to leave it hiding in a drawer. I have an idea what I will do with it," she said, smiling to herself.

"Marcia, did you know this is the house that Jack built?" Lulu asked excitedly.

"Is it? What do you mean?"

Lulu showed her the house plans and letter. "See? Jack Weatherly's family were the first people to live here, then your family. and now us."

"Maybe we should put a name on the front: Jack's House. I'll think about that."

Crystal, who had been out walking with Finn, arrived full of smiles. "Finn said mama and tata when we were out, isn't he clever."

'Yes he's clever and sooo cute, can I give him a cuddle? "asked Marcia, holding out her arms to take the baby. She took him and gave him a kiss on the top of his head. Finn looked up at Marcia and smiled which gave her a warm feeling and cheered her after the previous conversation about her brother.

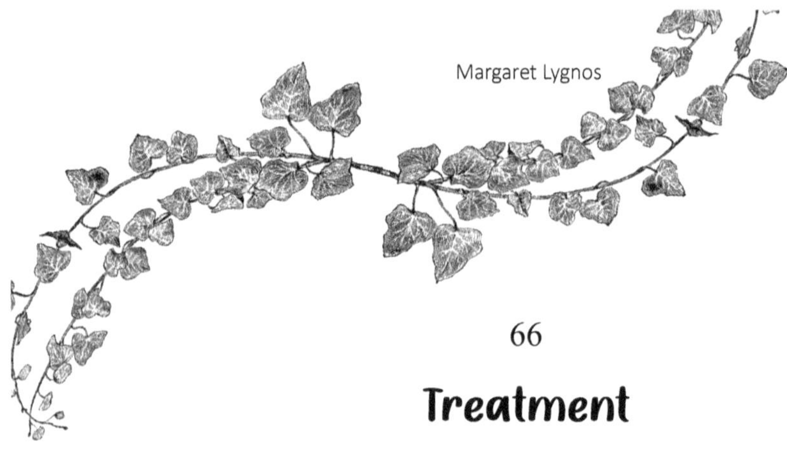

66

Treatment

After all the medical investigations were finished and the results were back, a consultation with the physician and the surgeon was scheduled for late Monday morning. Terry's nurse rang Bethany asking her to attend, which she was more than willing to do for her friend.

When the two doctors and the nurse entered the ward they found Terry and Bethany seated in arm chairs not talking, just staring out of the window down to the busy road below. Pedestrians were hurrying in all directions, cars were slowly moving forward and the trams clanged loudly as they routinely stopped to drop off passengers outside the front of the hospital.

Walking slowly to the window one of the doctors said, "The people look like ants from up here, don't they?" trying to begin the meeting on a light and friendly note.

"Yes and I never get tired of watching them rushing here and there," Terry answered. "I try to imagine what they are doing and where they are going."

Five of them sat in a circle and before either of the medical people could begin speaking, Terry cleared her throat and said, "I know I am very sick and I know that my prognosis can't be good, so I don't want you to mince words, I don't want you to stretch the truth and I don't want you to embellish the effectiveness of the treatment. I just want the cold hard facts — please."

The doctors and the nurse all exchanged glances then the physician began.

"We can do that for you Terry, but at the same time I would like you to consider the regime we have decided to present to you."

"Yes," said the other doctor. "We can help you quite a bit by concentrating on the symptoms we can treat, which will give you a little more time and keep you comfortable."

"How much time?"

"No one can ever predict that exactly, but with no treatment at all you will have less time than if you decide to accept some therapy."

"What sort of therapy?"

"Radiation therapy to the primary tumour to shrink it and some oral chemotherapy."

"Is that all?"

"No, we can surgically remove the tumour six or more weeks after the treatment has ended."

"Well I will have to think about it and as I am waiting to hear from my daughter and that will influence my decision. If she doesn't come home soon I might decide to do nothing, I'm not sure. It also depends on how I'm feeling."

The two doctors stood and prepared to leave then one turned to Terry and said, "I will be back to see you tomorrow, if you have any questions write them down and we can discuss it all then."

With a lump in her throat Terry replied, "Thank you doctor."

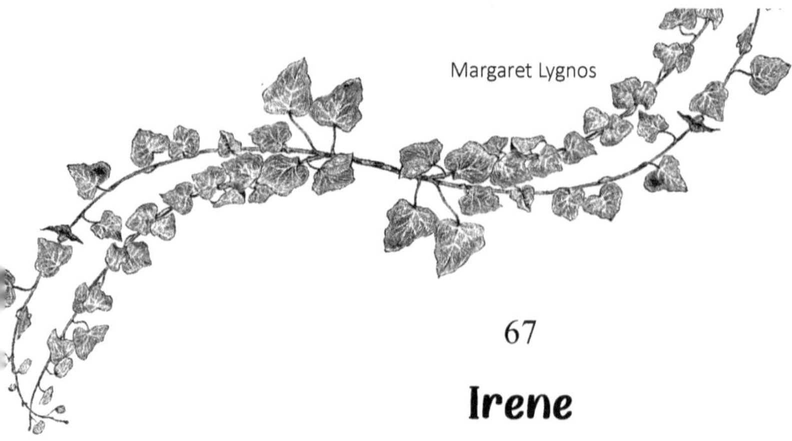

67

Irene

When Irene received and read the letter from her mother she was riddled with guilt. Her mother had always been at the back of her mind but because of her inability to stand up to Eric, which in turn had made her childhood miserable, she had felt a degree of bitterness towards her.

Now her feelings were confused, muddled and remorseful. She knew she had stayed away far too long and that she had not contacted her mother for ages, and now she wished she had been more forgiving, more understanding, and not so self absorbed.

68

Terry

When Terry had not heard from Irene one month after her letter had been posted she began to worry.

"It's quite likely she has moved, she could be anywhere in Europe. I might never see her again," Terry related to Justine.

"Give it a bit more time, Terry, your letter may have been sent on to another address. It could still find her."

Terry tried to be optimistic but it was getting difficult as she was about to commence the treatment she had almost consented to have.

Late one Friday night, a taxi pulled up outside the house and a young woman stepped out. After rechecking the address and seeing that it was correct, she paid the driver and walked onto the dark veranda and knocked on the front door. It was not long before her knocking was rewarded with a questioning voice from a woman inside, "Who is it?"

"It's Irene, I'm Terry's daughter."

A light was turned on and the door flew open, and Irene was welcomed by Justine and Bethany.

"Irene! Come in, your mother will be so happy to see you," Bethany said, followed by, "Terry, Terry, there is someone here to see you."

Dressed in an old pink dressing gown, Terry emerged from her bedroom. At the sight of her daughter she gasped and rushed forward, pulling Irene into her arms. Sobbing and patting each other on the back they hugged for a long time.

"Oh my darling girl, you have come, I'm so glad, I'm so happy to see you."

"I'm sorry Mum that I have stayed away for so long, I've been very caught up in my job and my life in London."

"It's okay, you're here now and I'm so glad."

The women all settled in the living room where Bethany made them a warm drink and toasted cheese sandwiches for everyone. It was late, so once they had told Irene all about Terry they went to bed, Irene in with her mother as that was the only room available.

The following Monday morning Terry was due to begin her treatment. After talking to Irene she decided she would go ahead with it as it would give them time together. Irene accompanied her, stayed all day, holding her hand during the painful procedure, and brought her home again. She did this each time Terry went to the hospital, even staying overnight when she was kept in.

Irene was shocked at the sight of her mother, her slim build now thin, her pretty face lined and pale and the obvious lack of energy she displayed.

Terry seemed to perk up now that Irene was with her. She looked and felt a little better in spite of her illness and the treatment. She said she felt more able to cope with whatever was thrown at her from now on. Irene decided to do everything she could for her mother to make her remaining time as comfortable and as enjoyable as possible. "I'm here for you Mum and I won't be going away."

When Terry was well enough, Irene took her out to the theatre, the movies, the zoo and the ballet; anywhere she thought would make her mother happy. Eventually Terry said, "I know you are trying to make up for the time we have been apart, but all I really want is to be with you doing ordinary things together at home. Plus all this gallivanting around the town is sapping my energy."

"Whatever you want, Mum, it's okay with me."

Irene was welcomed into the group of women and became fond of them all, admiring the way they supported each other and grateful for what they were doing for her mother. She played soccer with the children in the back garden and fed the hens when her mother was not up to it. Taking Pippy the dog for a walk one day, she allowed Sam to hold the leash. He looked up at Irene and said, "When Terry dies, who will look after Pippy?"

Irene was shocked because she was sure no one would have told Sam that Terry was going to die soon. Not sure what to tell him but not wanting to lie, she said, "If that happens, there are so many people in the house who would be happy to care for Pippy. Would you be one of those people?"

"Yes I would, I love Pippy but I don't want Terry to die."

"No, we don't want Terry to die."

69

The Ring

Crystal and Jason continued to see each other as often as possible and because there were many willing baby sitters available, they were able to go out together at night. After one night out to their favourite restaurant, Crystal came home bursting with happiness and exciting news.

"Look what Jason gave me," she said holding out her left hand for all to see. "He's given me the most beautiful engagement ring. I never ever thought I would have such a magnificent piece of jewellery!"

"That looks like the ring we found in the garage," said Lulu.

"It is, it's the same ring,"Crystal responded.

"How did he get it?"

"Marcia asked him if he would like to buy it so that it would be worn by someone and not left in a cupboard. He asked me and I said I would be happy to wear a secondhand ring, specially this one, so now we are really engaged. I love the ring and I love Jason for buying it for me."

Justine and Bethany exchanged amazed faces, knowing that Jason could never have paid the correct value of the ring. When Crystal was out of hearing they discussed the ring and both agreed that Marcia must have sold it to him at a very affordable amount.

Marcia had done just that, not wanting the ring to remain unused and shut in a box inside a cupboard. She had approached Jason telling him the story behind her brother's sad life and asking him if he would like to buy the ring for Crystal. Jason was more than happy to have it and paid the amount Marcia asked for. He was unaware of the true value and would have been gobsmacked had he known.

'After all, the initials engraved in the ring are J and C; it's made for them, so why not make a young couple happy?' Marcia said to herself, thinking of another idea she had thought up to help them.

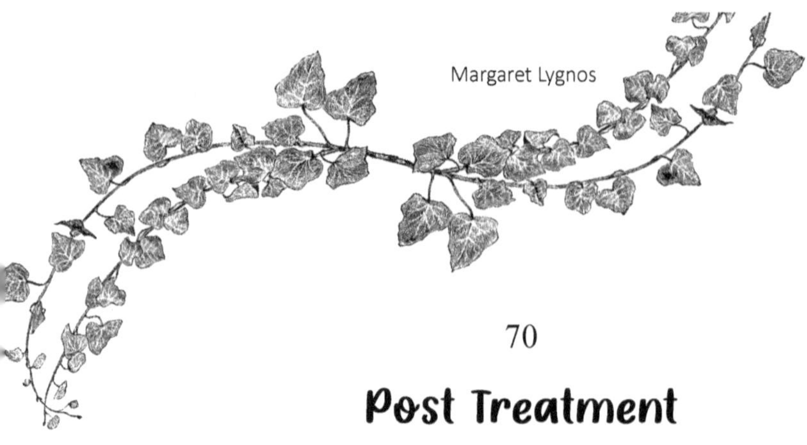

70

Post Treatment

Terry completed her treatment and looked and felt much better for a few months. Irene continued to live with her mother but as money was becoming a problem she began working two or three days a week for an agency providing admin work to city businesses. When Irene was not at home the women made sure there was always one of them at home with Terry. They had discussed the future as far as they could, but naturally no one knew how long it would be before Terry was unwell again.

Terry had made it clear that she would have no further treatment and that when her time came, she would like to die at home in the house surrounded by the people who had befriended her and made her happy.

Marcia, who was aware of the plans, wondered if she could add a little joy into the group. Jason and Crystal were planning to marry when Jason completed his study and had found a job. Marcia did not think she could help him find a job but she could give the couple a wedding to remember.

"There are two places you could have your wedding if you want my help," she told them.

"Really Marcia? That would be wonderful. We had thought we would go to the registry office and then go out for dinner. That's sort of what we had planned."

"Well, here are my ideas," she offered. "We could erect marquees here in the garden and have the wedding service and reception here, or we could do the whole thing at my place in the city. What do you think?"

Crystal spoke quietly to Jason and thought for a moment before replying, "We would like Terry to be present, so if she is not well it would be better to have the wedding here. That way she can take part if she feels up to it and maybe even have a rest during the celebration if she feels tired."

"Okay. that's settled," Marcia said, "We'll get together soon to finetune the details."

71

Sam

Now that Sam was at school he made a few new friends. One little boy called Toby was his best mate and he begged his mother to allow him to come and play on the weekend. Toby was dropped off by his mother at eleven am and the two boys jumped up and down with excitement being in each other's company away from school. Sam asked Terry if they could take Pippy outside with them to play in the back yard. They rushed out and began a noisy game of keeping the ball from Pippy, who leaped about, barking and trying to catch the ball. Bethany was pleased her son had a new friend and enjoyed hearing the sounds of laughter, squealing and barking coming from outside. Looking out of the window she noticed something brown and feathered flying through the air, squawking loudly; it was followed by another white squawking object flying in the other direction.

"Oh my goodness, the hens have got out!" Bethany raced outside, where the four hens were being pursued by Pippy who at that very moment managed to catch one of them in her mouth.

"No Pippy! No, put it down."

But Pippy was not going to put it down, she had been watching those hens for months and had always wondered what it would be like to catch one. Now she knew what it was like, and she knew by the smell it would probably taste good. She ran around the back garden with the unfortunate hen in her mouth followed by Sam, Toby, Bethany, Skye and Lulu all waving their arms and yelling for Pippy to drop the hen.

Eventually Pippy was cornered and reluctantly gave up the hen which was not badly hurt, just scared stiff. Lulu wrapped the hen in a towel, speaking comforting words and allowing her to calm down, Skye picked up Pippy and took her inside for Terry to calm her down and Bethany, with the help of Sam and Toby, herded the other hens back into the safety of their coop.

Turning to Sam, Bethany asked, "How did the hens get out?"

The two boys looked at each other sheepishly but said nothing.

"I think we need to have a talk about this, come inside and wash your hands for lunch."

It was not until Toby had gone home that Sam admitted to Bethany that it had been Toby's idea to let the hens out, but he had always wanted to see what Pippy would do if the hens were out so he had agreed.

"It was fun though Mum, wasn't it. Did you know that chickens could fly? I didn't know that chickens could fly and didn't they make a funny noise?"

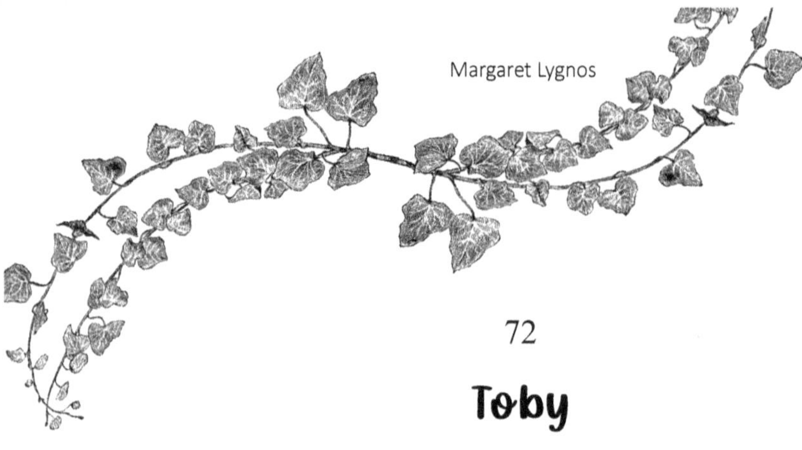

72

Toby

The next time Toby came to play with Sam, Bethany stressed that under no circumstances were they to let the hens out of their coop.

"We won't," said Sam "we're going to look for creatures today."

"What sort of creatures?" Bethany asked.

"Just any small creatures that might be looking for a home, we're going to build them a house."

"Okay, but why have you suddenly decided to look for creatures?" Bethany smiled.

"Our teacher told us that there are all sorts of creatures living everywhere, in the house, in the trees, in water, or in the back garden."

"Oh; well that sounds like a very good thing to do together, good luck searching for creatures."

Out they went on their expedition to find small creatures in the back garden.

Bethany was helping Terry, who had spread white satin fabric on the kitchen table and was about to begin cutting the material for Crystal's wedding dress. She was determined to make the dress but admitted that she would probably need some help at times. Cutting out the dress was one of those times as she would be on her feet for some time and also needed to bend and stretch over the table. Between the two women they pinned the pattern onto the fabric and Bethany began to cut. Outside the boys could be heard talking and laughing as they searched and dug in the garden.

Once the whole dress was cut out, Bethany decided she would check up on Sam and Toby. She found them both inside the chicken enclosure down on their hands and knees digging little holes inside the coop.

"Why are you in there?" asked Bethany.

"Because that's where the creatures are hiding."

"Oh, okay." Amused, Bethany replied, "I'm going to make you some lunch soon so I'll call you in shortly."

The boys continued their search until Bethany called them in for lunch. When they were seated at the table and eating contentedly, Bethany asked, "Have you found any creatures?"

"Only a few beetles and worms so far," Toby answered.

"Yes but I'm sure I heard something in there, we'll find out what it is after lunch," Sam added.

They finished eating and rushed outside. Sam returned about half an hour later asking for a container to put the creatures into.

"Will a shoe box make a good home for your creatures?"

"Perfect," Sam said taking it and returning quickly to Toby who was waiting outside the back door holding something in his hands.

Terry watched Sam take the box and said, "Dear little boys doing little boy things, it makes me so happy to see them enjoying such a simple thing." Terry smiled at Bethany as they began pinning and tacking the pieces of fabric of Crystal's dress.

Lulu and Skye had taken Pippy for a walk around the block and returned through the side gate and into the back garden. They entered the kitchen with broad smiles on their faces, obviously eager to tell something they had seen and found amusing.

"Have you seen the creatures the boys have found?" Skye asked her mother.

"No, but whatever it is, it has kept them amused for hours."

"I think you had better go and have a look," Lulu added.

Bethany and Terry went outside followed by Lulu and Skye, who had picked up the dog and was holding her close to her body. The boys were still inside the chicken enclosure where they had constructed a fort with old bricks and timber. The shoe box was inside the fort and the boys were talking to whatever creatures they had corralled in there.

"This is your new home." Toby said.

"You will be safe here," added Sam.

"I don't think they want to stay in there, they keep getting out."

Bethany bent over in an attempt to see the ungrateful creatures and began to laugh.

"What type of creatures do you think you have rescued?"

"We think they are pygmy possums."

"Or baby wallabies."

"Or perhaps we have discovered a new kind of animal."

Terry went closer and let out a little cry of alarm, "They are baby rats! Where on earth did you find them?"

"They were under the box where the hens lay their eggs," Sam replied.

"Well now we know why there are fewer eggs than we expect some days," Terry said. "Mummy rat has been feeding her babies with our eggs."

"Can we take them inside and keep them in the shoe box?" Sam pleaded.

"No, they will eat the shoe box for breakfast and run around in the house and by the end of the month we will be overrun with rats."

"They are nice though aren't they?" asked Toby.

"Yes, I suppose they're cute, but they are wild and are a pest so we can't keep them," Bethany told a disappointed Sam.

The boys looked upset as they had spent so much time looking for creatures and the ones they had found they were being forced to let go.

"I have an idea," said Bethany. "We can leave them in the fort you've made for them and we'll see if they decide to stay there. They might change their minds and probably their mother will come and find them anyway."

After Toby had gone home and everyone was busy Sam went outside to see if the baby rats were still in the shoe box. They were all still there, actually they couldn't get out because Sam had put a brick on top of the lid. He wanted to have a good close look at them and knew he could sneak them into his bedroom without being seen. Terry was having an afternoon nap on her bed with Pippy, Irene was out with Crystal visiting a friend and Justine and Bethany were in the kitchen preparing dinner. Hiding between the wall and the double bed he opened the lid and looked at the little rats. They looked harmless, very fluffy and cute, and Sam began to pick them up one at a time and inspect their bright eyes and long whiskers. Hearing someone walking up the hallway and not wanting to be caught, he grabbed the rats, shoved them into the box and pushed it under the bed. It was only Lulu going past the door towards her bedroom.

He put his head under the bed and pulled the box back towards him and noticed the lid was partially off and several of the rats had escaped. Diving back under the bed he grabbed two rats and stuffed them into the box followed quickly by the lid, which he held down firmly. When he was sure no one was watching he sneaked the box outside and returned it to the fort.

The following day Sam was disappointed the rats were nowhere to be seen, not in the shoe box, not under the nesting box, nowhere. As Sam was most upset at losing his creatures Bethany felt sorry for him and decided on a solution.

After school on Monday, Bethany took Sam and Skye to the local pet shop and told Sam he could choose a guinea pig as a pet. Sam looked about at the various animals but instead of the guinea pig he chose a brown and white rat called Raymond. Raymond was put into a cage and lived in the laundry except when Sam got him out to play. Raymond was a friendly little animal and sometimes sat perched on Sam's shoulder. If he ever ran away he eventually came back to Sam because, Bethany said, "he has been bred in captivity and he is used to people and he knows that you have the food." Sam was very pleased to have his very own creature.

73

Nadine

Nadine and Ari, together with Polly and Steve, travelled together from the western end of Crete to the east, stopping at many of the villages, beautiful beaches and famous sites of the island along the way. By the time they reached Sitia, Nadine and Ari were in love and had begun discussing their future together and how they could make it work back in Australia. Ari was from Sydney and held an important job which he really wanted to return to. Nadine had realised that it would not be prudent for her to return and work in Melbourne and was quite okay with the idea of living in Sydney.

The two couples parted company at Athens airport and Nadine and Polly returned to London where Nadine resigned from her job and prepared to return to Australia. She sublet the flat to her friend Polly, furniture and all. Nadine was sad to be leaving London but at the same time was looking forward to her future with Ari in Sydney.

Nadine did not contact her mother when she arrived in Melbourne, thinking she would just arrive and surprise her and Lulu with a knock on the door. The sight of the old house and the neat but ordinary garden shocked her but she knocked on the door, and was surprised when the door was opened by a young woman carrying a baby.

"Hello," said Crystal wrestling with Finn who was trying to get down.

"Hello," Nadine answered, "I'm looking for my mother, Justine; is she still living here?"

"Yes, come in. Oh boy will she be glad to see you."

Nadine closed the door and Crystal called out, "Justine, you have a visitor."

Justine appeared from the back of the house and almost fainted with the shock of seeing Nadine standing in the hallway. They hugged and hugged, Justine calling out to her other daughter, "Lulu, Lulu, Nadine is here." Lulu had been in the shower and emerged with a towel around her head. Rushing to Nadine she laughed and then cried with happiness. The towel fell on top of Pippy who had been disturbed by the noise and was barking and running around the three of them trying to get involved.

Justine took Nadine into the privacy of her bedroom and before she had shut the door Nadine asked, "Why are you still living in this old house with these strangers?"

"Don't get upset Nadine, they are not strangers, they are my friends, and I like living here."

"But why? It's like a refuge for homeless women."

"That's exactly what it is and I was a homeless woman. I was wretched after the house was sold and I became depressed and couldn't even work. I lost my job at the hospital but fortunately now I share a position as a receptionist with Bethany who you just met."

"Oh Mum why didn't you tell me? You could have been living in my townhouse in East Melbourne."

"I probably couldn't afford the rent."

"I own the townhouse, you wouldn't have to pay rent."

"Look Nadine, I can afford to live here. I don't have to pay rent and we share the expenses between us. It all works out well we have become very good friends and Lulu and I are really happy here. You can ask her."

"Really?"

"Yes, really."

"I don't know what to say Mum. Do you still have the car I gave you? I didn't see it out the front."

"No, your father took it after he sold the other cars. He has gone a bit loopy, Nadine, and I don't have anything to do with him. I don't *want* to have anything to do with him actually. He's out of my life and that's the way I want it to stay."

"I can't believe that my mother has been having such an awful time and I've been living it up and having the time of my life in Europe," said Nadine.

"I don't want you to feel guilty Nadine. Your father is the one who really caused the problem."

"But why did you have to give up your job?"

"I wasn't well; I had what Terry calls 'fire sickness'. I had severe depression and felt worthless. I could hardly get out of bed let alone leave the house. When our house was sold and I had to move I stayed with a friend for a short time then I was fortunate to be put in touch with Marcia who brought me here."

"I don't know what to say, Mum. What can I do now to help you?"

"I'm okay at the moment. I love these people I'm living with and I'm happy. I don't know what the future holds for me though because everything will change soon. Terry is very sick and she won't be with us for much longer and Crystal is getting married and will be moving out."

"What do you mean about Terry?"

"She has cancer and not very long to live. We're planning to have Crystal and Jason's wedding here so that Terry can be included in the day. Believe it or not I'm helping her to make Crystal's wedding dress."

"Oh Mum this is so much to take in. What about Lulu — is she still playing soccer?"

"Yes and doing very well thanks to her always having a pair of red soccer shoes that you have provided."

Nadine told her mother about Ari and that she planned to move to Sydney to live.

"We are going to live together and probably we will get married, but that's all ahead of me. I want to make sure everything is alright with you and Lulu before I take that step. Perhaps you could move to Sydney and live near me. What do you think?"

"Let's just see what eventuates in the next month or so. I can't make any decisions at the moment."

74

Terry

Most days Terry was given breakfast in bed, when she would take the morning dose of prescribed painkillers. After a shower she would feed the chickens, collect their eggs then spend the morning in the kitchen cooking. Still liking to contribute, if she felt well enough she baked biscuits and cakes for the whole household. After lunch she was usually so exhausted she needed to have an afternoon nap.

Lying on her bed with Pippy sleeping beside her, Terry gazed at the dust motes dancing through the shaft of sunlight which had managed to penetrate a slit between the window sill and the blind. From her childhood she had always been fascinated with the way dust motes were invisible until they were exposed by a strong ray of sun. Millions and millions of tiny bits floating in the air just like the stars in the Milky Way. She wondered if this was how aliens saw earth, just one of thousands of bits of dust floating in space. 'Dust is everywhere and is made up of all sorts of things,' she said to herself, thinking of a rhyme a woman had once told her.

'*Ashes to ashes, dust to dust,*
I don't do dusting
And that's a must
Could be an old friend
who has settled thus.'

With that thought in mind, her eyes were just about to close when she heard a shuffling noise at her door and it slowly opened, but she could not see anyone standing in the doorway. Lifting her head she saw that it was dear little Finn crawling into her room pushing the door before him. He continued to crawl towards the bed saying "Derry, Derry."

At the bedside he pulled himself to his feet and grinned at Terry, obviously very pleased with himself.

"You clever little boy, have you come to visit me?"

Finn laughed and began to pat Pippy on the head, waking her. Sitting up, the dog wagged his tail vigorously making a knocking sound on the bedhead, and licked Finn's hand. Terry reached for Finn and pulled him onto the bed, placing him on her other side away from the dog. Terry sang 'Twinkle Twinkle Little Star' several times, helping Finn to do the simple actions; he clapped his hands, pointed into the sky then settled into the crook of her arm and fell asleep. Terry closed her eyes and so did Pippy and soon the three of them were sound asleep.

Crystal walked down the hall calling softly for Finn and gave a sigh of delight when she found him asleep with Terry. Going to get her phone she returned with Bethany to see the sweet sight and take a photograph. They tiptoed out of the room leaving the door slightly ajar.

Finn awoke not long after, and moving to the side of the bed he lowered his feet onto the floor and walked sideways to the foot of the bed where he began to crawl towards the door saying, "Ma Ma Ma Ma Ma." Crystal had been listening out for him and met him in the hall, picked him up and returned to the kitchen.

Terry was slightly roused by the movement of Finn getting off the bed but did not wake. She dreamt that she was in the hospital having just given birth to Irene and that a nurse had taken her baby and put her into a cot beside her bed. When she woke she was distressed to find her baby had gone and began to call out "Where is my baby, who has taken my baby?"

Crystal and Bethany went running to her room and were distressed to find her in such a confused state. Crystal opened the blind to let in the light and Bethany sat on the bed reassuring Terry that she had been dreaming.

"But my baby was here with me I know she was, she was asleep here and I can still feel her warmth at my side."

"It was Finn who was on the bed with you," said Bethany.

"Was it?"

"Yes, you dreamt it was Irene but it was Finn."

"Oh that's really silly of me, of course it wasn't Irene."

"Would you like a cup of tea before you get up?"

"No, I will get up and come into the kitchen to have a cup of tea because I am going to put the zip into Crystal's dress today."

While they waited for Terry, Crystal and Bethany exchanged a few words quietly because this was not the first time Terry had woken and become confused and upset. Just last week she had woken the whole household calling for help during the night and one day recently she had became lost when out for an afternoon walk with Pippy. She had been gone for ages and Justine went out looking for her and found her more than a mile away walking further away from home.

"We will have to keep a close eye on her for her safety," Bethany said. Crystal nodded in agreement. "Poor Terry."

Terry was deteriorating and she was well aware of it but she was determined to keep going and finish Crystal's wedding dress. That evening she sewed the zip into the back of the dress and was relieved that the only thing left to do was the hem.

"Tomorrow you can put on your white shoes and the dress, hop onto the table and I'll pin up the hem," Terry said as she headed back to her room for an early night.

When Irene arrived home from work Bethany filled her in on what had happened to Terry today.

"I'll stay home with her if it's too much trouble for you," Irene said, thinking Bethany was complaining.

"No it's not too much trouble, we are concerned that's all," Bethany replied.

"When and if she needs nursing care I'm more than happy to take care of her."

"Do you think that will happen soon?"

"Well she was given only a short time to live but we don't know how short that time will be. I expect something will happen and we will see a change in her that will indicate a decline."

"Something like what?"

"Increased pain mainly, extreme tiredness, difficulty breathing or maybe lack of appetite."

"My poor mother, what an awful life she's had, and now she is sick and dying too young."

Irene went into the room she shared with her mother and looked at her as she rested on the bed.

"How are you today, Mum?"

"I'm fine, just a bit tired that's all," Terry lied.

75

More Creatures

Lulu took her muddy soccer uniform into the laundry to soak in a bucket of water. Glancing at the cage where Raymond lived, she noticed movement under an upturned plastic bowl which had been put there for Raymond to hide in. Raymond moved to the side of the cage and stood away from the bowl, which continued to move slightly. Raymond looked at Lulu expectantly and as there was no food in the cage, Lulu figured he wanted food. Either Sam forgot to fill the food bowl or Raymond's appetite has increased, she thought. After putting the clothes to soak in the bucket she opened the cupboard and took out the rat food. As she opened the cage Raymond ran under the bowl so Lulu picked it up to let him know there was food available, and there, all cuddled up together, were six little pink hairless baby rats.

"Oh!" squealed Lulu in a loud voice. "Raymond's had babies."

"What did you say?" Bethany yelled from the kitchen.

Louder she yelled, "Raymond has had babies, little pink rat babies, and they are so cute."

Everyone rushed to the laundry to see the babies.

"Well the first thing we have to do is give Raymond a new name and then we have to find out how he — she — got pregnant."

Everyone looked at Sam. "What you mean?" he asked.

"It looks like Raymond is a girl rat and for her to have babies she must have been visited by a boy rat. There has to be a mummy and a daddy to have babies," Bethany explained. "Could it be one of the rats we found out in the hen house?" Sam asked.

"Don't tell me you brought them into the house again."

"Only once, but not since the day we found them."

"Did any of the rats escape that day?"

"Yes but I put them back in the box and took them outside," Sam replied, suddenly remembering the rats running under the bed.

"Did you put them all back in the box?"

"I think so, I don't know," said Sam beginning to feel uneasy.

"I think one of them must have escaped that day and it has made friends with Raymond when he has been out of his cage and running around the house."

"I didn't know," Sam began to cry. "I thought they were all in the box."

"Don't cry Sam, it's all okay, it's done now. We can sort this out but we can't keep all these rats or we will have hundreds by the end of the year. Let's think of a new name for Raymond now. What name do you think would suit him, her?"

Sam thought for a moment and said "Mrs Rat."

"Right, Mrs Rat it is."

"What will you do with them?" Lulu wondered.

"If we can't find anyone who wants a pet rat I will give them to the pet shop," Bethany laughed, knowing full well that many people would drown them but she would not.

76

Terry

Terry was taking her pain medication more frequently and sometimes even increased the dose when the pain was difficult to manage. She knew the pain would get severe, much like the pain that had begun this awful situation and probably much worse. She was determined to enjoy Crystal and Jason's wedding which was now two weeks away, so she concentrated on that day and none after. Her plan was to have as much rest as possible and to leave as much to the other women as she could. She hoped that this would reserve her energy for the wedding.

The other women noticed and spoke about it quietly. Irene offered to speak to her mother.

"Mum are you feeling worse, are you having more pain? I have noticed you are taking a back seat which is unusual."

"Irene I want to have enough energy to enjoy the wedding and after that I will talk about how I'm feeling and about dying, not before."

"What do you mean?"

"I mean, I know I'm going to die soon, and when the pain becomes unmanageable I will probably want to die. If that's the case, I'll probably do something to bring my death closer."

"Do you mean you will kill yourself?"

"I suppose that is what I mean."

"But Mum that's awful. Surely you won't have to do that."

"Well, put it this way, I am not going to die in agony."

"You won't have to, your doctor has told you that you will have a choice of a hospice with palliative care or if someone can care for you at home, you can stay at home."

"It's not fair to ask you to do that," Terry said.

"I will be here," Irene argued, " but don't forget Bethany has offered to be your carer and she is a registered nurse."

Terry was finding the conversation tedious and with a large sigh she turned and walked to her bedroom.

"Let's just leave it for the moment. After the wedding we will talk about it and I will decide."

77

Wedding

The wedding day was wonderful, the sun shone, the garden was awash with colour and the birds were singing. Stepping into the garden Crystal lifted the hem of her beautiful but simple, close-fitting dress to reveal a pair of petit white satin shoes. A single crystal droplet hung above the scooped neckline and capped sleeves adorned her shoulders. Tiny pale pink and white flowers woven into a coronet enhanced her soft curls which fell around her pretty face. She walked towards Jason who was smiling as he waited for her in the decorated marquee. When she reached his side he took her hand and gazed at her with a look of love and admiration as they waited for the marriage celebrant to begin.

The guests were standing around talking, laughing and enjoying a drink as they waited for the service to begin. A lounge chair had been brought outside and placed in the shade for Terry to sit in so that she could hear and see everything. People soon heard that she had made the bride's dress and she accepted their admiration and compliments with grace. She had a big smile on her face and was proud of her dressmaking skills, knowing how good the wedding dress looked. Marcia and Jade sat nearby sharing Finn who was enjoying all the new faces and the general excitement.

Once the couple were pronounced man and wife they mingled with their guests and had photographs taken with everyone. The caterers began serving food to keep up with all the drinks that were being consumed. Terry was handed a plate of tasty savoury bits and pieces. As a waitress walked by with a tray of glasses filled with white wine, Terry looked at everyone enjoying the wine and said to herself 'It's years since I've enjoyed a glass of wine and as I'm going to die soon, what the heck. Will I have a glass or won't I?' she asked herself. 'Damn it, yes I will.' The next time the waitress walked by with the tray Terry asked for a glass and drank it slowly. 'That was so good and I can feel it coursing through my veins,' she thought to herself. 'It's making my toes tingle; I think it's giving me energy. It's doing something, that's for sure.'

So she had another and another, then began singing along with the mixture of music that was playing from speakers on the veranda. She slipped the empty glasses under the chair and tried to get to her feet. Bethany noticed her trying to get up and moved to help her. Smelling the wine on Terry's breath she said nothing.

"Have you had enough?" Bethany asked. "Are you tired?"

"No I'm going to dance."

She stumbled over to the DJ and asked her to play 'Dancing Queen 'by ABBA. When the song began she whooped out loud and moved to where others were dancing and began twirling and singing at the top of her voice. Bethany thought she should stay close by and was soon joined by Justine, Irene, Crystal, her mother Jade and Marcia who was still carrying Finn. One ABBA song followed another but eventually Terry was almost falling over, so Irene led her back to her chair and brought her a cup of tea. Terry drank some of the tea and spilt some onto the grass then promptly fell asleep.

Marcus offered to carry Terry inside where Bethany and Justine supervised her going to the toilet and putting her on the bed. The two women removed her outer clothes and shoes and covered her before turning out the light. Bethany placed a glass of water on the bedside table and kissed Terry goodnight.

Terry slept very late the next day and Bethany checked on her more than once, hoping she was okay. It was almost midday when finally she found her awake but not very alert.

"I'll get you a cup of tea, would you like toast?"

"I'll need the whole teapot to hydrate me and get me out of bed today."

"You don't have to get up if you don't want to."

"I'll see how I feel when I've had the tea, thank you Bethany."

Terry did not get dressed that day, and slept off and on until the following morning when she had a shower and sat in the living room all day. She carried her pain medication in her pocket, not wanting to get up and move about unnecessarily.

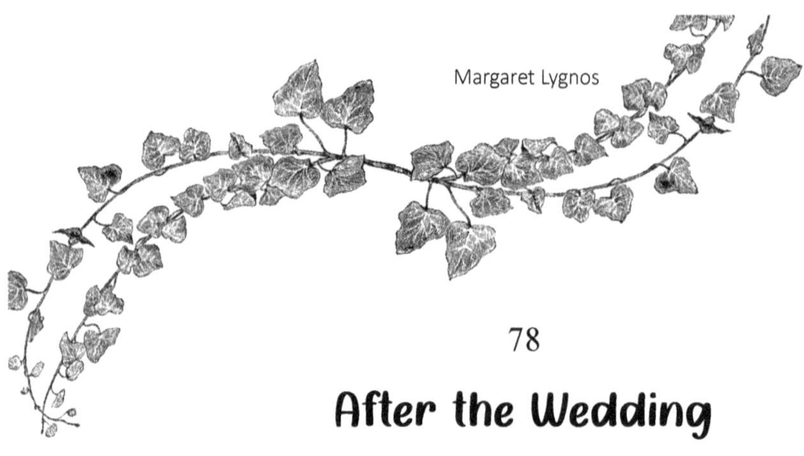

78

After the Wedding

For a honeymoon, Marcia gave Crystal and Jason the keys to her apartment which they had to themselves for three nights. Being in the city centre they were able to go to the movies, visit the beautiful gardens, the art gallery and eat out at good restaurants, or just stay in the apartment and enjoy the view. Marcia stayed at the house in Crystal's room and helped to care for Finn. She considered it a fair exchange as she felt such affection for the little boy. Knowing Crystal's room would become vacant soon she thought how much she would like to live there with these women of whom she had become so fond. Quickly she put that idea out of her mind because she already had two women whom she was considering for the room.

On the fourth day the newlyweds returned to the house, where they would stay for a week before moving away from the city so that Jason could begin his new job. Crystal packed up her few belongings and the gifts that had been given to them for their wedding. Most of her other bits and pieces she realised belonged to Finn.

Although Crystal was keen to begin her new life with Jason in their own rented house, she was also feeling sad at the thought of leaving the women and children who had become her close friends. Mostly she was troubled about saying goodbye to Terry, knowing that once she left the house she would probably never see her or speak to her again, so she decided to stay for just a little bit longer or until the dreaded day of Terry's death.

Crystal was well aware of Terry's deterioration as she spent most of her time asleep in her reclining chair, waking only when the pain returned. After taking her pain medication she drank half a glass of water, ate a very small amount of food and went back to sleep. Irene had bought a wheelchair and with Bethany's assistance they got her up in the morning and put her to bed each night, and twice a week gave her a shower.

Now and then after taking her medication Terry seemed to fall into a dream-like state in which she conversed with various imaginary people. Sometimes it caused her to get angry or sad, whereas other times she appeared to be involved in a happy conversation. On one of these occasions she woke suddenly and began laughing uncontrollably, grabbing at her abdomen because the jerking movement caused her pain.

Irene heard and, not sure what she was hearing, rushed to her mother's side, amused to see she was laughing.

"What's so funny Mum?" asked Irene.

"Oh Irene, I have to tell you and I will when I can get my breath."

"It must be really funny for you to laugh like that."

"I dreamt about a next-door neighbour who you probably remember, Roxanne."

"Yes I remember her, what did she do that was so funny?"

"Well she was a school teacher and a single mother with one child. The thing that is making me laugh so much only happened every second weekend when her child was with their father. Do you remember she was a fitness fanatic and she ran on Saturday mornings with a man who lived around the corner from us? I think they taught at the same school."

"I remember her but I don't remember her running."

"Well the first time this funny thing happened I was in the front garden pulling up weeds from under the hedge that ran along the side and front fence. She and her running mate had just returned from a run and were standing at her front gate puffing and panting. There was silence for a while then she said to him, "Want to come in for a fuck?"

He replied, "hell yeah," and I heard them running up the side path towards the back door. It made me smile."

"I suppose they were two consenting adults, that's okay isn't it?"

"No judgement, I haven't finished the story yet. Every two weeks after they went for a run they would stand at her gate and one of them would ask the other the same question but in a new and amusing way which made them laugh out loud as they ran up the side path to the house. They were like two naughty children running off to get into mischief."

"Mum! You were spying on them?"

"Not really, I was in my garden and it always made my day and would keep amused and laughing all weekend; don't forget I had your father to put up with, I needed a bit of humour in my life. Once her running partner said to her in a very pompous voice that mimicked an English army general, "I say old girl, you look like you could do with a jolly good rogering, how about it?"

"Yah, I'd love a rogering," she laughed out loud and off they went up the path to the door.

The last time I heard them was the funniest of all. This time she said to him in a voice that mimicked the clipped accent of the queen of England, "One is wondering, how does one feel about giving one one?"

They both laughed so much they set me off laughing as well and they heard me, which made them laugh even more. I went inside and giggled all day. Whenever I saw Roxanne after that we would look at each other and try not to explode with laughter."

"Were you dreaming about them just now?"

"I was just drifting off to sleep and the memory popped into my mind and tickled my fancy."

Terry settled down with a smile on her face but she could not fall asleep, there was something at the back of her mind. Aware of Irene and Bethany chuckling in the kitchen she struggled to sit up in bed and called to Irene.

"What is it Mum?" Irene said, assisting her mother to sit up.

"I've just remembered something important that I must tell you before it's too late."

"I'm all yours — fire away."

"It's a bit disjointed but I'll start at the milk bar your father and I owned years ago when you were a baby. One day a woman came into the shop looking for Eric saying that she was expecting a baby and that he was the father. After she left I never saw her again until years later, when I saw Eric leaning over the fence talking to her in Roxanne's back garden. I'm pretty sure it was her and she had a child with her, a young boy. I remember that Eric came inside, picked up his car keys and disappeared for the rest of the day. For the following three or four days I barely saw him and when he was at home he was silent. Eventually life resumed as before and he began to berate me for not giving him a son. I made every effort to keep quiet because I didn't want an argument and I didn't want to be hurt."

"What exactly are you telling me, Mum?"

"I'm telling you that you most likely have a brother."

"Wow, that's something I didn't expect, and it's very hard to hear."

"Yes I know but I think you should be aware of him. You could go to see Roxanne and ask her about the woman who was visiting her that day if you want to know any more. It's totally up to you what you do with the information."

"Won't that upset you if I become friends with these people?"

"No, not at all. Anyway I won't be here so I won't even know; besides, if he is your brother he is family and you don't have much in the way of family."

Unsure of her feelings Irene stood still, stunned by what her mother had just told her. As if to protect herself she wrapped her bright red cardigan around her slim body. Shaking her head from side to side she said. "Mum I'm shocked. This is so unexpected I hardly know what to say. I'll have to think about it before I decide what to do."

That was the last day that Terry was able to get out of bed without assistance. Overnight she had been racked with pain which the medication had barely touched. Bethany contacted Terry's doctor and arranged a consultation to deal with the next stage of her life.

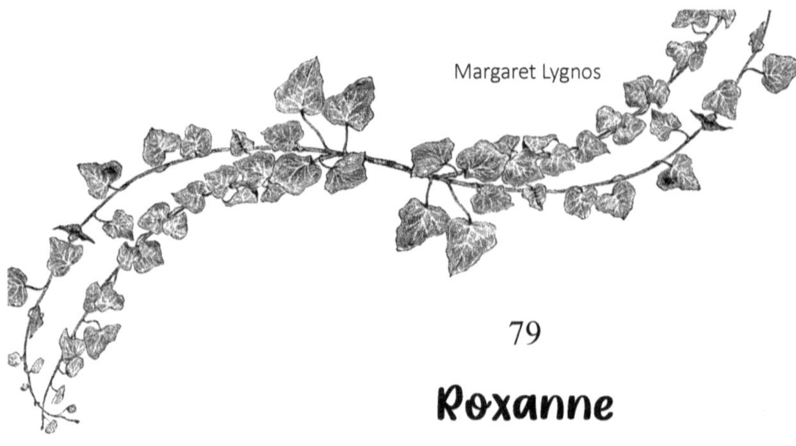

79

Roxanne

Although Irene decided to look up Roxanne to find out more about the woman and boy Terry had told her about, she was unable to begin until after Terry's death.

Fortunately Roxanne still lived in the same house and was happy to talk to Irene about what she was asking.

"I remember your family very well and I always felt sorry for your mother, I don't know how she put up with Eric. I'm sorry to speak that way about your father but -"

Irene interrupted, "Don't apologise, my father was an awful man and he treated my mother with disregard and disrespect and sometimes violence. God knows why she ever liked him, but in the end I know she hated him but was too scared to leave him. Well he left her in the end — he died."

"Yes I thought that was the situation but I never asked her anything about her marriage I didn't really know her that well. Plus she did keep her distance, giving me the impression she didn't want to get to close. It was more of a smile and a wave over the fence relationship."

"My father didn't like her having friends unless they were his friends; she was pretty sad and lonely and depressed. I feel guilty now because I left home as soon as I was able and that probably made her more miserable."

"Well, some people would say she made her bed and she should lie in it. But that doesn't mean you had to lie in it too. No one could criticise you for leaving — she should have left with you though. How is she?"

"Mum died a few weeks ago."

"Oh I'm sorry Irene, I didn't realise; poor Terry." Clearly upset, Roxanne shivered a little and picked up a bright green shawl that had fallen from the back of a chair. Draping it around her shoulders she added, "I'm shocked to hear that, she wasn't very old really, poor woman."

Roxanne made coffee which she served in her best English china cups and the two women sat at the kitchen table to talk.

"The woman you are asking about is my sister Cordelia, and her son is Gregory. They live in St Kilda and I see them about once every month. As far as I know Eric is the father of Gregory and the only time he spent with his father was the time that Terry told you about."

"Do you think my brother would like to meet me?"

"Probably, yes, because he knows he has a sister somewhere."

"So he knew about me but I didn't know about him."

Roxanne stretched her hand over the table and placing it over Irene's hand she looked into her eyes and asked, "Would you like me to ring her now — I can ask her if she will talk to you face to face?"

With her other hand Irene wiped her tear-filled eyes, "Yes, please."

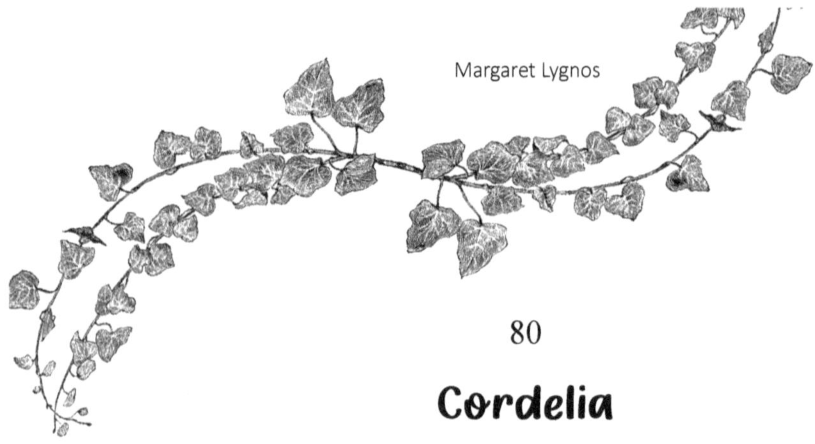

80

Cordelia

Cordelia was waiting by the window at the time she expected Irene to arrive and quickly opened the door before she even had time to knock. Greeting Irene in the open doorway she surprised her by giving her a warm hug. Smiling at each other, they entered the house and began to chat immediately.

"My sister has filled me in, so what do you want to ask me, is it about your father or Gregory?"

"My mother told me there is a possibility that I have a brother and after talking to Roxanne I think it's true," Cordelia said. "Do you think Gregory would like to meet me?"

"I know he would. He's known about you for quite a while and is keen to get to know you."

"Oh that's a relief! So did you tell him about your relationship with my father?"

"I did, and he spent a few days with Eric when he was young."

"Was that when you were visiting Roxanne?"

"Yes, and that's the only time they ever spent together."

Cordelia told Irene about the day she went to the milk bar looking for Eric and met Terry. Seeing baby Irene in the pram and Terry on her own trying to keep the milk bar going, she quickly worked out the situation and left not wanting to upset Terry any further. She did manage to find Eric but when she told him she was pregnant he said he didn't want anything to do with her or the baby so she gave up on him.

"I had the baby and managed on my own. It wasn't always easy but I'm proud to say I managed."

Cordelia held back further information about that time she and Eric had met over the fence, knowing there was no need to add to this young woman's sad story. There was also no need to tell Irene that when Eric found out he had a son he said he would leave Terry and begged Cordelia to be with him.

Cordelia had not been tempted in the least and after those few days she made sure she had no further contact with him.

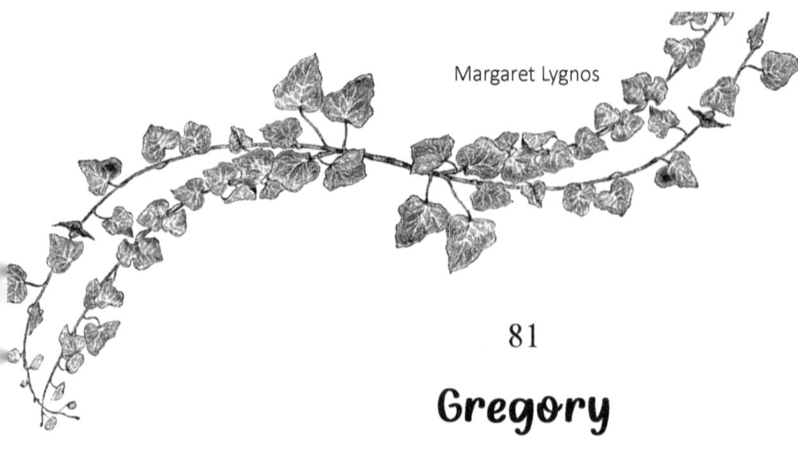

81

Gregory

Gregory lived nearby and knowing Irene was visiting his mother on that day, he half expected a phone call. As soon as he heard from Cordelia he jumped into his car and in less than thirty minutes was letting himself in through the front door of his mother's house. While the two women waited Irene found it hard to sit still; with her stomach doing back flips she stood and walked backwards and forward from the chair to the window. At last, hearing the door open, she turned and unexpectedly a familiar person entered the room.

"Oh! So you are my brother," Irene said, smiling broadly.

"Yes I am — what a surprise to see you again!"

Cordelia looked from one to the other and asked, "Have you met before?"

"Yes" they both said in unison. Irene laughed and said, "We were in secondary school together for a year. I was in year eight and Gregory was in year seven."

Gregory added, "Everyone teased us saying we were twins who had been separated at birth because we looked so alike. We both denied it and tried to ignore the teasing."

"When you didn't return after the Christmas holidays I forgot all about you," Irene said.

Cordelia watched as the pair, who really were very alike, smiled broadly as they moved towards each other and hugged. Laughing, Gregory said, "I moved to another school."

Irene moved from his arms and said. "Well here we are again and just look at us, we can't deny it now can we?"

"No we are definitely related and we must keep in touch. Do you live nearby?"

"I've been staying in my mother's accommodation but I have to move out as soon as possible because the room is needed."

"My wife and I have just bought a house and we're looking for someone to rent part of the house. I don't suppose you would be interested?" Gregory asked earnestly. "I won't lie, it's to help pay the mortgage."

"Possibly, give me the details," Irene answered him happily.

PART TWO

82

Another House

There was enormous change in the house when Crystal left and then Irene moved out, taking with her the few belongings her mother had left behind. After spending time with Gregory and his wife several times she decided to move into their house thinking it would give her a chance to get to know her brother better and time to decide if she would stay in Australia or return to the UK.

Bethany and Marcus were very much in love and keen to start living together. Marcus had a house of his own so Bethany and her two children along with Pippy the little dog and Mrs. Rat moved into his house.

The relationship between Crystal and Terry had been a godsend to both of them, filling an empty space in each of their lives. After Terry's death, Crystal felt an enormous void and lack of support which caused her to burst into tears at the slightest thing. Leaving the house seemed to be the best thing to help her move on. Jason, who had already moved to begin his new job, came to Melbourne for the funeral and to take Crystal and Finn back with him to their new house in the semi-rural town of Greenmount.

Marcia approached Justine asking her to remain as caretaker for the time being as she would be bringing more women into the house in the following weeks.

"I need you to help them settle in and to show them the ropes, is that okay?"

Justine perked up and smiled broadly at her friend, saying "I am more than happy to do that. I don't want to move at the moment although Nadine has offered me the town house or assistance moving to Sydney. I don't want to do either."

Lulu waved goodbye to the last of the house occupants, turning to look down the long hallway. A gust of wind blew through the open door and it slammed shut with a large bang. To Lulu it signified the end of a happy era of fun and friendship with an extended family. Justine came running to see what had caused the bang and found Lulu crying.

"Come here darling," she said putting her arms around Lulu, who spluttered, "I will miss them all so much. What if we don't like the new people who are coming, it will never be the same."

"Yes I know it won't be the same, we will find it very different, but it's not set in concrete; we can always change our minds, and we can always move if we are not compatible. At least we have options now."

After shedding a few tears and discussing how much they would miss their housemates, they went over the plans they had made to keep in touch with each of them, making Lulu a bit happier.

The house was eerily quiet for a short time, giving Justine time to clean and reorganise the house in an attempt to make it more suitable to accommodate four women. Lulu took over the care of the chickens which could forage outside the coop now that Pippy had gone. Lulu did miss Pippy but not Mrs Rat.

Lulu asked. "Could we get another dog or perhaps a cat?"

"Queenie from next door will probably start visiting again now that Pippy has gone, but I'll think about it," her mother replied.

83

nadine and Ari

Justine was alone in the house and she turned on some music and ramped up the volume as she mopped the floors. Singing along to a Queen CD, she swished the mop from side to side and sang at the top if her voice. 'Another one bites the dust,' swish went the mop, 'Another one bites the dust,' swish, 'and another one bites,' swish 'and another one bites,' swish, 'and another one bites the dust'. There was a knock at the front door, the swishing stopped and after rushing to turn the music down she hurried to open the door.

"Hi Mum," said a laughing Nadine. "Nice music."

"I didn't know you were coming, why didn't you tell me?" Justine yelled as she grabbed her daughter and kissed her.

"It was a bit spur of the moment. If you let me in I'll tell you why we are here."

"Is Ari with you?"

"Yes here he is, he's talking on the phone to his cousin." Ari reached the door and gave Justine a hug.

She beamed at him, "Come in, I'll make lunch."

Justine opened a bottle of wine and made a frittata and salad for the three of them which they ate outside in the shade. Draining the remainder of her wine she sat back in her chair and asked, "Well, why the surprise visit?"

"Ari and I have decided to get married and after telling his parents we thought it only fair that we come to Melbourne to tell you in person. So here we are."

"I couldn't be more delighted!" Justine grabbed her daughter then Ari, hugging them both. "And I really hope and wish for you to have a very good life together. You make a beautiful couple and I wish you every happiness together."

After lunch Nadine and Ari went off to visit his cousins, who lived in the Yarra Valley, and Justine continued with her housework, singing louder in an even better mood than before.

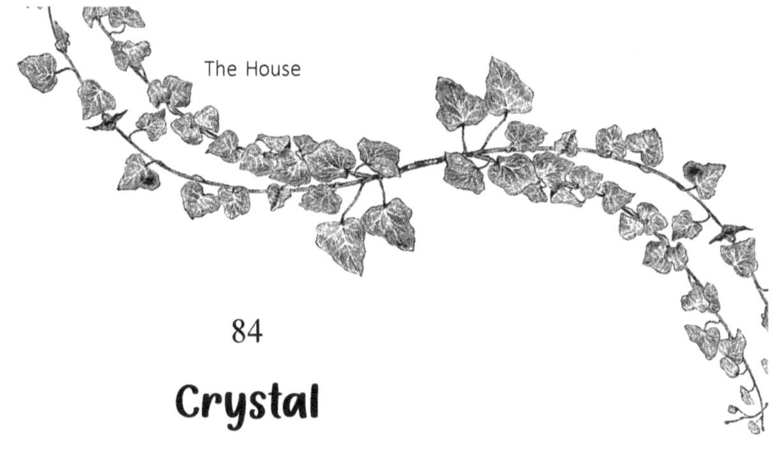

84

Crystal

Crystal had never had a home which was just her own, so moving into the simple two-bedroom brick cottage that Jason had found for them in Greenmount was beyond exciting. Jason's parents had given the young couple a few pieces of furniture and filled the pantry and fridge with everyday essentials. Walking through the house with Finn in her arms, Crystal was inspired with ideas for using each room. Although the house was old it had been updated and each window gave a view of the lush garden or the mountains in the distance.

Sifting through a pile of mail she found near the front door, she found a letter from a local group welcoming her to the area and inviting her to join their community meetings and casual gatherings.

"We don't know anyone here except Jason so we will probably go and see what they have to offer, what do you think?" she said to Finn, who smiled at her and said, "Mama."

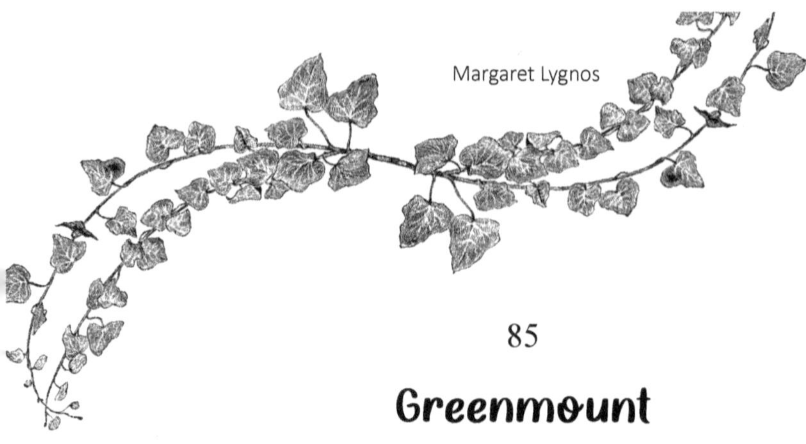

85

Greenmount

Greenmount, an old village in the Macedon Ranges, had recently been rediscovered by people wanting to experience a tree change. People of all ages and types had made it their new home, bringing demand for everyday essentials and new business and therefore more money into the area. Weekends saw the local cafes, shops and wineries thriving as tourists from nearby Melbourne visited in droves. It was a particularly busy place in the autumn when thousands of European trees displayed their autumnal colours, bringing people from Melbourne and further afield. Altogether a pleasant place to live, semi-rural, not quite in the country but more importantly not in the city.

A diverse number of women living in the village had established a support group some time ago in an effort to help newcomers blend in and make friends. It was such a success that they laughingly called their gatherings Group Therapy.

Once Crystal had the house organised she decided to seek out the women's group in the village hall. Entering the old timber building she was met by an older woman who was pinning an advertisement for an art exhibition on a noticeboard. With a broad smile she warmly welcomed Crystal and introduced herself as Mandy, telling her she was one of the founding members of this particular group, explaining why it existed and what their expectations were. Ushering Crystal into a large room, she introduced her to a number of women who were sitting in a semi-circle at a low table overseeing several small children playing on a mat before them.

"This is a good place for you to begin," said Mandy. "These women all have little children like you do so you will have something in common."

Crystal smiled at the expectant faces as she removed her coat and sat down. Although feeling nervous, she was determined to try to fit in with these people, this town and her new life as a married woman and wife of Jason. This could be where it all begins, she thought.

The morning went well and she eventually relaxed and enjoyed the casual conversations with the friendly group. One of the women, who was also new to the area and a new mother, had been experiencing the usual frequent waking and feeding problems when two of the women assured her it would soon settle down. Crystal nodded in agreement, making her feel included. There was talk of the art exhibition which was to be held in the village hall in conjunction with the next farmers' market.

Suddenly there was a loud bang as something was dropped nearby, and Crystal looked up, noticing a pretty blonde woman standing in the doorway of the kitchen staring at the table of women. Bending down, the woman picked up the tray which she had just dropped, flicked her long hair behind her shoulders and walked over to the group of women.

One of her companions smiled and said quietly "That's how she announces morning tea time."

"What do you mean?" Crystal asked in a whisper.

"She always makes a noise of some sort to let us know she's coming."

The woman, who shyly introduced herself as Kathy, stood at the table asking each of the women what they would like to drink. Taking the orders, which she wrote down on a pad, she sauntered off to the kitchen and returned with the tray carrying tea, coffee and biscuits. One of the women at the table, Jane, explained that Mandy, who seemed to be running the place, had offered Kathy the opportunity to work at the group house. Mandy thought if she worked several mornings a week it would get her used to working as a waitress and perhaps allow her to build up the confidence to apply for a job. Kathy liked being there but was far from ready to venture out into the cafes on the High Street. She found the women intimidating, although most of them treated her kindly. Not knowing how to approach them, she used the guise of dropping the tray thereby creating a noise to alert the women that she was about to approach them. Mandy had told her that although it did announce her approach to the tables, she wouldn't be permitted to do that if she was working in a restaurant. So far Kathy had not been able to heed this advice.

Crystal departed from the group house at the same time as Jane so they walked over the road to the local shops together. She'd had an immediate liking for this woman who was a good ten or fifteen years older than her.

"Have you lived here for long?" she enquired.

"Quite a long time now," Jane replied. "I moved here with my two older children and my ex-husband. We divorced and I have remarried a wonderful man called George. Actually he is Mandy's son — Mandy is my mother in law."

"Oh wow, that's quite a story. I suppose everyone has a story I certainly do."

"Yes it's true, we all have a story and each of the women you met today is included in that, particularly Kathy. She's had a very sad and depressing life but it seems she is making an effort to turn her life around. Mandy is always trying to help her."

"I have a friend called Marcia who is like Mandy, a giver or helper I suppose."

"Yes, Mandy's determined to help rehabilitate her and has asked me to give Kathy a job in my business."

"What is your business?"

"I make cakes, tarts and desserts which I supply to local restaurants and cafes."

"What job would Kathy do for you?"

"We thought she could do deliveries but we haven't tried her yet. She might start next week. Mandy is very keen but I'm still not sure."

The two women walked to where Jane had parked her car and Crystal continued her walk home happily thinking over all she had learned today, and thinking about the strange behaviour of Kathy.

86

Kathy

Kathy was a woman who'd had a very troubled time in the recent past. She had married at a young age, given birth to three children, developed an eating disorder and gained a lot of weight. Following her marriage breakdown and her husband leaving her, she had custody of the three children but following some awful neglect and abuse of them she lost custody, and the children now lived with their father and his new wife. Kathy had not seen her children or her ex-husband, Wayne, for several years yet still she regularly told Mandy that Wayne and the children would be back with her soon.

After treatment and discharge from a psychiatric institution she lived with her parents in Melbourne, but suddenly decided to return to her own home in Greenmount. Her parents were against the move but Kathy insisted and despite her parents' advice she just went ahead and moved.

"I have to go back there otherwise how will Wayne find me?" she had insisted.

Her mother told her many times. "He knows where you are Kathy, he knows you are living with us."

"I don't think so Mum. I think he is more likely to come and get me if he knows I am in my house in Greenmount."

Kathy's parents could not convince her to stay with them and when she departed her mother said, "I wash my hands of you Kathy; if you leave, don't come back."

Kathy remembered the women in the group who had befriended her when she had lived in Greenmount and quickly made herself known to Mandy who was surprised and concerned to see her back in the village.

Of course Wayne did not appear in Greenmount but Kathy kept looking out for him. Eventually she did have a new boyfriend, Chris, who she met in the local beer garden during one of her searches for Wayne. Chris was the first man she had been with since Wayne, who had been her only sexual partner. She found the way Chris treated her unpleasant and confusing but being naive she allowed it to continue, hoping Wayne would come and rescue her from this aggressive, demanding man. She imagined telling Mandy about him pushing her around and bringing his friends to watch them have sex but was reluctant because he had begun to hit her if she refused his demands. When he insisted she get into bed with his friends she really got upset, which caused more arguments and distress for her.

She wanted to tell Mandy about the situation she had found herself in, but just could not get up the courage. She often thought about what she would say: "Chris is not like Wayne, he is nasty and he hits me if I don't do what he wants. I don't like his friends to see us in bed together but that makes them happy. Sometimes I don't care too much because he gives me a tablet to take and I get sleepy. I still remember though and I don't like it. I'm not happy, I'm sad and lonely. I can't go home; my parents told me I couldn't go back to live with them. I don't know what to do. What will I do Mandy?"

She did not have this conversation with Mandy, but in the end she did not need to — Mandy visited her and found her groggy, battered and bruised.

"What has happened to you Kathy?"

Averting her eyes, she lied, "I fell over and hurt myself."

"Are you sure Kathy? Did your boyfriend hurt you?" Mandy asked.

"No."

Mandy became angry. "It's Chris isn't it? You have to kick him out, get rid of him, tell him he can't live with you any more," she advised. "Or go to the police if he won't listen to you."

"Yes I will," Kathy replied unconvincingly, keeping her eyes averted from Mandy.

Mandy went away not persuaded that Kathy would or could get him to leave, so planned to return a few days later.

Chris came home in the evening after spending some time drinking with his friends. Arriving dirty from work and drunk from too many beers, he continued to use and abuse Kathy in spite of her telling him that Mandy said he should leave.

"Who's Mandy anyway? She's just an old busybody. Tell her to mind her own business," Chris taunted, and pushed past her.

Mandy did return and found Kathy in an even worse state than before. Taking in the new bruises, the upturned furniture and untidy kitchen, she felt the rage rising within her. Drawing herself up to her full height of 180 centimetres, taking a deep breath and with shoulders back, Mandy prepared to speak out. Anyone who knew her could see it coming. This was one of those times.

"Okay Kathy, enough is enough. If you won't do it I will. I'm going to the police station and I'm going to report Chris. Are you coming with me?"

Visibly intimidated, she replied, "No. When I told Chris I would go to the police he laughed at me and said they don't care and wouldn't be interested."

"They will be interested and do care, so let's go," Mandy insisted in a less authoritive voice.

Taking a step back Kathy wrapped her arms around her body, "I can't go out looking like this," she said, beginning to cry.

Realising she had been too heavy-handed Mandy put her arms out to Kathy in an attempt to console her.

It was at this moment that Chris returned to the house and was surprised to find Kathy being comforted by Mandy. At the sight of the tall, older woman his eyes shifted from Mandy to Kathy and back again.

Taking a step backwards, "What's going on here?" he asked gruffly.

"I'm advising Kathy to kick you out. When are you leaving?"

"Yeah, yeah alright, I hear you," he retorted slinking off to the bedroom. Emerging with a small suitcase he made for the front door. Mandy was aware of a strong stench of stale alcohol and cigarettes on his clothes as he passed her.

Following him to the door she spoke quietly but firmly to him. "Don't come back."

Mandy stayed with Kathy after Chris left helping her tidy up the house and to make a simple meal. Seeing her safely in bed she prepared to leave, saying "You can ring me if you need to Kathy, I'm not far away."

Driving home Mandy was not aware that she had passed Chris's car parked nearby in a side street.

Although relieved to be at home, Mandy could not get Kathy out of her mind. Knowing her to be alone and vulnerable, small and childlike lying in her bed in the house on her own, made her feel guilty and worried that she had left her. "Stop worrying," she growled at herself.

Putting her hands around her cheeks she stared in the mirror aware that her face reflected the way she felt. Worried, exhausted, pale and dishevelled. Concern for Kathy was taking its toll.

Picking up a basket and a pair of scissors she entered her vegetable garden to harvest greens to make an omelette for her dinner and was met by a little brown rabbit nibbling on the lettuce.

"Get out of my vegie patch Peter, and don't come back."

The little animal ran at top speed into the nearby bushes.

"So that's what has been eating my greens," she muttered under her breath.

After cutting enough herbs and spinach leaves and gathering eggs from the hens, Kathy was still on her mind so she decided to give her a ring before cooking her omelette. Allowing the phone to ring out twice she became even more concerned.

"Oh damn this." Driving back to Kathy's house she rang the police on her mobile phone and arrived at the same time as a police car. No surprise that the car belonging to Chris was sitting in the driveway.

Parking her car behind Chris' car, she and the policeman approached the front door, which was ajar. They could hear Chris yelling at Kathy, who was crying loudly.

"Please leave me alone, Chris, please go away, don't hurt me."

"You're an idiot! You were on your own before I came along, you need me."

"I don't need you, I don't want you, go away."

Mandy called out, "We're here Kathy, I have brought the police with me."

Mandy and two uniformed policemen entered the bedroom where Kathy was sprawled on her bed. Rushing to Kathy's side Mandy sat on the bed to comfort her. Chris was dragged away from the room and put into the police car.

Following this awful episode Mandy felt she had to get more involved so she took Kathy under her wing and asked her to work at the village hall with a promise of more work experience in the future.

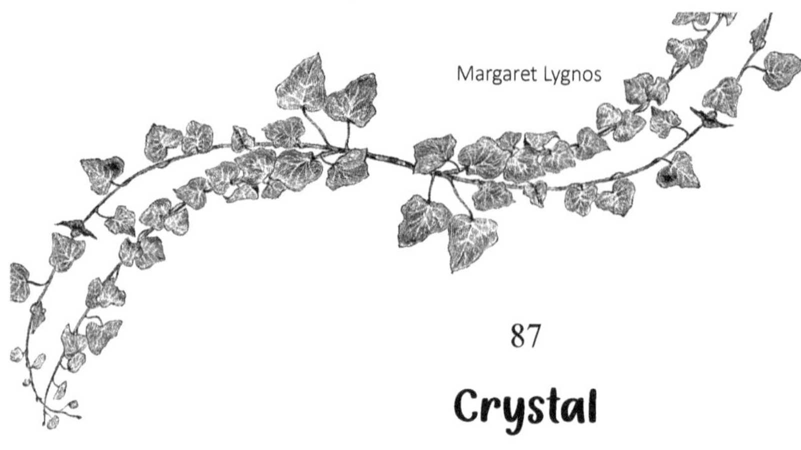

87

Crystal

Crystal continued to go weekly to the casual meetings at the village hall and became friendly with Jane and the other women. She volunteered to help prepare the hall for the upcoming Greenmount Art Exhibition which gave her a chance to ask Jane if she had decided to give Kathy the delivery job.

"Yes, and so far so good. She's been doing a good job up until today, there've been no complaints. I did have my doubts but I'm quite happy to be proved wrong."

"Is she still coming to make morning tea here as well?"

Turning Jane replied, "Yes, here she is now."

Crystal lifted her head and watched Kathy enter the kitchen.

"Wait for it," murmured Jane.

Next they heard the loud clang of a metal tray being dropped onto the wooden floor. Kathy knew Mandy did not like her dropping the tray but she was determined to stick with her weird idea. In her mind it was still a good way to let people know she was about to approach and offer them morning tea. It worked didn't it? Everyone knew she was coming, they were always smiling when she reached the groups, so she continued to drop the tray each morning.

The art exhibition was to be held the following weekend at the same time as the local craft and farmers market. Crystal was keen to go hoping to buy at least one thing to hang in the house. Jason agreed to go with her and hoped they could afford to purchase at least one of the exhibits.

88

Farmers' Market

The sun shone, making it a perfect day for the market which was very busy drawing crowds from all over the area. Children squealed with delight as they rode on the merry-go-round, mothers pushed prams, dogs strained on leads, coffee drinkers drank coffee and people shopped for fresh produce from the local farm stalls. Crystal stopped to view a truck full of young 'point of lay' chooks for sale at thirty dollars each. Thinking of the chooks and the fresh eggs she had got used to eating in Melbourne, she decided to ask Jason to build them a coop to house a few of these endearing birds.

Crystal and Jason sat under a tree to eat their lunch and were unexpectedly joined by one of Jason's workmates, resulting in their having a discussion about one of their work projects. Wanting to look at the art exhibition Crystal stood up and said, "I'll leave you two to talk. Jason I'm taking Finn and heading to the village hall, you can meet me there later, okay?"

Crystal could see Mandy and another woman at the entrance passing out information and accepting payment for sold items of art.

Excitedly Mandy clasped Crystal's arm, "Hello Crystal, I'm so glad to see you, and I think you are going to be very surprised when see some of the pencil sketches inside."

Laughing Crystal asked "Why what are they?"

"Just go and have a look you will be amazed."

Pushing the pram inside she walked cautiously around the exhibition until she found what Mandy was so excited about. On a separate wall hung three A4 size pencil-sketched portraits of a young woman. Each picture captured her looking in a different direction, her long hair either to the left or right of her face and in each sketch she was wearing the same earrings but in a different colour. The only colour in each sketch was the same dangling earrings. As she was turning to the left her right earring was red, as she turned to the right her left earring was green, and in a full-faced portrait two blue earrings were visible.

Gasping Crystal threw her hands up to her ears where the same blue earrings were dangling from her ears.

"Oh my god, where did these pictures come from?"

"I thought you'd be interested," Mandy laughed.

"Who brought them here?"

"They were entered by the mother of the artist. They were both here earlier, they're probably still around somewhere. I'm sure they'll be back later to see if they have sold any."

Rushing out of the hall Crystal felt she had to find Jason. She began to run to where she had left him but instead of Jason she was met by the familiar figure of a tall young man with a memorable smiling face; Finn's father Simon.

"Crystal," he said, then his eyes lowered to Finn who was sitting up in his pram and he said, "Did we make a baby?"

With gaping mouth and heart racing, Crystal stared at Simon, the last person she had expected to see. If truth be known she had not expected to see him ever again after the day in North Melbourne when he had walked away from her to his mother's car, walked away without even a glance back at her.

"Hello Simon, how are you?"

"I'm very well. Is that our baby?" he persisted.

Not knowing what to say she just stood still looking at him, wishing that Jason would appear but he did not — Simon's mother did.

"Hello there," she said to Crystal, who did not recognise her at first having seen her only once briefly. Then the penny dropped — the sketches.

Turning to Simon, "I see you have met a friend?"

"Yes it's Crystal," he replied happily.

"Oh I see," she said in a cooler voice, finally understanding who the young woman was. "Hello Crystal."

"Hi," came a croaky reply.

"Well come on Simon, we have to go, your father is waiting for us, say goodbye to Crystal."

Once again Simon willingly walked away with his mother only this time Crystal was glad to see him go. Spotting Jason in the distance she called to him and he was soon by her side. Immediately aware of her distress he put his arm around her and brought her close to him.

"What's wrong Crystal, what's upset you?"

She tried to tell him but she was crying and it was all mixed up so he was not sure what it was all about.

"Come with me, come and look at the sketches of me that are in the exhibition," she finally said. It was easier for Crystal to explain once Jason saw the drawings of her that Simon had done more than two years ago.

"So these were done by Finn's father Simon? They are an excellent likeness."

"Yes that's fine but he saw Finn and asked if we had made a baby."

"Hmm, he must live somewhere around here, do you think he'll be back to see you again?"

"No I don't think so, not if his mother has anything to do with it."

With his arm around Crystal's shoulder Jason began pushing the pram. "I think we should go home, perhaps that way we can avoid another meeting. Come on, let's get going"

Crystal agreed but was sad to see Simon under those circumstances. He had helped her and been her only support when she had lived in the squat in North Melbourne. They had literally clung to each other and Finn was the result of that. Crying off and on as they walked home she had never been so glad to get inside their house and close the front door.

89

Simon And His Mother

On Monday morning Jason was reluctant to leave Crystal alone but she was feeling calmer and assured him she would be okay. "I won't go out, I'll just stay at home with Finn; anyway the exhibition is over so Simon and his mother have probably gone home now."

Kissing his pretty wife, Jason added, "Ring me if anything at all happens to worry you."

Crystal smiled gratefully, "Thanks Jason, I'm sure I'll be okay."

Having decided to work in the garden she was soon outside, with Finn toddling around on the grass behind her. Down on her hands and knees she began to pull out weeds along the front fence. There were some nice ground covers planted under roses and with the weeds gone and a fresh sprinkling of water the garden looked wonderful. Crystal picked a bunch of roses, took Finn by the hand and was about to go indoors when a car pulled up at the roadside. Emerging from the driver's side of the car she was shocked to see Simon's mother Carol walking towards the gate.

Viewing each other over the gate, Crystal was aware of how alike Simon and his mother were. "Can I come in and talk to you Crystal? I won't keep you long."

Heart racing Crystal answered, "I suppose so but you will have to be quick, I'm busy this afternoon," she lied. She didn't see how she could refuse to at least speak to this woman, and anyway she did not know what she wanted yet.

Holding the door wide, Crystal said, "Come in." She did not offer Carol tea or coffee because, feeling uncomfortable, she wanted to get this over and done with as soon as possible. Simon's mother sat at the kitchen table and immediately began to say what she had come for.

"Simon has told me about your relationship when he was in North Melbourne and I know that you slept in the same bed. He has told me that you had sex several times and we have come to the conclusion that Simon is the father of your little boy. Is that correct?"

At first Crystal was not sure what to say. She knew it was easy to count the months and guess Finn's age. Thinking there was no point in denying it she said "Yes. Simon is Finn's father."

"I thought so, he looks just like Simon as a toddler."

"Yes he does look a bit like Simon." Crystal agreed.

"Well all of that means he is my grandchild, doesn't it?"

"Yes, technically."

"I'm very keen to have Finn in my life and in Simon's life also."

"But I'm married now and Jason has adopted Finn; he has our name."

"All that aside, he is still Simon's child and Simon should be able to have a relationship with him."

"Why isn't Simon here asking to see Finn?"

"You must have realised that although Simon is very clever and artistic, he is very young and unsophisticated. He can draw, paint and play music but he is very childlike. He is on the autism spectrum, that's why I'm so protective of him. I have always had to be."

Beginning to feel concerned Crystal picked up her phone and said, "I'm going to call Jason."

Jason advised her to ask Carol to leave the house. "Get her details and tell her we will seek legal advice."

Carol heard the conversation and prepared to leave. Taking a pen and paper from her bag she wrote down her phone number and handed it to Crystal. Before leaving the kitchen she picked up Finn, kissed him on the cheek and said, "Goodbye Finn. I'm your grandmother; I'll see you another day."

Finn looked at her then wriggled, eager to get down from the strange woman.

Crystal lifted Finn into his highchair, wiped his face and hands and put a bowl of food in front of him. She watched him with tears in her eyes as he ate a little, playing with some, various bits landing on the floor. Crystal was unable to eat anything at all. 'Oh god, what next,' she thought.

On his way home Jason called in to the local police station then a solicitor's office and made an appointment for the next morning. The next day they were advised that grandparents have no legal rights to their grandchildren in most normal situations, but the father of the child certainly has. The solicitor advised Jason and Crystal not to panic and to wait until they had been contacted by Carol's solicitor or Simon, because he was the only one who could make a claim for access to Finn.

The solicitor's words helped to placate Crystal and after a day or two with no contact from Simon or Carol, she began to settle down and resume her happy life with Jason and Finn.

90

Calm Before the Storm

Crystal went frequently to the village hall, meeting up with the women she had become friends with. Together with her new friends she chatted and laughed made arrangements for weekend catchups with husbands or partners, and was generally happy. The two people she was closest to were Mandy and Jane but she had also made an effort to connect with Kathy, for whom she felt great sympathy having been told a little of her sad story. The thought of another visit from Carol or Simon was no longer uppermost in her mind.

Leaving the hall after a happy morning with her friends, Crystal pushed the pram over the road to the little shopping centre. The sun was out, currawongs carolled from the nearby gum trees and the sky was the bluest of blues. Feeling content and full of the joy of living in this stunning semi-rural setting, she gazed at Finn who was sleeping soundly in his pram and said, "I'll just pop in here and get some milk then we'll go home for lunch."

Inside the shop she chatted for a few minutes to a woman while they each waited to pay for their purchases. Emerging from the shop Crystal looked from left to right and back again to where she had left Finn asleep in his pram. The pram was gone and he was nowhere to be seen.

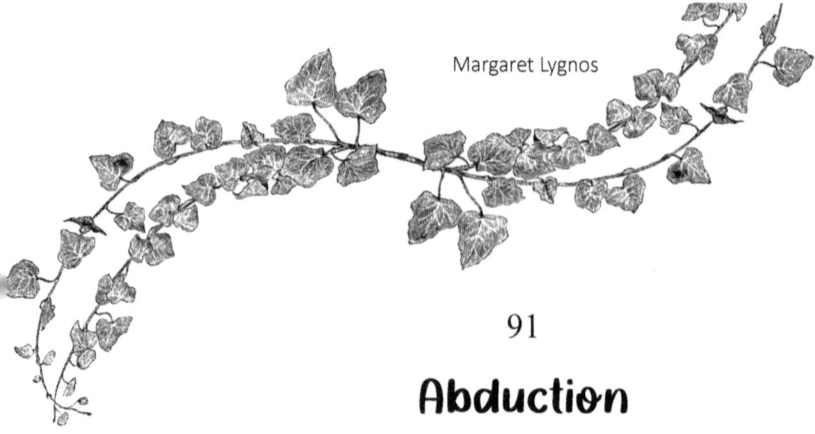

91

Abduction

A woman saw an abandoned child sleeping in a pram which was parked outside a shop. Without a second thought she grabbed the pram and began to push it towards the corner, where she turned and almost ran down the hill.

Picking up the sleeping child she pushed the pram into an overgrown garden and rammed it under an overhanging branch of a big tree, then proceeded quickly towards home.

92

Panic

"Finn, my baby, Finn!" screamed Crystal, running from shop to shop, yelling into each of the shops as she searched desperately for her child.

"Has anyone seen my baby?" she yelled, "He was in his pram just outside this shop."

Crystal ran down the street to the side road, looking down the hill and back again, yelling at the top of her voice. People began to stop, stunned by the sight of the panic-stricken young woman tearing around in circles. The sight of her manic behaviour kept one or two people away whereas others, seeing her wide-eyed terror, were quick to get involved, asking her what had happened, when she had last seen her child, why she had left him alone, how they could help and where could they look.

One of these people, a woman who frequented the local village hall, rang Mandy who quickly appeared at Crystal's side. Joined by some of the other women from the village, Mandy began to take things in hand.

"I'm ringing the police," said Mandy. "Crystal, ring Jason," She ordered.

Jason arrived at the same time as a police car and they hurried to where Crystal was still standing outside the shops, surrounded by concerned people. With his arm around her, Jason and the policemen asked everyone to stand back as they questioned Crystal. Quickly the police car left the area and began to drive around the village searching for the pram containing Finn. There was no sign of him or the pram. Two more policemen from an adjoining village were contacted and quickly drove into the area and began to consult the others.

Jason and Crystal were advised to go home and wait, hoping that someone had acted impulsively and would bring the child back. The afternoon went by slowly and with no news of Finn or any sighting of an abductor Crystal was inconsolable.

Several hours after Crystal and Jason got home a police car pulled up. Rushing to open the door, hoping to see Finn, Crystal fell back into Jason's arms crying when she did not see her precious boy.

"You haven't found him — where is he, who has him? I want my baby back."

Speaking over Crystal's distraught figure the officer said to Jason, "You gave a report a few weeks ago asking for advice about a woman who was taking an interest in Finn. Do you know who she is? Do you have her name or address?"

"Yes," said Crystal. "I know her, her name is Carol and her son is Simon. They were here because he had sketches displayed in the art exhibition. I was friends with Simon some years ago and he is Finn's father."

"Oh I see, that makes it more interesting; maybe she has taken Finn. The report you gave us just said that she wanted access to Finn."

"Yes that's most likely what has happened," Jason added hopefully. "How can we get her address, we don't know where she lives, we don't know anything about her really."

"I did have her address but I threw it out," said Crystal. "I was angry and upset with her. But I do remember she lives in Bendigo."

Spinning around to face Jason and the policeman, Crystal said, "If Simon entered the sketches in the exhibition, surely the organisers will have contact details of all the exhibiters?"

It was easy for the police to obtain the required information and discovered that Carol did live in nearby Bendigo, where she and her husband owned a newsagent and gift shop business.

93

Looking for Finn

Two uniformed policemen approached the tall, attractive woman who was dusting and replacing beautiful handcrafted ceramic objects onto a shiny glass shelf. At the nearby counter a young man stood singing quietly to music playing on a radio. After speaking to the two men for a few minutes Carol called out, "Simon, can you put the Closed for Five Minutes sign on the door and shut it please?'

Simon looked quizzically at his mother but did as he was asked then walked to his mother's side.

"Why Mum, what's wrong?"

"Finn has been abducted and we are prime suspects," she answered incredulously.

"Finn? Crystal's baby?"

"Yes. Crystal's baby has been taken by someone and the police think it could be us." .

In astonishment Simon said, "We wouldn't do that."

"No we certainly would not and did not," Carol added firmly.

The more senior policeman said, "We have a report that names you as showing an interest in Finn and wanting to have access to him, and it caused considerable anxiety to his parents. So much so that they reported the conversation you had with Finn's mother to us and we advised them to seek legal advice."

"Well yes, I did say that we wanted access to Finn, but that was as far as it went at the time. I am intending to get some legal advice also I just haven't had time yet."

"Where were you this morning at 11am?"

"I was here with my son, Simon."

"What about your husband?"

"He was out for a few hours but returned home about 11am, I think."

"Where is he now?"

"He's still at home; he'll be back here soon."

"We'll need to go to your home now and look around for any signs of Finn."

"You won't find any signs of Finn because he has never been at our house; in fact we have only seen the child once and that was a few weeks ago on a weekend when Simon's sketches were in an exhibition in Greenmount."

''None the less, we have to do everything we can to find this missing child."

Leaving the shop closed, Carol and Simon drove the five-minute journey behind the police car to their beautiful Victorian house in a tree-lined street in an old area of Bendigo. They were asked to remain outside where they paced up and down in the lush garden while Simon's father showed the two police officers around inside. After a thorough search they found absolutely no sign of a child or any child's things inside or outside the house.

Carol, by now feeling quite upset for what they had been accused of and for the disturbing news of Finn's disappearance, put her arm around Simon's waist and leaned her head on his shoulder.

"Oh darling, I'm beginning to wonder if it would have been better had we not seen Finn."

Then to the two policemen," We'll do anything we can to assist you to find Finn but I can assure you that we have nothing to do with his disappearance. I would never dream of doing such a thing, never, ever."

During this exchange Simon was looking bewildered had nothing to say.

Sadly Crystal and Jason received the news that Finn had not been located at Carol's home but they would keep watching the family.

Everything Simon's family said was checked and found to be accurate. The story of an abducted child spread like wildfire and was on all the television and radio news throughout the state.

Jason's parents drove up to be with the young couple as soon as they were told the awful news and shortly after that Justine arrived with both her daughters, Nadine and Lulu, hoping to assist in some way.

94

Marcia

Finn had been missing for a week before Marcia was able to get time off to join Crystal and Jason to offer moral support. Observing Crystal's cheerless face Marcia cried in sympathy for the girl she had become so fond of.

Imploringly she asked. "Is there anything at all that I can do to help you? I feel so useless."

"We all do, Marcia." Justine added.

"Yes I suppose I should have realised that. What are the police telling you?"

Jason joined in, "They are keeping in touch with us daily but so far they have nothing new to tell us. It's heartbreaking."

Marcia had brought some beautiful flowers and a hamper of delicious food and wine. With Justine's help she prepared a wonderful meal hoping to persuade Crystal to eat something but she hardly touched a thing. After dinner there was a knock on the door and Jason ushered Carol into the living room.

"I won't stay for long," she said, "I just wanted to see you and add my support."

"Thank you," Jason replied.

"Please get in touch with me if I can help at all. That's all I wanted to say."

Jason showed her out and returned saying, "That was nice of her. I think she is genuinely concerned and I don't think it was easy for her to come here."

"Who is she?" asked Marcia.

The story of the art exhibition and meeting Simon was told to Marcia, who said, "What a coincidence. Did you buy the sketches?

Thoughtfully Jason said, "No we forgot all about them, didn't we Crystal?"

"Yes," she replied. "I haven't thought about them at all."

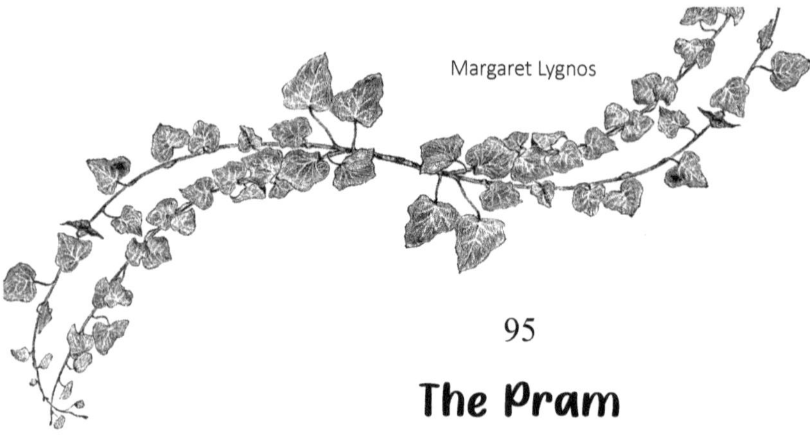

95

The Pram

Just after lunch time an elderly woman who lived around the corner from the shopping centre went out to check her mailbox. Her garden was like a jungle with overgrown shrubs and trees covering the whole area, providing a perfect place to hide anything or anyone. Pushing the low-hanging branch of a tree to the side to gain access to her mailbox she found a perfectly good pram shoved up against the trunk of the tree.

"Well I never," she muttered. "Why would that be discarded? There's nothing wrong with it, such a waste, young people these days are so wasteful."

Pulling it out of the foliage she pushed it onto her front veranda, thinking it would do nicely for her to carry her shopping home and she would try it out later that afternoon.

Very pleased with herself and her newfound shopping carrier, the elderly woman set out later for the local shops, thinking about the benefits of the pram she now possessed. Instead of two potatoes I can buy a large bag now and more than one day's shopping at a time. Smiling at one or two acquaintances as she walked up the hill she was surprised to be stopped by several people who wanted to know where she had got the pram.

"I've been unwell for a week and yesterday, when I finally went out to check the mailbox, it was in my garden," she replied more than once. "Someone threw it out and it's mine now; I found it in my own garden," she insisted. "Why are you all pestering me?"

The police were called and quickly arrived to interview the confused woman, who by now was quite upset with all the attention. She was requested to walk home with them and show them the place she had found the pram, where it was still quite obvious that something had been pushed into the garden. It had broken several small branches of a tree and flattened the long grass. The house and garden were searched and nothing else was found and according to a neighbour the elderly woman was usually not out of bed until midday on most days.

"She is very slow in the morning and usually has breakfast at lunch time. I don't think she was anywhere near the shops on the day the child went missing."

The poor old dear, visibly upset, shaking and crying, was taken inside by her neighbour who rang her son, who arrived promptly helping to reassure her that she was not in trouble.

It was more than a week since Finn had been abducted and so far the only two leads had gone nowhere, and the police putting out requests from the public to ring Crime Stoppers had received very little if any helpful information.

96

Going Nowhere

Crystal was unable to sleep and was eating virtually nothing, and seemed to her adoring husband Jason like a ghost of her former happy self. After a week he decided to resume work as his mother and Justine were with Crystal every day, and he felt he needed to have a little respite. He cared deeply but found his inability to do anything to help was almost as distressing as the loss of Finn.

"You ring me the minute you hear anything at all," he told Crystal.

Looking up at him through sad, swollen eyes she nodded. "I will."

Justine suggested a walk to the local shops as a diversion, hoping some exercise would be good for all of them. The sun was shining and it was warm but not too hot, and a slight breeze shifted through the trees as they walked the short distance to the centre of the small township. Crystal, weak from little nourishment and sleep, felt light-headed and needed to rest when they reached the village centre cafe. After a cup of coffee and a small cake, she said she was okay to walk back.

"I feel better now. Let's go past the village hall and see Mandy," she suggested. "She's there most days."

Waiting at the door Mandy watched the three women as they approached the village hall. The bright bubbly girl whom she had become so fond of was flanked by the older women giving her obvious physical support. Crystal looked so miserable. She appeared to have lost her glow.

Mandy murmured to herself, "It's as if her inner light has been extinguished."

Mandy took the girl in her arms and hugged and kissed her cheeks, murmuring, "You poor darling girl."

Greeting each other, they all sat inside one of the larger rooms where a small group of women were sewing or knitting and laughing together.

"Can I get you a cup of coffee?" Mandy offered.

"No thanks, just water; we just had coffee over the road."

"Well we can just sit for a while and you can tell me what has been discovered about Finn."

"Nothing," gulped Crystal, her eyes filling again. "Nothing has turned up, he's gone and I'm scared I'll never see him again."

Mandy took Crystal's hand, adding hopefully, "I'm sure he will be found. The police are looking everywhere and a missing child is a top priority for them."

Crystal nodded, then looking around the familiar room she noticed someone else bringing the tea and coffee to the nearby group. "Where is Kathy, I thought she worked here every day?"

"She's sick and hasn't been able to come for a few days." Mandy replied, then laughed, adding. "We miss her but we don't miss the tray clanging on the floor. Then again, she has helped to bring some of the community together, some people were coming in just to hear and see the tray being dropped."

"What's all that about?" asked Justine.

Mandy related the story, explaining the way she was trying to help Kathy learn to be a waitress in the hope it would help her find future employment.

"She'll get there in the end, I'm determined to make it work," Mandy said, but even she was beginning to wonder now that Kathy was absent yet again.

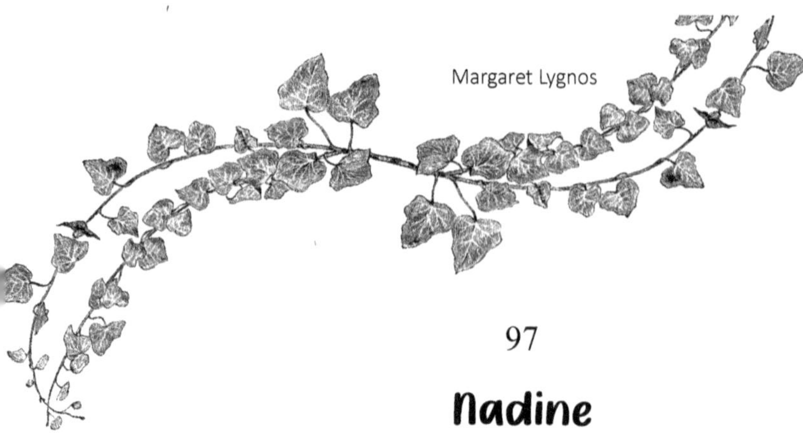

97

Nadine

Justine offered to stay a bit longer when her daughters went back to Melbourne after the weekend so that Lulu would not miss any more school.

"It was so good of them both to come all the way to see me," Crystal said.

"We all think of you as family now, and Nadine will stay with Lulu. Actually Nadine is staying with us for a while. She didn't want to stay on her own with the new women in the house, she doesn't know them yet. I'm still getting to know them myself; they seem to be a nice bunch but nothing like our original group."

"Is Nadine moving back to Melbourne?"

"Maybe, she isn't quite sure."

"Why, what has happened to change her mind?"

"A bit of an upset with Ari, something I'm hoping they will overcome."

For just a moment the thought of Nadine and Ari not getting on gave Crystal something else to think about. The disappearance of Finn took a slight shift back for just a second as a look of surprise was mirrored on her face. Pulling her hair back behind her head, she secured it with a red scrunchie that had been around her wrist.

"They're not splitting up are they?"

"I'm not sure," Justine answered looking at Crystal. She wondered whether or not to tell her and went over in her head what had happened the night Nadine had returned to the house sobbing. When she'd asked

Nadine what had happened, Nadine related the afternoon's events, stopping and starting between periods of obvious distress. Eventually the whole unfortunate story was told and Justine hardly knew what to say as it was something she had dreaded since she became aware of the unmentionable dancing her eldest daughter had once been engaged in.

"I hope they won't split up," Justine said, "but it's not looking good at the moment."

98

Nadine Tells Her Mother

"Ari and I went to his uncle's house where his cousins were waiting for us. We had a lovely dinner together and were all enjoying ourselves when two old friends of Ari's called in to see him. They were only there for a short time when one of the men spoke quietly to the others and beckoned them outside, taking Ari with them. They were outside for about half an hour before Ari came back in and pulled me aside into a bedroom. He was red-faced and obviously really upset about something. I could tell just by the look of him that something very serious had happened. He grabbed me hard on both arms, shook me and asked if it was true that I had been a dancer in a club and naturally I had to admit that I had. Two of his friends had sworn it was me they had seen dancing and as I had never told him, he was completely bowled over."

"I can't marry you, my family will never accept you, I'll be exiled from them," he yelled at me.

I told him I was sorry, that I can't change the past and that I always intended to tell him but the right time had never come up.

"He kept harassing me, I think I should have denied it but stupidly I didn't so I had to leave, I couldn't face his family. I called a taxi. Oh my god, what have I done?"

Justine's heart sank as she led her shattered daughter to the couch. "My advice is to sleep on it. Yes you danced but that was all, you were a dancer only and if he can't see around that well I suppose you will have to get over him."

"I love him Mum."

"I know, but how much does he love you?"

"He says he can't live without me."

"Well we will see then, won't we? Time will tell," Justine added not really feeling too hopeful. "Time will tell."

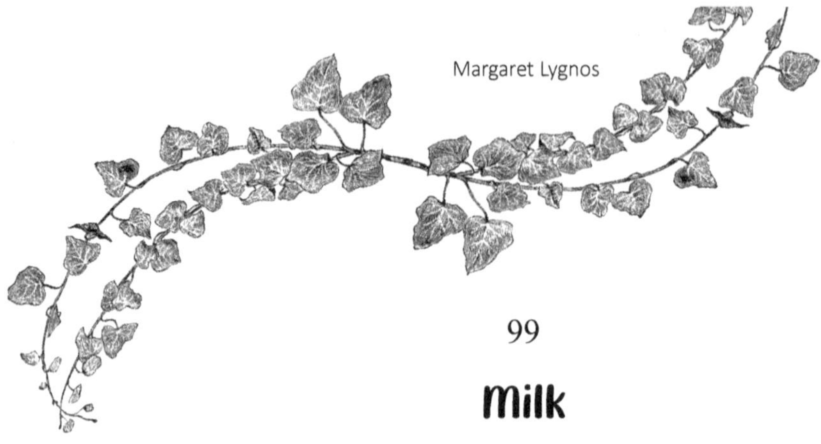

99

milk

Mandy filled the kettle and pushed the button to start the boil. Placing a tea bag in a cup, she opened the fridge and reached for the milk.

"Damn, no milk, I forgot all about it when I was out today. Damn it, I'll have to go out again, I'll need some in the morning."

Mandy pulled on her coat and drove to the local shop where the lights were partially dimmed as the shop was just about to close. Hurrying through the door she almost collided with a young man whom she knew from the village hall yoga class. "Hi," they both said, laughing as they did the awkward dance stepping around each other. Waving to each other they carried on with their respective tasks. There were very few people in the small shop doing last-minute shopping as she was. Grabbing the milk she hurried to the counter to pay. Being quite tall she was able to see over the top of some of the shelves. A familiar head appeared in an aisle over in the corner of the shop. Because a few lights had been turned off in anticipation of the shop closing, visibility was poor so she was not really sure. Leaving the cashier she walked to where she had seen the familiar head but there was no one there, just a plastic shopping basket containing grocery items and disposable nappies that had been left on the floor. I must have been seeing things, she said to herself, paying for the milk and returning to her car to drive home.

The following morning at the village hall she prepared two areas for the morning groups, a book club in one of the small rooms and a large room for the twice-weekly yoga class.

The young man whom she had almost collided with last night burst through the door saying, "Any chance of a coffee before we begin?"

"Yes but you will have to help yourself, Kathy isn't here, she's still not well."

"That's okay, I can do that, but I thought she was well again: I'm sure I've seen her recently. Actually it was last night, just before I saw you. Didn't you see her?"

"No—well I'm not sure."

Mandy stood thinking as she looked out of the window. The grevilleas in the garden bed were moving with the weight of eastern spinebills drinking nectar from the elongated flowers. Her mind raced and she felt a cold shiver ripple through her body as she recalled memories and visions of a little boy called Tommy who had been abused and neglected by his mother some years ago.

Holding her hands up to her cheeks she said out aloud. "Oh my god!"

Grabbing her phone and car keys, Mandy ran to her car, driving out of the car park in a cloud of dust. As she drove she rang Jane, asking her, "Has Kathy done your deliveries this week?"

"No she's sick, I had to do it myself."

"Okay thanks, got to go."

When she arrived at Kathy's house it looked much the same as usual: grass in need of mowing, windows dirty, curtains closed and an old rusty car parked in the driveway. Knocking loudly on the door she called out "Kathy, Kathy are you there?"

There was no answer. She walked to the side of the house and peered over a locked gate into the untidy back yard; nothing to see there. Back to the front door, bang, bang. "Kathy, Kathy!"

Why didn't I think of it sooner, she said to herself as she began to dial Kathy's phone number. Inside the house she heard a phone ringing until it rang out. Immediately she rang the police.

A police car arrived promptly and two policemen joined Mandy at the front door where she quickly filled them in on what had just happened with the phone, the suspected sighting in the shop last night and the abandoned shopping basket containing nappies.

"I have banged on the door and yelled out for ten minutes and she doesn't answer! I hate to think what is going on in there, can you force the door?"

The door was easily forced open and the three of them hurried inside. Mandy ran to a bedroom where she remembered there had been a cot. Finding it empty she ran her hand over the sheets which were slightly warm. About to move to another room she heard the tiniest sound coming from the closed wardrobe. Sliding the door open she found Finn sleeping on the floor on top of a pile of old clothes and shoes.

Picking Finn up into her arms she said to him "Finn, Finn, wake up darling, wake up."

One of the policemen came running and at the same time the other called out 'eureka' as he located Kathy curled up in a broom cupboard in the laundry.

An ambulance was called to assess Finn who had been mildly sedated, but attention soon turned to Kathy who had difficulty walking and talking, making it obvious she had taken something. In the meantime Finn began to rouse from his slumber and stared confused at Mandy. Carrying him to the kitchen she gave him a drink of water then rang Crystal. By this time he was fully awake and had begun to cry for his mother.

When Crystal answered her phone the first thing she heard was Finn crying then Mandy's voice exclaiming, "I have found him and he is safe! I'll take him to the medical centre, meet me there in ten minutes."

100

After

Finn was seen by a doctor and as there were no obvious injuries, was able to go home with his parents. Crystal cried with relief as she took her son into her arms and repeated over and over again, "I'll never leave you alone again my darling boy, not even for a minute, never ever."

Finn was very clingy and would not allow his mother out of his sight, Crystal didn't mind, she didn't want to let him out of her arms anyway. Kathy was taken to hospital for assessment, and once she was properly conscious she was arrested and charged with kidnapping. This being her second offence meant she was in serious trouble. Mandy was beating herself up over her part in aiding Kathy to befriend Crystal and Finn, and felt she had trusted her too much.

"I feel I'm partly to blame," she said. "I should not have tried to help her. It was a disaster waiting to happen."

No one blamed Mandy, after all it was she who worked out where Finn was and it was she who had rescued him from the cupboard, from the house and from goodness knows what.

Justine spoke up, saying, "If Kathy had died alone in the house from an overdose Finn might never have been found, and it's obvious Kathy has very serious psychological problems; it's hardly your fault."

"Yes but I still feel partly to blame."

"What's her story anyway?" Justine wondered.

"It's quite sad really. She came to live here when she was married with three little children. Her husband left her for another woman and she never coped with the divorce, always thinking that he would come back to her.”

“That must have been hard, poor woman.”

“Well to get her ex-husband’s attention she made her son sick so badly that he was hospitalised and her husband always rushed to see the little boy.”

“How did she make him sick?”

“Firstly she didn’t give him his medication and allowed an asthma attack to progress to a dangerous point where she had to call an ambulance. This happened at least twice. Then she sedated him and called an ambulance telling the medics that he’d had a fit. This is why she lost custody of her three children and became even more disturbed.”

“My goodness that’s serious!”

“Yes, very serious, and her other two children, twin girls only six years old, were neglected and often left alone in the house. I think they lived on jam sandwiches most of the time. Such dear little girls, and now thankfully living happily with their father and his second wife.”

“Did she go to prison?”

“No, but she spent quite a long time in a psych hospital and once discharged was supposed to be living with her parents and being supervised.”

“What happened to that arrangement?”

“She walked out and they have given up on her. I don’t know what else they could have done.”

101

Kathy

Kathy once again was incarcerated in a psychiatric institution with very little chance of release as the possibility of her reoffending was too great. Her medications were reviewed and changed and she was seen frequently by a psychiatric team. At first she was mystified by the restrictions placed on her and could not understand what she had done wrong.

Remembering the day she had been found in the cupboard she recalled the banging on the front door which had scared her. She had picked up the sleeping Finn from the cot and put him in the bottom of the cupboard, then running to the laundry she had curled up behind the vacuum cleaner in another cupboard. Drifting off into a medicated sleep she had barely heard the bells and sirens of a police car as it arrived at her house, the phone ringing, the banging and yelling. In the distance, Mandy talking loudly to someone, "I've found him, I've got him, he's okay." That was all she remembered until she woke up in a hospital bed where she told the psychiatrist, "I thought it was my baby Tommy. I found him in the street. No one else wanted him. I wanted him to love me. I thought Wayne would come back to me now that I'm slim and pretty again and if I had Tommy. I'm sad and lonely, even my parents are cross with me and they don't visit me very often."

As a courtesy Mandy quickly got in touch with Wayne letting him know of Kathy's arrest, saving him from hearing about it on the television news. He was shocked and saddened and felt just a little guilty again, as he felt it was their separation that had been the catalyst for Kathy's deteriorating behaviour. Getting off the phone after speaking to Mandy he took his son Tommy in his arms and hugged him hard for quite a long time, making Tommy fidgety and keen to get down.

"I love you, Tommy."

"Yeah I know you love me Dad, but next time don't squeeze so hard." He giggled, getting to his feet and running off to play.

102

After

Eventually Crystal regained her confidence and would go out alone. She rejoined her friends twice a week at the village hall and enrolled in an online course to complete year twelve. Jason's mother and Justine had returned to Melbourne and Crystal was determined to keep her promise to visit them soon. Marcia had given them an invitation to stay with her whenever they were in Melbourne. Her friendship with Nadine had blossomed and she rang her frequently, always hopeful Ari had been in touch with her to mend their relationship.

Sadly Nadine did not hear from Ari; there was just deathly silence. He had even done something with his phone making it impossible to contact him. Crystal and Jason spent a weekend in Melbourne and stayed at Marcia's city apartment and Crystal spent some time with Nadine.

"Have you decided what you will do?"

"Well I suppose I'm luckier than most people, I have three choices, I can go back to Sydney and work in the same company, stay in Melbourne and find a new job or I could go back to London where I was very content, I'm not sure yet. I'm really very disappointed in Ari, I thought he would at least get in touch with me, even if it is to tell me it's over."

"Yes you'd expect something from him."

"Yes. But I'm not going to cry over him any more even though I'm very hurt."

"Yeah it's pretty weak of him," Crystal sympathised.

"Gutless, I think you mean," Nadine responded.

"At least you know where you stand with him though."

"Yeah, and when I talk to Mum I can read her face, it says. 'I told you so.' She never says it, she doesn't have to."

"What do you mean by that?"

"When she found out about my dancing job she went into meltdown. To her it was about as bad as soliciting on the streets of St Kilda."

"I'd love to see you dancing, I bet you were good."

"Well that's another option for me I suppose, returning to dancing."

"Would you?"

"I don't think, so the hours are awful. I prefer nine to five. When I was at uni it suited me because I could go to lectures during the day and the money was good, that's really what kept me there, No, that would be going backwards, I need to go forward. Anyway I had my heart broken for the first time there and the man, Nick, is probably still involved. So no, I don't think so."

103

Finn

Finn was turning two and crystal decided to have a party. All the usual people were invited and also Simon and his parents. When they arrived they brought with them the three sketches of Crystal which had been exhibited in the recent art show. Jason got a hammer and nails and he and his father hung them over the fire place which seemed to be the perfect spot. Simon was complimented on his artistic ability. Finn looked up at the pictures and said "Mama."

Nadine announced that she was returning to London and had been offered a job in the same company she had previously worked in. Justine was sad her daughter was going away again but secretly thought it was probably the best choice.

"When are you leaving?" asked Crystal, feeling a little disappointed.

"After Christmas, I'm due to start work early in January."

"Okay, so still a few weeks to go."

"Yes I need to go to Sydney to tie up some loose ends then I'll spend Christmas with Mum and Lulu, then I'll be off to spend New Year's Eve in London."

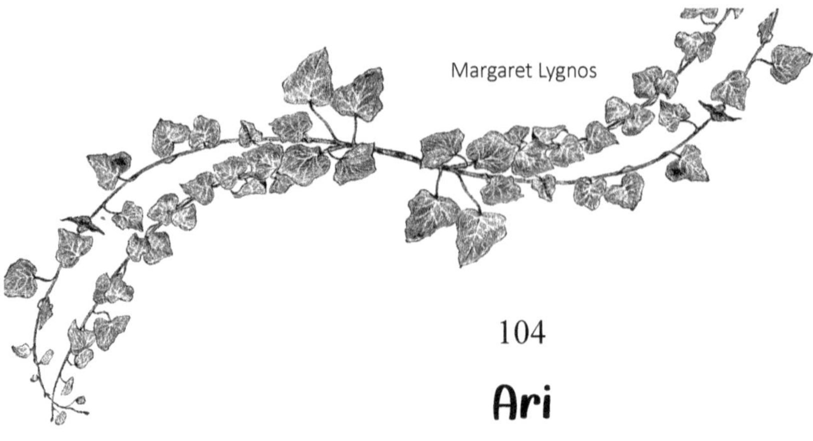

104

Ari

On Monday morning as Justine swept the front veranda, her eyes were drawn to the sky by the sound of an aeroplane climbing into the heavens. She imagined it could be the plane that was carrying her daughter Nadine away from her back to London. It was a feeling she had felt before several years ago, when Nadine had gone on her first trip to Europe. Stopping and leaning on the broom handle, she felt a wave of sadness realising she may not see Nadine for a long time.

In the process of closing the door she was aware of a car pulling up in the driveway, and pulling the front door wide open she watched as a man exited from a taxi with difficulty. Getting his footing and aided by crutches he walked unsteadily towards her. Noticing his long hair and his unshaven face she waited to see who he was and what he wanted.

"Probably someone we don't want here,' she thought, 'someone who is out to cause trouble for someone.'

"Can I help you?"

"Yes Justine, I've come to see Nadine."

She peered at him, suddenly realising that the man was Ari.

Shocked at his dishevelled appearance she cried, "Ari, is that you? Where have you been for the last month? What has happened to you?"

Hobbling towards her he replied, "Can I come inside?"

Ari sat at the kitchen table watching as Justine made coffee and opened a cake tin to offer him a slice of cake. Her heart was in her mouth as she thought of Nadine up there in the sky hurtling towards Europe, determined to forget this man sitting in front of her. Saying nothing she sat down and looked at the sad injured man.

Fighting back tears she asked, "Ari what has happened to you?"

"I'll tell you, but first, where's Nadine?"

"Oh Ari she's gone, she waited to hear from you, why didn't you answer your phone?"

"Gone? Where has she gone?"

"This morning she got on a plane for London. She has a job over there and has no plans to return for a long time. She was heartbroken when you blocked her calls."

"I didn't block her calls, my phone was wrecked in a car accident and I've been in hospital ever since. I don't have your phone number or address so I had to come here physically. I discharged myself this morning against medical advice because I had to see her. I've thought of her every day since I regained consciousness; I miss her so much. I love her and I need her to love me and help me to get over the accident."

"Oh Ari, why didn't someone get in touch with her?"

Putting his head in his hands, his shoulders began to shake. "I was unconscious and no one realised, no one thought of her," he replied, trying not to succumb to tears.

Justine was moved by the sight of Ari being in such a distressed state. Moving to his side she put an arm around his shoulder and took one of his hands. "Nadine couldn't contact your cousins in the Yarra Valley because she had no idea of their address and she didn't get in touch with your parents because when she didn't hear from you she assumed it was all over."

"What a mess."

"Ari this can still be fixed; I will get in touch with Nadine in the morning or maybe tonight. I'll send her a text message and when she lands she will get it."

Ari nodded as he fought back tears. "Thank you Justine."

The hand she was holding was warm and clammy and his face was losing colour. "You are not well Ari, come and lie down on the couch."

Managing to get to the couch he lay back. Justine lifted his feet up and covered him with a light rug which they had used for Terry during her illness. She brought him a large glass of water and said, "Drink this and just rest, you can stay as long as you need." Leaving him alone she continued with her chores, checking on him frequently as he slept.

Lulu came home after school and gasped when she saw Ari asleep on the couch. She was about to make herself a toasted sandwich and thought Ari might like one.

"Mum will I ask him if he wants something to eat?"

"Yes he's been asleep for hours now, wake him gently, he must be hungry."

Lulu touched his shoulder and said "Ari." But he did not wake.

"Ari, would you like a sandwich?"

No response at all. "Mum, he's not dead is he? "she yelled.

"No just out of hospital too soon, I think," she replied moving to his side to take his pulse, which was weak and thready. She felt his forehead which was hot.

"I think he should go back to hospital he signed himself out this morning to come here and see Nadine, it was the wrong thing to do for his health."

"Do you think we should ring an ambulance Mum?"

"I'm going to ring Bethany, she will advise us."

Bethany was there in a flash bringing a BP machine and a stethoscope. After a quick examination she said, "His blood pressure is very low and I think he has a high temperature; I think he should go back to hospital. Did he bring any medications with him?"

"No nothing, I don't think he was thinking clearly when he left the hospital."

Picking up her phone Justine rang for an ambulance.

"We don't want to take any chances now that we have found him—well, he has found us."

105

The Accident

Ari's friends informing him of Nadine being a dancer in a gentleman's club was the catalyst for a series of events which led to a disaster. If only she had told him before he could have been prepared for what the men had told him. He did not like what they had to say but he loved Nadine and he knew he could live with it once she talked to him about the circumstances. Plus it was in the past wasn't it, and he had been to one of those clubs himself on a bucks' night anyway, so he could deal with it. Unfortunately he had not realised all of this soon enough and what he said had sent the wrong message to Nadine. Imagining her future with Ari shattered she called a taxi and fled in tears. He returned to the house, picked up his car keys and sped off down the road hoping to catch up with the taxi.

Driving through an intersection as the lights were changing he was hit by a car that was turning early. His car was hit on the driver's side and Ari was knocked out and sustained a head injury and chest and pelvic fractures. He spent days in an induced coma and when allowed to wake was confused and drowsy. His phone was wrecked and he was too confused to remember Nadine's phone number — in fact he had never had to memorise the number. Because of his confusion and needing to sleep so often, his concentration was all over the place. No one knew how to contact Nadine and did not bother trying to find out as they were more concerned with Ari's health and recovery.

106

Nadine

Nadine was surprised to receive the message from her mother when she landed at Heathrow airport. She had been walking along with all the passengers who had just disembarked from the plane when her phone pinged several times. Pulling it from her handbag and reading the message brought her to a stop, causing several people to bump into her.

ARI CAME TO SEE ME, HE WAS IN AN ACCIDENT, HIS PHONE WAS WRECKED, HE IS NOT WELL, STILL IN HOSPITAL, LOVES YOU. RING WHEN YOU GET THIS MESSAGE. MUM.

Heart beating wildly she continued to stand still until everyone had passed her by and she was almost alone. She moved to a nearby seat and rang her mother, aware that she would still be asleep. The few people passing Nadine were aware of the emotional woman both laughing and crying as she fired rapid questions at her mother, "Mum what happened? How did you find out about the accident? Is he going to be okay?"

"He is going to be alright but he's still unwell. Get yourself into the hotel and ring me in four hours. I will be with Ari in the hospital and you can speak to him then. Darling he still wants you and he loves you so much."

"Oh Mum I don't know what to say, I blocked his number before I left Melbourne and I put my engagement ring in your rubbish bin. Can you fish it out please?"

"Just the way I wanted to spend the morning, going through the rubbish bin. Of course I'll find it for you." She replied laughing.

"Thanks Mum, I love you."

107

Reconciliation

Justine entered the hospital at 7am. Taking the lift to the fifth floor, she spoke briefly to a nurse at the ward desk. Ari had already spoken to Justine and was sitting out of bed waiting for her, freshly showered and cleanshaven.

Justine smiled at the handsome man whom she hoped was soon to be her son-in-law, noticing that he looked so much better than the previous day. Altogether happier and healthier, she thought to herself as she pulled up a chair to be near him. Sitting down she handed him a takeaway coffee and said, "I thought you would like a decent coffee while we are waiting for the phone call, Nadine said she'd ring at 7.30."

Ari removed the lid and breathed in the aroma of the freshly brewed coffee, "I've missed that almost as much as Nadine." Noticing Justine's exaggerated face of disapproval, he laughed and added, "Just joking."

The phone rang, it was Nadine. Justine handed the phone to Ari and left the room to give the couple privacy. About an hour later she returned to see Ari on his feet gazing out of the window as he still spoke on the phone to Nadine. Hearing the door open and close he turned and smiled at Justine. He was a different man, his whole demeanour had altered and his dark brown eyes were sparkling again. Ah look what love can do for you she thought. After a short conversation with Nadine, Justine said goodbye to Ari and with a smile on her face she headed for home.

108

Ari and Nadine

Ari was discharged to his uncle in the Yarra Valley and planned to stay a week or two then fly back to Sydney to convalesce with his parents. Having acquired a new phone, he and Nadine spoke daily. After many discussions they decided Nadine would stay in London until Ari was well enough to fly to London where he would find a job and they would live there for the time being. Justine once again was sad about the decision but agreed it was their decision and she had to accept it.

The flat in Earls Court that Nadine had previously rented had been taken over by her friend Polly, who was shortly to marry and move to Scotland. Nadine moved back in with her friend and began work in the city. Everything was fine except she missed Ari terribly. If it was not for the daily phone calls she wouldn't have been able to cope, but the thought of him joining her soon in London kept her going.

109

London

Ari arrived at Heathrow airport mid-morning and when he finally got through baggage pickup and border control he rushed out to look for his beloved Nadine. Where is she, he wondered looking left and right. Then he spotted her standing to the right of the crowd. She was holding a large placard on which she had drawn a large red heart and written inside the heart in bold letters 'ARI'. He ran to her and they embraced, causing the placard to fall to the floor. They were one of many couples or family groups greeting each other but Ari and Nadine were oblivious to everything and everyone around them, they were lost in a world of their own.

They caught the train to Earls Court and much to the amusement of the other train travellers they gazed into each other's eyes, kissed and laughed for most of the journey. After the five-minute walk to the flat they stood at the doorstep where Nadine pretended to have lost her key. Ari was standing behind her with his arms around her waist.

"I'll break a window if you can't find your key."

"I'm just pretending. It's here," she laughed as she inserted the key, opened the door and they rushed inside. They grabbed at each other, almost falling over as they headed for the couch. They had not made love for several months so it was over fairly quickly.

"You have a sleep and a shower while I cook dinner then we can go to bed and catch up on what we've been missing," Nadine said, laughing as she watched Ari struggling to keep his eyes open. He slept, she cooked, he woke, they ate, they made love again and then they both slept.

"Oh Nadine, you have no idea how much I've missed being with you, I thought I'd lost you."

"I do know Ari, I was in the same situation and it was awful. Let's make a promise to never part again."

"Yes I agree, we should never be apart again."

"Well that's settled."

"Ari, there is something else we need to settle."

"What's that?"

"We have never talked about having children. Do you want to have children?"

"Yes naturally, that's the way it goes. Marry and have a family, I would love to be a father one day."

"That's good because we will be parents in about six months time."

"What? Are you sure?"

"I'm sure."

"Wow, I didn't expect that."

"I didn't plan it. I was taking the pill as you know, but I had gastroenteritis once, I'm sure you remember, and I suppose the pill wasn't digested. Now I have our baby inside me."

"Do you want to get married at once or do you want to wait?"

"I don't really care but it would probably be better if we just get married quietly here in London with as little fuss as possible."

"Yes we could do that and have a big family celebration at a later date."

"Do you think our families will be upset if we do that?" asked Nadine"

"Yes and no; we're a long way from home and it's up to us really. Plus it's a lot of expense and trouble for everyone to come here and you might not be up to it when you are further into the pregnancy."

"That's true, and you have to find a job, so let's just take it easy and be kind to ourselves; a quiet wedding here, tell the family after, greet our baby and then maybe a trip home next year, no pressure. Agree?"

"Agree," Ari said smiling at Nadine. "Oh, and I forgot this." He handed Nadine the engagement ring. "You left it with your mother."

"Oh yes," she said, putting it on her finger. "I suppose I had better tell you about that too; no more secrets."

Nadine gave birth to a beautiful brown-eyed baby girl who they named Petra. They returned to live in Australia but chose to make Sydney their home for the time being.

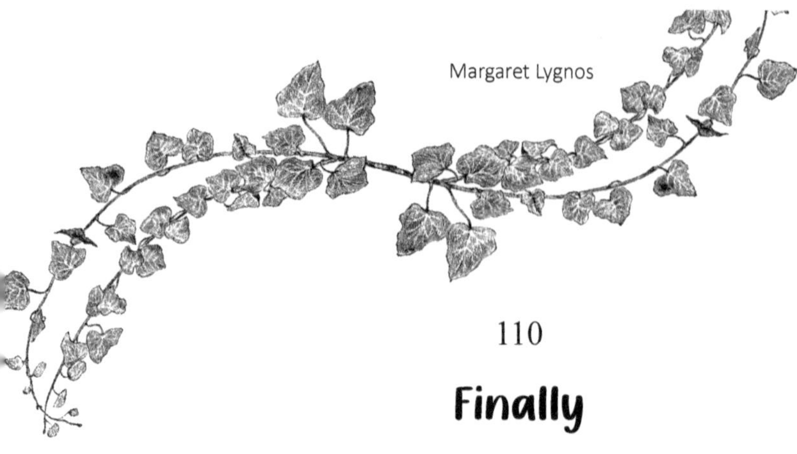

110

Finally

Marcia continues to help homeless women.

Mandy still tries to help people, always seeing the good in each one.

Kathy remains in a psychiatric institution.

Simon and his mother continue to see Finn occasionally, more or less like an aunt and a cousin.

Marcus and Bethany married and are very happy together.

Bethany finally completed her nursing refresher course and has returned to nursing.

Lulu has qualified for the Australian women's soccer team.

Crystal and Jason stayed in Greenmount and had two more children. Crystal discovered she loved the quiet of the semi-rural township where she was surrounded by trees, birds and other wild life. It had a calming and embracing effect of security which she had felt a little when she had lived in the share house. Now she had really found her happy place with Jason and her children. She completed her secondary education and hopes to do further study when her children are older. In the meantime, she began to write poetry, something she had done when at school. One of her English assignments had called for a descriptive, emotive rhyming poem which she had mused over for weeks before finally writing something she was happy with which expressed the peace and refuge she felt living in Greenmount.

Everything I love is here

Everything I love is here
I see it every day
the flora and the fauna
nature on display.

Tall majestic eucalypts
shading all around
bending in the gusty wind
almost touch the ground.

The large and raucous
mountain birds
flocks are flying by
tiny wrens and finches
just visible and shy.

Gentle-faced kangaroos
grazing 'neath the trees
joeys peeping out the pouch
eating grass with ease.

At night time there are possums
occasionally an owl
koalas moving through the trees
famous for their growl.

Sky is vast the air is fresh
the mountain stands on high
weather changing suddenly
embellishing the sky.

If you are fortunate
you may get a treat
half a dozen little birds
in front of you will meet.

They'll dance and sing and
flit about
they tantalise and tease,
just as soon as they began
they fly back to the trees.

Everything I love is here
I see it every day
I am never leaving
I am here to stay.